The Girlfrier
Jack Carteret

Copyright : Jack Carteret 2017

Published by : Jack Carteret

Cover Design: The Cover Collection

Visit my Facebook page at www.facebook.com/JosieCloverfieldBooks

Chapter One

When Hannah Davenport first went missing, I'd been kind of glad. I'm not proud of it; it's just the truth. I didn't like Hannah, and with good reason. As far as I was concerned, she had taken over my little world.

Liam was all that I had, but she just *had* to make him hers. I didn't fancy Liam. I wasn't in love with him or anything like that. It was just that he was my best friend, and had been since we were just six years old.

Sometimes Liam was like my brother; other times, a parent. He was a small island of security in the chaos of my life. Mostly, he was the right arm to my left arm. It had always been that way.

Then Hannah, rich, pretty and totally entitled, just walked right in and swiped my right arm away. And there I stood; just a left arm dangling there, not really knowing what to do with itself. If I'm brutally honest, I hated Hannah Davenport.

So, I guess it was kind of strange that I more or less led the charge in the search for Hannah. It even gave me a reputation at Grantstone University as something of a private detective.

I was actually a mechanical engineering student, so it was a weird reputation to have, but you go with the flow. Anyway, had it not been for my best friend becoming number one suspect – being the boyfriend and all – then I doubt I would have gone to such great lengths in my own investigations. But I'm jumping ahead. I'll start at the beginning.

On a fairly routine sort of a Monday afternoon, I was heading in the direction of a calculus tutorial when I got a text from Liam. I rolled my eyes as I looked at it.

"Dude, where are you? I need to see you right now."

I sighed for ages, until there was no air left in my body. I don't know why Liam calls me *Dude*, but he's done it for so long that I don't question it. I actually *daren't* question it; Liam's explanations can be long-winded and confusing, whatever the subject. I long ago adopted a policy of *need to know*, and reckoned the whole Dude thing was in the list of things I *didn't* need to know.

My tutorial was kind of an optional extra, but I really wanted to go to it. I wasn't struggling or anything. In fact, I actually excelled at calculus. The thing was, I didn't like to miss anything. I'd dreamed of going to uni since I was really little, and I didn't want to miss a bit of it. I guess I'm kind of a geek or a swot or what-have-you, and I had been right through school and sixth form.

Anyway, Liam's trauma-by-text-message would, I had no doubt, put the nutcrackers on my attendance at the calculus tutorial. I love Liam to bits, but knew that if his trauma was anything less than life or death, I would strangle him.

"I'll meet you in the canteen."

"Thanks Dude."

I did a complete one-eighty and headed back in the direction of the canteen. I had that persistent grumbling thing going on, you know, muttering under my breath about how much I needed to be at my tutorial and how this better be serious or else. I was moaning into thin air right up until the point at which I started to get on my own nerves.

Finally, I reached the canteen. It was more or less deserted, and I could pick Liam out immediately. He'd already got himself a cup of coffee, and nothing for me. Still, I couldn't really blame him for that. Liam knew that I carried a flask of tea in my rucksack at all times.

You see, if I'm totally honest, I would have to describe my upbringing as, amongst *many* other things, *dirt poor*. Something inside me bucked wildly and ranted to itself every time I read the hot-drinks price list in the university canteen. I'd had so little growing up that I just couldn't buy a cup of tea which cost the same as a *whole box* of tea bags.

Anyway, I dropped my rucksack with exaggerated gusto onto the table and began to root around in it for my flask. As I did so, I looked at Liam. He was kind of pasty and worried looking, and that wasn't really his everyday countenance.

"Liam, what's wrong?" I said, feeling the first fluttering of concern.

"I can't find Hannah." He said, and looked up at me.

"You can't find….. seriously, Liam? I missed a tutorial for this!"

"Dude!" He said. "I don't know where she is!"

"That's the same thing just worded differently." I said, totally exasperated. "Why is this newsworthy?"

"It's *newsworthy*...." He said, with an air of sarcasm, "because Hannah is missing!"

"Just because you cannot find someone does not make them a missing person, Liam." I said, sloshing hot tea into one of those really little cups that you get with a flask. Naturally, much of it ended up on the table.

"No Dude. Hannah's been missing all night. She hasn't been seen since yesterday."

"Oh, I see." I was struggling with enthusiasm.

"I'm serious."

"Alright, Liam. I'm sorry." I said, and was beginning to mean it. Liam really did look concerned and he should have been able to turn to me of all people. "Look, where did the two of you go last night?" It was time to wind my neck in and help.

"We didn't. I mean, we were supposed to, but we didn't. She had a *thing* and kind of called off our plans at the last minute."

"A *thing?*" In Liam-speak, someone having *a thing* was an actual explanation in and of itself.

"Yeah, she had a thing. We were only going to see a movie or get a pizza or something. Nothing, like, *firm*, you know. Then she called me and said she had to go somewhere to collect something and it was kind of a surprise so she couldn't tell me. I sort of thought it was a surprise for me, so I didn't get upset about her cancelling. Anyway, that was the last I heard of her until her mum called demanding to know where she was." Liam took a gulp of coffee and looked at me expectantly.

Looking at each other expectantly is what Liam and I have done for years. In times of crisis, we could always rely on each other to pick up the slack and come up with the right solution, whatever was going on.

It's just how it had always been. In our own ways, we had both experienced the kind of childhoods that didn't tend to end up at university. The common links we shared were poverty and dysfunctional, alcoholic parents. Or *parent*, in my case. It was just my mum and me, and whichever low-life loser she was currently clinging to like the last piece of driftwood after the sinking of the Titanic.

Liam, on the other hand, came from a large family with a huge reputation for thievery and thuggery. His care worn and rarely sober mother had spent an entire life struggling to cope with a husband who had eaten more meals in prison than at home, and four sons, three of whom were constantly in and out of Police Custody.

Liam and I hadn't just clung together, though. We were actual friends, with loads in common and a real caring for one another. We'd met as six year olds in what Liam still rather cutely referred to as *little school*.

Liam had kind of rescued me really. You see, our teacher had bought a special colouring book and nice crayons for the whole class. Every night, one kid would get to take the book home and colour in one of the pictures.

When my turn came around, I'd spent ages neatly colouring a rolling meadow covered in sheep. Without going into painful, long-winded detail, my mum had been beyond drunk, and had torn a great chunk of pages out of the book. When the teacher saw it, she totally shredded me in front of everybody.

Of course, anyone worthy of the title *teacher* should have realised that a shy and unkempt little girl, who was so withdrawn she was practically mute, would never have done anything to have drawn such attention to herself. Still, she wasn't one of those teachers. She was one of the kind whose life was made very much easier by not finding out a damn thing about mine. Enough said. Anyway, as I sobbed under the bombardment of teacherly scorn, a little boy who sat a few desks away stood up for me.

"She didn't do that on purpose, did she? Leave her alone." Yep, you've guessed it. It was little Liam.

I'd never paid much attention to him back then because my head was mostly down and my attention seriously averted from all other life forms. Anyway, that day I had a good look.

Liam was really little for his age, and his hair was the darkest sort of a brown, just one notch up from black. And it was a great, unruly mop, which looked kind of funny perched on top of such a little boy. His clothes made mine look almost new and, if I'm brutally honest, he was kind of whiffy.

Anyway, my soon-to-be best mate in all the world stood up for me that day, and I never forgot it. He got himself into so much trouble that the teacher totally forgot about me and the ruined colouring book. I've loved Liam ever since.

As I turned my attention back to Liam, I thought of the brave, somewhat stinky little boy he'd been, and I felt ashamed of my tutorial related snottiness.

"Ok, we'll work this out." I said, suddenly all encouragement. "Where and when did you actually last see Hannah?" I studied Liam as his eyebrows knitted together in deep thought.

"Erm….it was last lecture. We had an art class with Matty Jameson. It finished around half past three."

Matty Jameson was a kind of clichéd excuse for a university lecturer, in so far as he was *exactly* what you would expect. Bohemian; long woollen scarves in garish stripes, big hair, even *bigger* hat, long coat... you get the picture. He was actually only, like, late twenties or something, so there really was no excuse in my opinion.

"So, you finished at three-thirty?"

"Yeah. I was going to the library to look for a copy of The Count, and Hannah said she was going home to get showered and changed for our date later."

The Count of Monte Cristo. God knows how many times Liam had read that book, yet oddly had never actually *owned* a copy. Liam felt the same way about paying for books as I felt about paying for hot beverages. He had libraries, I had my flask.

"Where were you supposed to be meeting last night? And what time?"

"Erm.. Around six at her place. I was supposed to pick her up and then we'd decide what we were going to do."

I was floundering, really, but kind of becoming more determined to help him.

"Liam, has she ever ducked out on you before? You know, like changed plans at the last minute?"

"Nope."

"And you didn't think that was *odd?*" I knew I'd made a mistake as soon as I saw him raise just the *one* eyebrow.

It was the *you and me are about to fall out* eyebrow of doom, and I was heartily wishing I hadn't provoked it. It was a great big hairy thing with a life of its own.

"What do you mean?" Liam's voice was quiet, but the eyebrow was still way up there.

"I mean, well, didn't it get you *thinking?*" I was taking it a bit more cautiously.

"Jeez, Dude! I haven't killed her and abandoned her lifeless corpse somewhere!" It was just a mini-outburst. Once assuaged, the eyebrow relaxed into the *off* position.

"Liam, like I said *that!* For God's sake, I'm trying to help. I hope you're not this touchy when the *Police* ask you. And, by the way, please don't rattle on about *lifeless corpses* to them."

Liam's jaw dropped. He looked totally upended. I couldn't work out if it was the thought of being questioned, or if the idea that the Police being involved would make the whole thing serious; *real*.

"Police? God, I hadn't even thought about the Police being involved. Well, maybe, if she doesn't turn up.... but... she'll turn up. She *has* to."

"Liam, I'm just going through the basics. Come on, we've had enough Police encounters between us to last us a lifetime." "Yeah, but none that were actually about *us!* About our families, *yes*. But none where we were actual *suspects* Dude!"

"*We* aren't suspects." I corrected him, realising my mistake immediately. "I mean...." He cut me off.

"Oh, I get it, you mean *I am* a suspect!" *Eyebrow back up.*

"Liam, you're putting words in my mouth. I'm trying to help, remember? And it will help greatly if you can get your recollections in order. It might even help to *find* Hannah. Never mind about the Police for now. Let's not get going on the subject of *suspects* when Hannah might just be sleeping off a hangover at a friend's house."

He visibly relaxed, and our friendship returned to its normal, easy footing. I was doing my job, albeit a little shaky on the offence management side of things.

"Liam, I don't suppose she actually *could* be sleeping it off somewhere? Have you thought about that?"

"Erm, no, I hadn't. I don't know... She doesn't really drink, I don't think."

"You don't *think?* Liam, she's your girlfriend, you must know." He looked defensive, spreading his hands.

"I've only been seeing her for five weeks, Dude. It's not like I *know* her... I mean, I know her, but not the way I know *you*, you know?"

Five weeks? Wow, was that all it had been? It had seemed to me to have been so much longer. I'd felt this horrible, dull... I don't know, something....this *feeling*. It was almost as if I'd been abandoned. Had it *really* only been five weeks since Liam had hooked up with Hannah?

I remembered well how I'd seen it coming. Hannah was so irritating. I didn't share any classes with her. I was studying Engineering after all, and she was arty. In fact, she and Liam had met in one of their art classes.

Despite his rough edges and distinct lack of table manners, Liam had a very honest and direct way of expressing himself, and a fearless sense of humour, all of which had clearly impressed Hannah.

Hannah came from a clique who had been together right through school. They had that confidence that came from knowing you had your tight little crew all around you, and it had probably made starting university in September a piece of cake. They were clearly locals. They knew their way around and none of them seemed to live on campus. Obviously, they were not from the same part of town as me and Liam. Their clothes, hair and subtle-yet-expensive jewellery spoke volumes. As did their accents. Compared with them, I might as well be from another planet.

When Liam and I wandered onto the Grantstone University campus for the first time, we had no such feelings of confidence. There was no happy group waiting to join us in the canteen, or desperate to tear around the campus with us on fresher's week finding cool groups and societies to join.

Nope; things were the same as they had always been. It was just me, Liam, and a whole lot of social-misfit angst.

We'd only been there just over four months by the time Hannah went missing, but it has to be said that Liam had done very much better at finding friends than I had. Liam's a much more trusting and outgoing person than I am.

I sometimes look at him and wonder what it would be like to *be* Liam. Then I remember that he occasionally still lights his own farts and laughs like a drain, and I am reminded to be grateful for my own evolution.

Anyway, for some reason, and I'm assuming that she'd never been introduced to the whole *fart-lighting* thing, Hannah had decided that she wanted Liam in the rosy sphere that was her life.

To be honest, Liam is probably quite good looking. He's not small for his age anymore. Quite the opposite, in fact. He's well over six feet tall and is pretty broad. He's muscular in a way that would lead you to suspect he plays a lot of sports, if you didn't know him well enough to know that *that* would never happen.

Liam still has that really dark hair, and it's still thick and kind of mop-like. Happily, he's not an *all-over* hairy dude though, like *arms* and *hands* and stuff; mostly it's just his thick mop-top and his aforementioned super-expressive eyebrows.

Liam's skin is a bit on the pale side, and he has pale blue eyes. He reminds me a bit of the lead singer of Green Day, only younger and minus the tattoos and eyeliner. Oh yes, and he smells a lot better than he used to; quite nice, actually.

So, I'm sure Liam's looks had plenty to do with Hannah's singling him out for her attentions, but there was something else there too. It's hard to explain. I had wanted to tell Liam about it from the first, but I just knew I would never make myself understood. There was something about the way Hannah interacted with Liam which made me feel like he was her project or something.

Maybe like an outreach thing, or a pseudo Lady Chatterley thing, or a *look at me dating the boy from the bad part of town* chic thing….. whatever it was, I always felt kind of patronised on Liam's behalf. Liam himself did not seem patronised, and I knew that this feeling had a lot to do with me. I suffered badly from inverted snobbery, and had a huge problem trying to like, *or even just be polite to*, people who'd had a much more privileged upbringing that I did. The problem was that this group included a massive swathe of people.

Anyway, I say *suffered from* in the past tense. I like to think that my recent experiences have taught me a thing or two about that.

So, Hannah started appearing in the canteen whenever I was meeting Liam, and she began to invite herself to sit with us more and more. For the most part, Hannah ignored me. Her reason for joining us at break times clearly wasn't to get to know *me* better, put it that way. Most of her lunchtime chatter went something like this…..

"Liam, you were *sooo* funny in art. Even Matty Jameson laughed!" *Said with squeaky admiration.*

"Really, you must meet some of my friends. They'd simply love you!" *Yes, in the same way that kings love court jesters…..*

"Oh dear! Why don't you just *buy* a meal here? I'm sure they sell chips and beans or something that would suit you." *Said to me in horror whilst looking into the lunchbox of miscellaneous items picked out of the fridge at home before they went out of date.*

Honestly, I don't know if it was my fault or Hannah's, but I cannot say I enjoyed her company. Oh, but, horror of horrors, Liam seemed to.

At first I was just convinced that an overload of arty pontification had dulled his senses and that normal service would soon be resumed. However, within a matter of just a couple of weeks, Hannah was a fixture, as were her somewhat bemused group of friends. Suddenly my world had gone from the known and the relatively comfortable, to the unknown and the distinctly *uncomfortable*. Liam had a way of letting the world bounce right off him, leaving him totally unaffected.

Not me; I caught every snotty comment or eye roll that passed between Hannah's girlfriends, Fliss and Amelia. I felt every cell of my skin warm up as I was treated to the surreptitious once overs I generally got as soon as they came over to us. I wasn't scruffy by any stretch of the imagination, but most of my stuff came from charity shops and such the like. And Hannah herself had a way of looking me up and down that made me want to dissolve with shame.

Fliss had a boyfriend called Richard Allencourt, who tagged along behind her everywhere she went. Despite being what I would have called *one of them*, he was actually alright. By which I mean he didn't spend ages trying to come up with the sort of comment that could put you in your place but be completely denied if challenged. To be honest, that was enough for me. He was the best of a really crappy bunch, in my opinion.

All in all, the last five weeks had not exactly flown by. I knew it had a lot to do with my world being altered and my inner puppy objecting wildly and cocking its leg everywhere. Liam was *my* friend, my very *best* friend and, at that point, my *only* friend. I'd been suffering from the dull ache of the unknown which kept prodding at me and telling me everything was changing.

So, it is with a certain amount of shame – well, a rather sizeable helping of shame, actually - that I shall openly admit that, for a good few moments, I pretty much *wished* that Hannah had gone missing. Not Liam's kind of missing, but News at Ten's kind of missing.

"Dude? Where'd ya go?" Liam was staring at me and picking his empty polystyrene cup to bits.

"Sorry, I was just thinking. Look, have you called either Fliss or Amelia? Maybe she was out with them?" I was back on the detective track.

Even my self-involved bout of victimhood knew that wishing a young woman was *really* missing was beyond wrong.

"No, I don't have their numbers. Still, I reckon Hannah's mum will have called them."

"Really? Whose mums have the phone numbers of their kid's friends?" I was thinking of my own mum, I guess.

I could be consorting with Lucifer himself and still not hear so much as a *mind how you go, sweetheart* from my beloved parent.

"Well, she had *my* number." Liam looked up at me with this kind of dopey expression he gets from time to time.

It was a mixture of things, and I knew them all by heart. Hunger mixed with confusion mixed with anxiety. Well, I could help him with *one* of them, at any rate. I rummaged in my rucksack and pulled out a foil wrapped cheese and marmite sandwich and a packet of crisps.

"Here you go. Eat them, and then *focus*, ok?" I smiled at him.

"Dude? What are these?" Liam looked up in horror. "*EuroSaver* crisps? I never heard of them before. What are they, like, *five pence?*" Liam had opened the bag and was peering in doubtfully. "*Dude!* They're totally shining with grease and really, *really* small!"

"Seriously, Liam, at a time like this you're gonna become a crisp snob?" I looked at him in mock horror.

"I'm not a *crisp snob*, Dude. I'm just…. what's the word?....*discerning!*"

With that, we both burst out laughing. It wasn't that Hannah was forgotten, it was just that we had always faced life's traumas this way. Liam had a way with him that always made me laugh.

No, Hannah wasn't forgotten, she was just on hold for a few seconds whilst we let humour do what it had always done for us. Still, that was probably *not* the best moment for the Police to show up, if I'm totally honest.

"It's the cops, Dude!" Liam hissed at me through his teeth. We were immediately silent, which probably made us look as guilty as sin. I peeked out from under my overgrown fringe and felt momentarily relieved to see that one of the two uniformed officers approaching us was PC Dale Webb.

Dale Webb was actually a nice guy, but he knew way too much about the seedy horrors of my home life for me to be comfortable seeing him there at the university. As much as he'd helped me out at home when things had been at their worst, somehow his presence at the university made me feel angry.

This was my place of learning. This was a different world where I had opportunities and the sort of inner peace that came from order. Suddenly Dale Webb felt like a man standing on my bridge, and that bridge was joining two worlds which should *never* be joined. I wanted to pound on the bridge with my knurled staff and scream *You shall not pass!* in the style of Gandalph. But I didn't; I just pulled myself together and smiled politely at him.

"Hey Josie. How's it going?"

"Not bad. How are you?" I felt kind of surly but was determined to battle it.

Dale Webb had been good to me over the years. Whenever the police attended my house, and it was usually some *mum's drunk again* episode, it had always been a time of high stress and high embarrassment for me. Quite often, the cops who came into my home almost dismissed me with the assumption that I was likely to be a *mini-me* version of my mum, which I most certainly am not.

I know the training they get these days is all *touchy-feely* and geared towards ensuring they make the right noises in any given social situation, but if the cop who actually turns up to your particular crisis is judgemental by nature, then no amount of training will cover it up.

Trust me, I know. I've had loads of them trotting through my home since I was a little kid. I've seen enough police officers to be able to write a thesis on the various types.

Anyway, my point is, Dale Webb *never* judged. He'd first appeared in my world when I was about thirteen. Dale had joined the Police at just eighteen, and he'd *looked* it then. God knows how he'd managed to get older people to behave themselves when he'd looked like a giant schoolboy, but somehow he had.

Dale was pretty calm and patient and it seemed to work. My mum has called him some truly appalling names over the years, names which I *cannot possibly* repeat, yet he never seemed to take it to heart. Every time he met my mum, it was like the first time. Dale never held her past behaviour against her. Amazing, really, because *I* certainly do.

The very first time I met PC Dale Webb was when my mum had called the police to tell them that I was trying to kill her. Let me just tell you that she was drunk. I wasn't *actually* trying to kill her; I'm not that sort of a daughter. I was simply trying to get on with my homework.

I'd hidden away upstairs in my room, throwing across the bolt which I had fixed on myself to keep her out, and had put cotton wool in my ears to drown out the noise of her shrieks. I had always been a keen student, and I *always* made sure my homework was done properly and in on time.

My mum never really *got* that. It was weird, but my conscientiousness seemed to make her angry for some reason. She just couldn't understand where I was coming from with that one.

Anyway, she had demanded that I go down to the off-licence and get her some more vodka. Oh yes, at just thirteen years old they served me booze alright. For most of my childhood, I hadn't even realised that selling alcohol to a child was illegal. Anyway, I had refused to go out and get the vodka because I had homework to do.

By the time I'd reached thirteen, there wasn't a great deal else left for my mum to do to me, so I had grown pretty used to saying *no* to her. Anyway, on this particular occasion, when she found she couldn't distract me or get into my room, she resorted to calling the police and telling them that I was trying to kill her, complete with death screams and desperate cries for help.

I'd heard the blues and twos from a mile away, and knew that they were coming to our house. So much for getting my homework done. Anyway, I waited in my room until there came a most polite and gentle knock at the door.

"Hello? I'm looking for Josie. It's alright, love, I'm a police officer." *And there was me thinking it was Santa come to drop my presents off early.*

I un-bolted and opened the door without speaking. I was a bit taken aback to see him standing there, since he didn't seem to be so much older than me. Well, you know, five or six years, but not like *some* of the crusty old fossils that the Grantstone Constabulary routinely sent round to our house.

"Can I come in and speak to you for a minute?" He was one of those *big* police officers, you know, the sort that was *always* going to be a police officer purely because the giant uniform would fit him perfectly.

PC Dale Webb was kind of rugby player shaped and, to my thirteen-year-old self, epitomised all that a young man should be. For one thing, he was sober, for another, he was in gainful employment. In my world, two minor miracles.

"Yeah, come in." I'd gone back to sit down at my tiny desk, purely because I didn't know what else to do. Dale Webb did what every other police officer before him had done when they came into my room. He looked about him, and let his mouth gape open in wonder. He had seen the rest of the house, and the terrible disarray that was to be found there. So, when he had walked into my room, a tiny oasis of order and respectability, he'd been unable to contain his surprise.

"So, getting on with your homework then?" Dale had said, clearly casting about for a way to open the conversation.

"Yes, I know, *shocker*, right? Chav kid has aspirations." I laughed without any real humour, and waited for him to turn against me for being snotty.

"I'm sorry, I suppose you've seen and heard it all before, haven't you? Well, I just want you to know that I'm not like that. I'm not *amazed* that you would have aspirations, I'm just amazed that you are able to follow them when your mum is behaving so badly." Dale Webb had parked himself on the edge of my tiny single bed.

He was a big guy, and I was really hoping that he wouldn't wiggle about much, because the bed no longer had legs at the bottom end and was propped up on books and stuff. Even *I* had to get in with a certain degree of caution and remember not to turn over with too much gusto in the middle of the night. If one of the makeshift legs went down, I kind of slid down the bed slowly, as if I was on a sinking ship.

"Oh, right. Ok, I'm sorry. That was rude."

"Look, you have nothing to be sorry for. Your mum is behaving like a child and you are behaving like an adult. That's got to be so stressful. I get that you're annoyed, and I don't blame you. Anyway, since *you're* the adult in this house, I'm going to ask *you* what it is that you want to happen next. Now we can take your mum in for a Breach of the Peace, or something along those lines, but that means either Social Services for the night, or an appropriate adult for you to stay with. I can see how *that* would be a nightmare for you if you're trying to get your homework done, but I also can see that your mum would be a nightmare too if we leave her here. Just tell me what it is you want us to do, and I'll do it."

"Just leave her downstairs. I'll put these back in." I lifted my two pieces of cotton wool, and Dale began to laugh. "I'll just lock myself back in here, and I can get on with my homework just fine. I'm used to it really. She'll either go out and get her own damn vodka, or she'll whine until she falls asleep. Now that she's had her little bit of revenge on me, she'll more or less forget I'm here."

"Cool, we'll do that for you. But call us if you need us, ok." Dale Webb began to rise, and the bed shifted in a way which made me wince. Fortunately, he didn't seem to notice. "By the way, what are you studying?"

"Oh, it's just my maths homework."

"You like it?" He was smiling, clearly expecting me to grimace or say *no*.

"Yeah! God, I love maths. I'm going to go to university one day." I knew my exclamation had come out in a most dreadful, dorky way, and my cheeks went from peaky-pale to beetrootblush instantly.

"Good for you, Josie. Don't let *anything* take you off your path, you understand?" I understood perfectly.

He wasn't patronising me at all. Dale Webb had meant every word of what he just said and, for reasons I could not understand at the time, it had kind of brought tears to my eyes.

"So, I'm guessing you know we're here about Hannah Davenport?" Dale took a seat at the table next to me.

I'd totally drifted off, but I was glad I had. My little hop and skip down memory lane had reminded me that PC Dale Webb was one of the good guys, and it dragged my hostile demeanour back into check.

"I know, Dale. Me and Liam were just talking about it, wondering if she might have gone out with Fliss or Amelia."

"Oh, that's …. Felicity Hardcastle and Amelia Ledbetter, is it?" Dale was looking through his notebook, reading off the names.

"I suppose so. They've never introduced themselves to me exactly, so I never got surnames. They're Hannah's best mates, I suppose."

"Yep, they're the ones. No, they haven't seen her either. Liam?" Dale turned to look at Liam, who now seemed grateful for the distraction of the Euro-Shopper crisps he was picking out of the bag. "When did you last see her?" From any other police officer, it would have sounded like the preamble to a lifetime in prison.

However, as always, Dale Webb spoke in a way that didn't accuse.

Liam went through the same as he'd told me. It wasn't until I heard him explaining, *we were going out, but then she had a thing, and I thought it was a surprise thing for me, and so we didn't go out and I haven't seen her since…*. that I realised how confusing Liam must appear to the uninitiated.

Whilst Dale Webb knew Liam well and wasn't at all fazed by his explanation, the other police officer he had come in with might well be. There was an *air* about this police officer; she had the kind of frame and bearing that made you feel that you wouldn't argue with her on a dark night in a deserted alley.

However, there was also something in her face which struck me as being very sensible. Almost as if she was the kind of woman who would give a person a fair hearing before pummelling them into non-existence.

"As Liam told it to me, they had been due to go out, either to the cinema or for a pizza. Hannah called and said she couldn't make it, because she had something to pick up, which was a surprise. Liam was all smiles, because he thought that this *surprise* might be something for him. I'm sorry, I'm not trying to put words in his mouth, I'm just kind of translating Liam-speak." I smiled at the policewoman, all the while hoping that she wouldn't pick me up in one paw and bite my head off like I was just a tiny lollipop. Muscles I hadn't even realised I'd been tensing all relaxed at the same time when the policewoman laughed heartily.

"It's alright, love, I've got a teenage boy myself. You never get a story in a straight line from him either. It's the testosterone." She reached out and softly patted my shoulder. Immediately I warmed to this woman. In that moment, if I'd been given the choice of having any mum in the whole wide world, *she* would have been it.

I was sure she'd be the type of mum who would look after me like a lioness with her cub. She'd always make sure I had enough to eat, and she would *mutilate* anyone who messed with me.
That's what mums were supposed to be like. I smiled back at her, like some sort of goofy idiot.

"I'm Josie Cloverfield, by the way." I held out a hand to her.
I could feel Liam's eyes on me, and hoped that his mouth wasn't hanging open. At least I stopped myself from saying *please will you be my mum?*

However, I thought it might be prudent to introduce myself since, sooner or later, she was bound to end up at my house. Best get the introductions out of the way now.

"I'm PC Elizabeth Butler, but you can call me Betty." I had never, ever met a policewoman called Betty before.

"And Betty when you call me, you can call me Al." Dale sang from the old Paul Simon song.

Betty rolled her eyes, and smiled at me with the most amazingly straight teeth I'd ever seen in my life. Seriously, they were the sort of teeth that you saw in toothpaste commercials.

"Funny, isn't he?" She laughed. "Well, at least *he* thinks he is." Betty shrugged, and I wanted to curl up in her lap and go to sleep until it was time for her to give me my tea. "So, you don't know where she was going to get this *thing*, Liam?" Betty turned back to Liam.

"No, I didn't even ask actually. Anyway, she said it was, like, a surprise or something. I suppose it might not even have *been* for me." Liam was chewing his bottom lip, thinking hard. "I suppose I just kind of assumed it was."

"And she didn't say if she was meeting a person to collect the thing, or going to a shop for it?" I was in quiet amazement; Betty really *did* speak Liam.

"No, she didn't. I didn't really ask enough questions, but I hadn't realised at the time that she'd be going missing. Not a lot of help, am I?" Liam looked down at the little pile of polystyrene pickings that he'd left on the table.

He seemed to sag a little, and I realised that he was suddenly thinking that this was very real. If Fliss and Amelia had no idea, and Liam had no idea, and Hannah's family had no idea, then where the hell *was* she? Suddenly, the theme tune to the News at Ten began to march a beat through my head, and I felt like the biggest git on the planet.

"Not at all, you've been very helpful Liam. At least we know where she *wasn't*, and that all goes towards helping to find out where she *is*." Dale gave Liam's shoulder a manly punch, and followed it up with a smile of encouragement.

"Yeah, Dale is right. Look, don't go thinking all sorts of terrible things right now. Hannah could have gone off of her own accord. After all, she's a grown woman." Betty began, and it felt really strange to hear someone of my own age been described as a *woman*. I mean, I know that, strictly speaking, it's true, but somehow, I still felt like a little kid. "Was anything getting to her just lately?" Betty changed tack altogether, and I sat up with interest. Betty was a proper copper.

"No, I don't think so. She just seemed like she normally seems, you know?" Liam shrugged a little. "The problem is, I've only been seeing her for about five weeks, so she might not even *tell* me if there was something upsetting her."

"True enough. So, you guys hadn't rowed about anything? She couldn't have stomped off somewhere, trying to frighten the life out of you?"

"To be honest, I don't think we know each other well enough for that sort of thing yet. I dunno, it just seems to me that people don't start arguing about stuff until they're really comfortable with each other and, like, taking each other for granted and whatnot. We weren't really *there* yet, you know? We've been out on a few dates and stuff, and I've even been round to her house, but I'm still on my best behaviour, you know, minding what I say and everything."

"How do you get on with Hannah's family?" Dale chipped in.

"How do *you* think? They weren't exactly thrilled, were they? I mean, I'm at the *same* university, doing the *same* courses, getting *better* grades than Hannah, but I'll never be good enough, you know?" Liam shrugged again, and it hurt me to know that sometimes this stuff *did* get through. I would have to stop assuming that his apparently nonchalant appearance meant that he was impermeable to hurt.

Betty was smiling at us both in a way that made me like her even more. It wasn't a patronising smile, it was a smile that said *I know what you're going through, guys, but you'll get there in the end*. In truth, Betty was my new hero.

Chapter Two

Liam and I got off the bus on the edge of the estate. There was no bus stop in the heart of the Moss Park estate, and where we were dropped off was right over the other side from where we actually lived. Still, we were well used to it. The twenty-minute walk at the end of the bus journey was nothing new to me and Liam.

"It's weird, I keep trying her mobile, expecting her to answer it. But Dude, it's not even *ringing*. It's been switched off since last night."

"Have you ever known Hannah to switch her phone off?" Betty's nifty line of questioning had not only *impressed* me, but it had made its mark.

"No, not in the time I've known her. I mean, I've text her almost in the middle of the night before now and still got a reply. So, I don't suppose she ever really turns it off. Most people don't, do they?"

"No, I don't suppose so. Unless she ran out of battery."

"But where could she be that she doesn't have electricity to charge her phone up with?" Liam looked suddenly horrified.

Ever since Dale and Betty had left us, with a promise to keep us informed if they found anything out, Liam had been a different person. It was clear that he now realised that Hannah really *was* a missing person.

Even for me, a person who, as I've already said, did not like Hannah one little bit, the whole thing felt pretty surreal.

"Don't think like that, Liam. She might have even just left it somewhere, you know?"

"Dude, I know you trying to help, but everything you say is making me feel worse."

"Alright, I'm sorry. I'll stop speaking, Liam." I linked my arm through his, and we walked silently along through the Moss Park estate.

I should have had a better night's sleep than I did. My mum had hardly been around for the last two weeks, mainly because she had a new boyfriend.

She had met Snatcher Harris in the Dalton Arms, and they had seemingly been inseparable ever since. Don't ask me why he's called Snatcher; I really don't want to dwell on it.

At that point, I'd only met him once, and that solitary meeting was enough to have me hoping that it would be the last time I ever set eyes on him. I could tell almost immediately that his addictions ran to a little more than simple booze.

He was a good ten years or so younger than my mum, and when I'd found him sprawled on my couch one day, watching my telly, he barely even spoke. I had just come in from uni, and was looking forward to a nice cup of tea and five minutes of quality late-afternoon viewing on the box.

Mum had been nowhere to be seen, and this greasy heap who looked like he'd accidentally wandered into the wrong house, just smiled at me as if he'd always been there.

The smile had been something I would never forget. In amongst the brown and rotten mess, there was clearly only one good eating tooth. Such a set of gnashers I had never seen in all my life, and hope never to see again. Not for the first time I had wondered why it was that so much of what orbited around me was so very grubby.

Anyway, if Snatcher Harris had one redeeming feature, it was this; my mum spent a lot of her time around his place. It's hard to explain *exactly* what it is I feel for my mum, so I might just leave that one for a bit.

Anyway, after I'd left Liam and gone home, I felt oddly restless. I kept wondering where Hannah might be, and if she really *was* a missing person. I mean, I knew she was *missing*, I just didn't know if she was missing against her will.

The thought of it suddenly whacked me; what on earth must it feel like to be taken away, and realise that nobody knew where you were and who had taken you? I was in the realms of imagining all sorts of awful things and, what was worse, I was putting myself in the shoes of the victim. It freaked me out so much that I set about doing some serious housework.

Restoring order and cleaning up always made me feel like a real, normal person. Since my mum had been out of the way for a couple of weeks, I had actually managed to make the place look quite nice. I had, of course, been here before. I couldn't count the number of times I had made the place look nice, only for mum to return, bringing her special brand of chaos and grubbiness with her.

I spent almost two hours scrubbing shelves and rearranging stuff in the kitchen. By the time I had finished, I was very much in need of a shower. I had managed to put the nutcrackers on my imagination for a little while, but as soon as I stopped the cleaning, the morbid fantasy-land returned. In the end, I gave in and sent Liam a text.

"*How you doing?*" As I waited for a response, I sat perched on the edge of the sofa, almost as if I wasn't in my own home.

"*Not good. I feel sick, Dude.*"

"*Mum is still gone. Do you want come over?*"

"*Normally I'd say yes, but I'm feeling really bad. Just gonna go to bed Dude.*"

My heart sank a little bit at his response. I hated the idea of Liam being at home and feeling so worried. His home life was even noisier than mine at times, and I very much doubted that he would be getting any kind of support from either his three rotten brothers or his careworn mum.

However, I *also* wanted the company, and for that I felt really selfish. I had this weird kind of creepy feeling, and I couldn't really get to the bottom of it. I think it was the idea that whilst I was at home scrubbing shelves, Hannah was out there somewhere, possibly suffering in some way. I know it was a morbid way to think, but I guess that's the way we all go when something like that happens and it's unexplained.

"*Ok Liam. Get a good night's sleep and see you tomorrow. Phone's on, so call if you need.*"

"*Thanks dude. I'll see you in the canteen about half ten.*"

In the end, I decided to go and take a quick shower and head to bed myself.

Once showered, I sat up in the dim lamplight reading *An Introduction to Thermodynamics*. The sheer weight of the book alone was enough to tire you out and make you ready for bed. However, that night, sleep seem to be totally elusive.

What was worse, I wasn't taking in a thing of what I was reading. It was funny, I had managed to study through some of the noisiest parties and most appalling domestics you can imagine.

I barely had any sort of peace for studying, and I had always managed to block out everything. And yet, that night, for the first time ever, I found myself unable to study. In the end, I put down the book, shut off the light, and stared at the patterns which the streetlamps made on the ceiling of my bedroom.

Fortunately, I had gathered myself enough by the next day that thermodynamics was making sense again. I was tired, yes, but I was still firing on all cylinders.

Having been struck by the idea that there was absolutely nothing I could do to help find Hannah Davenport, I had come to the conclusion that to pay attention in my lecture wasn't exactly blasphemy. However, that's not to say that I didn't have niggling doubts.

At the end of the lecture, I wasted no time in gathering up my stuff and speeding away to the canteen. Liam was already there, nursing another polystyrene cup of coffee, and looking like hell.

"I take it there's no news?" I don't know why I said it; I think it was more or less the first thing that sprang into my brain.

"On the contrary, Dude, Hannah's sitting in her art history class, and all is right with the world. What do *you* think?"

"What *I think* is that you shouldn't bite my damn head off for asking a simple question. I'm a human being; I say the wrong things. Get used to it." As I dropped my rucksack down onto the table with a bang, I realised that I was actually pretty tense myself.

"I'm sorry." We both apologised at exactly the same time, and then smiled at each other. Little spats like that were nowhere near being deal breakers in our lifelong friendship. Usually, by the time we got to apologising, any argument we had was already over, and mostly didn't come up again.

"How did *you* manage in art history? I can't imagine it was easy to focus."

"No not really. Especially when people kept turning round to have a little stare at me."

"Stare at you?" Another question I wished I hadn't asked. I already knew what was coming.

"Yeah, seriously. Fliss gave me a couple of looks that could have curdled vinegar, and didn't say a single word to me the whole time. Anyway, the way she went about it got everyone else doing the same sort of thing, you know? It's like she was determined to have everybody think that I've had something to do with Hannah going missing."

"You're kidding."

"No, Dude, I'm not. Honest to God, she made me feel like Rose West or something."

"Maybe *Fred* West?" I smiled at him as I reached out and patted his hand. Liam was thoroughly miserable, and it gave me physical pain to see it.

"Oh, cheers Dude!"

"Without even seeing what happened, Liam, I know what Fliss is up to. Already, she is working out how she can get the most amount of attention out of this. It's not even about Hannah going missing, it's all about Fliss. It's not about a young woman's safety, it's about *poor Fliss*, and how her best friend's sudden disappearance is affecting *her*. Just ignore her."

"A bit hard to ignore her when she's silently turning everyone against me." Liam looked at me, almost helplessly. "Nothing changes, does it Dude? Something goes wrong at school, and the

council estate kids get the blame."

"Don't add that to the list of things to worry about, Liam. Leave all the social inadequacy stuff to me, you know I'm much better at it."

"Thanks Dude. I don't know what I'd do without you." Liam reached out and took my hand.

"I don't know what I do without you either. We're a team, Liam, and we'll work this out together. We always do, right?"

"Oh Christ. Here comes Rich Richard. Well, I wonder what he's got to say for himself." Liam said, miserably.

I looked up and Richard was, indeed, approaching. Richard Allencourt was studying economics, like any good stockbroker's son. He was effortlessly good-looking, in a kind of irritating way and, as much as he always tried to dress down, Rich Richard couldn't help looking well... *rich*.

I was just gearing myself up to tell him to *get lost* when he surprised me by smiling at us. Obviously, he hadn't spoken to Fliss or Amelia that morning, for why else would he be making his way over?

"Hey, Liam, how are you doing?" Richard dropped his bag down onto the table next to mine, and took one of the empty seats.

"Not brilliant, to be honest. But thanks for asking, Richard."

"Do either of you want a tea or coffee?" Richard stood up again, and thrust his hand into his pocket looking for change.

"I'm ok, thanks, I've got this." I tapped my finger gently on my flask.

"I've still got one here, thanks Richard." Liam added.

Since we were sitting so close to the serving counter, Liam and I couldn't even have two minutes' surreptitious conversation about why Richard had come over to us. Instead, we sat in silence and waited for him to return. In the end, I just needed to be upfront.

"Have you spoken to your girlfriend this morning?" I barked. Without even looking at Liam, I could actually feel him wincing. "Yes, I have." Richard looked down for a moment, clearly indicating that he knew what was going on with Fliss. "Look, Fliss is just a drama queen, and she loves the attention. Sooner or later everyone will get bored with her and realise what her motives really are. Anyway, I've pretty much preferred to have lunch and stuff with you guys these last few weeks, rather than be stuck with Fliss, Amelia, and Han….." Richard went scarlet and I felt really sorry for him.

He'd put his foot in it *big-time*, but I'd had some experience of that myself, and I had a certain empathy for him.

"Yeah, I know what you mean. The three of them can get a bit much when they get going." And that was why I loved Liam so much; there was no way he would capitalise on a simple human error.

Almost everyone I'd ever met would have felt duty bound to leap on that one and make the most of it. Liam was just cut from better cloth than everyone else.

"You know what, Liam, I didn't really mean that." Despite the fact that Liam had let him off the hook, Richard seemed determined to apologise nonetheless. Something about that made me actually like him. "I just wasn't thinking. It kind of popped out. I mean, Hannah's your girlfriend, and you must be really worried about her."

"I am, Richard, but that doesn't mean you need to turn yourself inside out worrying about a slip of the tongue. Seriously, I'm just grateful that you're not looking at me as if I was some kind of serial killer. Everybody else here seems to be."

"They won't for long. Look, it will blow over. I'll have a word with Fliss and get her to rein it in a bit."

As I saw two suited men striding towards our table, my belly did the sort of flip which told me that this was *not* about to blow over. If the two guys coming towards us weren't plain clothed police officers, then I was a belly dancer.

"Liam Attwood?" The taller of the two said, whilst they both flashed their warrant cards.

Liam, who had been about to take a sip of his coffee, almost dropped his cup. My heart was thundering like the hooves of twenty charging horses, and I felt sick.

I just knew what was coming. Their whole demeanour just screamed *you're coming with us, son*.

"Yes?" I could tell by the look on Liam's face that he was thinking exactly the same thing.

My hands were shaking so badly that they felt like they belonged to somebody else.

"You're going to need to come with us." The taller officer raised his eyebrows, as if to say *up you get*.

Despite numerous encounters with law enforcement, neither Liam nor I had the wherewithal to ask if he was actually under arrest for a crime.

"Oh, ok. I'll just get my stuff together." Liam looked at me desperately, and I'm ashamed to say that my eyes had filled with tears.

I would have given anything for him not to have seen that; I felt as though I was sending him off to the gallows.

Liam got to his feet, put his jacket and woolly hat on and picked up his rucksack.

"I'll call you when I get out." Liam said quietly, his face flaming red and his eyes showing the purest shock.

Despite being one of the infamous Attwoods of the Moss Park estate, Liam had never been taken into a police station in his life, and it showed.

"As *soon* as you get out." I replied, not even acknowledging the CID officers.

I couldn't even look at Rich Richard; all I could do was watch helplessly as my best friend in all the world was led away from me.

The way they did it was totally unnecessary. Liam was flanked on either side by the burly officers, making it very much look like they had him covered if he decided to make the big guilty *break for it*.

For a few moments, I was left wondering why it was that some people went through their whole lives trying to prove themselves. I mean, it was clear that Liam wasn't under arrest. Looking at the two goons who came to collect him, I'd say that if he *was* under arrest, they'd have made a big deal out of hand-cuffing him.

So, just to make themselves feel like *real* men, they had behaved in a way which might very well ruin a young man's university career, and therefore his life. I was so unutterably tired of people using the lives of others to prop up their own damned egos that something inside me snapped.

It wasn't like a big, noisy snap. No, it was a little internal one. It was a *quiet* snap, but it was profound. I wasn't going to sit around helplessly waiting for the Grantstone Constabulary and Fliss Hardcastle to ruin the life of one of the best humans on this crappy planet.

I'd find that damned Hannah Davenport if it was the last thing I did. I'd lie, cheat and break all the rules if I had to, because I realised at that point that the rules are only in place for the people who meekly keep them. People like me and Liam. Well, not anymore.

"Uh, Josie?" Richard's voice was tentative, as was his little pat on my forearm.

If he hadn't been uncommonly nice for a man who was dating Fliss Hardcastle, I would have swatted his hand away and loudly told him to *go to hell*. As it was, I just looked at him impassively.

"Josie, look, he's obviously not under arrest. But the way the police just handled that was appalling. They could have made it a *lot* less public." To realise that Richard was appalled, rather than entertained as the rest of the canteen seemed to be, made me feel better disposed towards him.

"Thanks Richard." I smiled as best I could.

"Look, if there's anything I can do….." Richard tore a scrap of paper off his notebook and scrawled down not only his mobile number, but his home number too.

I took it gratefully, although I could not begin to imagine how Rich Richard could help me now. Still, it was an *offer*, and one which I decided to stow away for future use.

"Thanks Richard. I appreciate that." I could feel the eyes of the whole canteen on me.

There I was, the girl who consorted with the crazed killer. I felt like Myra Hindley, minus the shocking hair-do. Every cell of my body was trying to force my head down and cast my eyes away from the crowd.

However, I had been doing that my whole damned life and I wasn't going to do it anymore. I had *snapped*, remember? The rules had changed now. As I defiantly stared around the room, making eye contact wherever I could, I noticed that it was the crowd, and not me, who were forced to look down.

Well, there was a turn up for the books. I was making people feel uncomfortable, instead of it being the other way around, for once. I rather enjoyed it. Anyway, as I looked about me with the cool, calculating stare of my new and somewhat peculiar persona, I spied PC Betty Butler through the window, striding along with purpose in the direction of the Arts Faculty. I rose and hurriedly stuffed my flask into my rucksack before launching myself into my duffle coat.

"Richard, I've got to go." I said, as I was preparing to make a dash for it.

"No problem, Josie. Just text me or something and let me know how you're doing, ok?"

"Will do." I called out over my shoulder as I dashed out of the canteen.

No doubt the crowd had thought I was suddenly overcome with embarrassment and had run away. Well, I didn't have time to worry about the development of my strident new personality at that moment, and instead cantered out of the room with all the grace of a pantomime horse.

Chapter Three

Once I hit the cold January air, the old Josie seemed to return. Well, not entirely; I was still going to make the whole disappearance of Hannah my personal business, but I was probably going to do it as the *real me*.

I ran around the outside of the canteen building in the hopes of seeing the disappearing rear of my hero as she made her way to the Art Faculty, but was disappointed. For a few seconds, I stood undecided, looking about me. I could head in the direction of the Art Faculty, but Betty could be anywhere by now.

As I was casting about somewhat helplessly, I spotted Betty's police car some distance away in the car park. I decided I would go and see if Dale Webb was in it and, if not, I would wait by the car until Betty came back. I had to start somewhere. If anyone would help me, it would be Betty and Dale.

So, still in the style of the pantomime horse, *I've never been a keen athlete*, I set off once more. My rucksack was bouncing against my shoulder blades, and I was seriously hoping I had screwed the flask top back on properly.

Breathless and strangely sweaty for a winter's day, I arrived at the car. As I almost fell against it, I could see the somewhat startled expression of PC Dale Webb, who was perched in the driver's seat. He scrambled out and looked at me, his concern really obvious.

"Oh, Josie." As he came towards me, I knew that he was very well aware that Liam had been taken away.

So, with my new resolve still burning bright within my soul...... I burst into big, *wailing* sobs. Yep, I was *definitely* going to do this thing as the real Josie Cloverfield.

"I know, I know." Dale soothed, as if speaking to a sobbing child.

He scooped me into his arms and didn't seem at all bothered that my hefty, handkerchief-less crying was leaving a trail of destruction all down the front of his police body armour. Instead, he just let me lean there and hugged me tightly.

In the five or six years that Dale Webb had attended horrible incidents in my home, not once had I cried. Although my life had contained a certain amount of horror, it had been a familiar and predicable horror.

This, on the other hand, this *snatching* away of an innocent man who also happened to be about the only person in the world I cared about, *this* horror was brand new. Brand new, and shocking.

"Josie, he's not under arrest. Come on, sit yourself down in here." Dale released me and opened the passenger door of the police car.

He sped around to the driver's side and got back in. As we sat there, I could just hear snippets of radio traffic. The radio was turned down so low that it was mostly just an unobtrusive auditory backdrop.

However, there was one dispatcher whose nasally whine could more or less be made out. She started every sentence with the word *yeah*.

"Yeah, all patrols, I need a code one response to the Dalton Arms. Disturbance in progress."

The whole thing was oddly comforting.

Dale reached under his seat and came out with a family-size box of tissues. They were the sort of tissues I bought, you know the ones; so rough you could actually rub gloss paint off door frames with them.

"Thank you." I sniffed, as I took a huge handful of the tissues and prayed my skin would survive the ordeal. "I know he's not under arrest, but the way they did it! Those officers frog-marched him out of the canteen, and now everyone thinks he's a psycho!" I was still furious about it, and I could feel my teeth kind of gnash together as I pictured it again.

"Yeah, all patrols, I need a code one response to Hackett's Audio-Visual. Theft in progress."

"I'm so sorry about that. Those CID blokes can get a bit, well….you know, they think they're *big-city-jacks*, like something off the telly. But listen Josie; we both know that Liam hasn't done a thing and the truth of that will come out. It's a rotten time for you both, but it will pass, I promise."

"Honestly, Dale, I feel so sorry for Hannah and I can't imagine how awful it is to be missing and no-one know where you are. But I really wish Liam had never met her. I can't help feeling this horrible thing inside where I'm blaming her for what's happening to Liam. I know that makes me sound like a crap person. I don't want anything to happen to her but, to be honest, I can't pretend to have ever liked her. I wish he'd never set eyes on her." I set off crying again.

"Yeah, I know." Dale laughed, and I remembered that I had given him chapter and verse on how I felt about Hannah already.

It had been a few weeks before. My mum had been caught on CCTV in the local Euro-Saver stealing bacon, and Dale had volunteered to come and pick her up. Whilst two other officers shoe-horned my screaming banshee of a parent into the back of a transit van, Dale had shot upstairs to my room to see if I was alright.

"You ok, lady?" Dale had popped his head around the door and grinned. He knew by then that my mum being locked up for stealing would barely ruin my night, never mind ruin my life.

"Yeah. Same old same old." I'd shrugged. "You know, why *bacon,* Dale? Seriously. I mean, I'm not actually trying to *condone* shop-lifting to an officer of the law, but if a person's going to risk getting locked up for stealing, why not do it properly? I mean, why steal a quid's worth of bacon from a crappy little convenience store? Why not get yourself down to Marks and Spencer's and steal something worth stealing? Like some really expensive anti-wrinkle cream or something. I mean, the offence is the same, and the penalty is the same, right?" I chewed the end of my pencil somewhat ponderously.

"You mean that you might as well be hung for a jar of antiwrinkle cream as be hung for a packet of bacon?" Dale's shoulders began to heave as the roar of laughter made its way up.

"Yeah! Precisely my point!"

"Josie, I think you might just be too rational for your own good!" Dale wandered into the room and perched on the end of my bed. After five years, he'd got the hang of the *no-legs* thing, and took it cautiously. "Anyway, how's life?"

"Crap, Dale. Liam has started seeing an annoying *well-to-do* girl at uni, and she's taking over my world."

"Oh, really? You're not *jealous,* are you?" Dale winked.

"No, I'm not. You know me and Liam are just friends. But he's my *best* friend, and I get the horrible feeling that *Miss Snotty* will be edging me out of his life at the earliest opportunity." I'd looked down sadly.

"Look, just because she's got a few quid, doesn't make her bad."

"I suppose not. But she doesn't like me, I can tell."

"But you don't like her either."

"No, I don't, to be honest."

"Look, Liam is a smart lad. If this….what's her name?" "Hannah Davenport!" I spat the words out, and Dale laughed again.

"If this *Hannah Davenport* tries to push you out of Liam's world, he won't put up with it."

"But Liam seems so impressed by her. And I don't trust her."

"You don't have to trust *her*, Josie. You have to trust Liam. Believe me, he will put your friendship first if it comes to the crunch."

"I wish I could believe that." I knew I was overdoing it.

In my heart of hearts, I knew Liam would always be my friend, I just didn't want to accept change. I wanted to resist it all the way.

Dale waved the box of tissues at me, gesturing for me to take another handful and successfully dragging me out of memory lane.

"Yeah, Control to Alpha-X-ray Four-Three, there's a Mrs Sneddon at the enquiry desk to see you regarding a statement." "Look, don't beat yourself up about this. It's pretty natural for you to think like that. After all, if Liam really *had* never met Hannah, then this wouldn't be happening. I mean, she'd still be missing, but Liam wouldn't be at the police station over it all. So, you're *not* a rotten person, Josie. You're just human."

"Thanks Dale." My tears had more or less dried and I was calming down. "Do they think Liam did something to her?" I was ready to ask questions.

"I doubt it. He's just *the boyfriend*, you know? They always bring in the people closest to the missing person."

"But Dale, he wasn't *that* close to her. They've been seeing each other for five weeks. That's, like*, thirty-five days*. He doesn't even know if she drinks or anything. God, he's such a buffoon; I'm totally freaking about how he will come across in the police station. I mean, Liam's bright. Like, really, *really* bright. But it's not *my* kind of brains. It's not rational or even vaguely linear. It's arty intelligence. It's really right-brain. He can paint such amazing things and he's read everything under the sun, but he still comes across like kind of a ding-bat, you know?"

"Jose, I know that the CID guys didn't come off too well, but there are some good guys in the police, you know. There are even some right-brainers in there. Liam will be just fine, you'll see."

"But he might be interviewed by *those* two. There's no way they will be open-minded. They just want a lock-up, I could see it in them. You forget, I've made a pretty good study of cops over the last nineteen years. I've probably seen more than you have!" I tried to laugh.

Just as Dale was about to respond, his mobile phone trilled loudly. He took it out of the top pocket of his body armour and squinted at the caller ID.

"I have to take this. Unrelated case, though, Josie. Look, wait here, ok?"

"Sure."

As Dale sauntered away from the car, I heard his voice disappearing to nothing. I took the opportunity to give my nose a genuinely fulsome blow. You know, the kind of nose-blowing you just can't do with another person present.

"Yeah, Control to Alpha-X-Ray Five-Five. DI Thorn is requesting that you meet him as soon as you're clear. He needs a team for the search at the Davenport address."

Suddenly, I was on high alert. The Davenport address? Surely the dispatcher was talking about Hannah's home? Casting the briefest of guilty looks at the retreating back of PC Dale Webb, I reached out and turned up the volume.

"Alpha-X-Ray Five-Five to Control. Received that. Can you pass the address please?"

There was a moment's pause before Miss Nasal came back on.

"Yeah, it's 355 Westmorland Drive, Grantstone."

"Received. ETA twenty minutes."

Hastily, I pulled my notebook and a pen out of my rucksack and scrawled the address down. Seeing Dale slot his phone back into his pocket and slowly make his way back, I thrust the notebook back into my bag and turned the radio down again.

"Sorry about that." Dale concertinaed his mighty frame back into the police car.

"No problem." I smiled, wondering how quickly I could get away.

I didn't know what I'd achieve by going over there, but I just had to do *something*. Obviously, I wasn't going to, like, present myself at the front door. I planned to find a place to watch from.

As futile as that seemed, if I was going to get to the bottom of this and help Liam, I wasn't going to pass up any leads at all.

Leads! Like I was a real detective or something.

"Thanks for listening to me blub and stuff, Dale." I was gearing up for a hasty *anyway, thanks and see ya later*.

"No problem Josie. Look, if you need anything, just call me ok? Here's my own mobile number." Not for the first time that day, a man had scrawled his phone number on a piece of paper for me. Wow, on any other day, a minor miracle. "I'm not supposed to, so don't mention it to Betty or anything. Just call if you need, ok?"

"Thanks Dale. I really appreciate it." I took the scrap of paper and suddenly felt a twitch of guilt at the way I'd taken advantage when Dale's back was turned.

Still, as I said before, rules are only there for the people who intend to keep them. I got out of the police car and turned back to give him a watery smile, all the while itching to get away.

"Take care, Josie."

The area around Westmorland Drive was not a part of Grantstone that I knew particularly well. I had needed to use the GPS maps on my phone to get there, almost wiping myself out on a lamppost that I was *this close* to walking into. Totally *suave* detective, right?

Anyway, I arrived long after good old *Alpha-X-Ray Five-Five* had been due to get there, but I'm guessing he didn't have to take two busses. As I wandered down Westmorland Drive in what I hoped was a nonchalant manner, I stared over at the front of Hannah's house and tried to take in as much as I could.

There was a large police van and two police cars outside, and I wondered how many coppers it took to search a house. I also wondered what they could be searching for. I mean, it wasn't like Hannah was ripped out of her bed and spirited away out of an open window. What on earth could they be looking for?

I tried to think of the numerous police dramas I had watched over the years. Usually, when someone was murdered or missing, the TV cops asked the forlorn parents if they could look around the victim's room for clues.

Maybe they would take her laptop, thinking she had met someone online? Or maybe they were looking for something incriminating that Liam had left there? Maybe his detachable horns and cloven hooves?

Anyway, I had more or less decided that they weren't looking for forensic type clues, but maybe lifestyle ones. So, I had my *first piece* of information, but absolutely no idea where that would take me.

Fighting the awful feeling that I was being ridiculous and had no chance of making a difference, I looked about for a vantage point from which to watch the goings-on. The problem was that most of the neighbours were peering out from behind blinds and lacy net curtains, so I would, sooner or later, stand out.

The police officers might even come out to move me on, thinking I was a reporter or something. Well, it wouldn't have done to be found there, what with my new-found Myra Hindley status and all.

I carried on up the street at a fair old clip, wondering what I should do next. I kept going until I reached a crossroads and looked left to see if there might be a way of getting around the back.

I could have dropped to my knees and kissed the ground in gratitude. Seeing the long line of rangy, leafless trees, I realised that Hannah's house must back on to the canal footpath. I totally realise that this makes my GPS map reading skills look poor, but I was exceptionally stressed at the time, *ok?*

Anyway, I picked up the pace and had landed on the old canal tow-path in under a minute. I began to head back down in the direction of Hannah's house with a rather inappropriate frisson of excitement.

The canal bank was strewn with the sort of low, spikey foliage that refuses to die back, even on a cold January day. Still, the path was well beaten and easy to walk down. No doubt it was a favourite with the local dog walkers, so I made a mental note to mind where I put my second-hand Converse.

I was able to amble along and look about me without the same sense of standing out like a sore thumb that I'd felt in the street. I tried to work out which of the houses would be Hannah's, but could only narrow it down to four possibles.

Every so often, I looked up and down the canal to make sure I was alone there. The path on the other canal bank was as mercifully deserted as the one I was on.

The fencing which ran along the back of the houses was only about five feet tall, so I could have peered over if I'd wanted. However, I didn't want my disembodied head being seen to skate along the top of the fence by anyone inside.

In all honesty, I could see *less* from the back of Hannah's house than I had seen at the front, and could feel that disheartening dullness return to my chest.

Just as I had been about to hang up my imaginary PI badge, something in the foliage caught my eye. It was in the area of the four possible houses, and I hurried over to it. Again, I looked up and down the canal. Still alone, I crouched down and peered at what turned out to be a small book. Not a reading book, but a journal-come-diary type of thing. It was bound in a sort of shabby-chic floral design and practically *screamed* young woman's diary.

I'll be honest, my heart rate doubled, if not tripled. Could it be a clue? I felt like Columbo or Magnum PI or something, just for a moment. Of course, if it wasn't for the daytime TV *flog-em-tillthey're-dead* channels, I wouldn't have a clue who these people were. Still, that's what I felt like just then, so there it is.

Anyway, as I leaned in close, I could see that the book was wedged into the spikey tendrils of the shrub, like it had landed hard and gone deep. Once I had stared for long enough, I realised that I could learn no more without actually *touching it*.

So, it's fair to say that I had reached some kind of pivotal moment. Firstly, if I took this book away, assuming it *was* Hannah's, then I would be removing vital evidence which might help to find Hannah. Secondly, I could get into absolutely *massive* trouble for it.

As I crouched there on the canal tow-path in an agony of indecision, I suddenly pictured the look on Liam's face as he'd been marched out of the university canteen by two of the most careless oafs on God's green earth.

In a heartbeat, I'd dug my woollen mittens out of my rucksack, aiming for *forensically aware*. I thrust my hands into them, and picked the book out of the thorny foliage before stowing it away in my bag. Without looking to see if it was even Hannah's, I quickly looked around me, then stood up and set off at speed.

My heart was hammering wildly. It wasn't too late to simply turn back and fling the book back into the undergrowth, and yet I couldn't. As I tore along the canal bank, I justified my actions like this; *one*, Liam had been treated like dirt, and *two*, if I found anything helpful in it, I would call the police and tell them I had innocently found the book on the canal path when I was out for a walk. Simple. *Unbelievable*, but simple.

As soon as I got back on the bus, I decided to head for the university campus. I still didn't know if the diary was Hannah's; I was too scared to even open my rucksack in front of witnesses. Anyway, if the diary *was* Hannah's, then I needed a plan. I knew I would have to either return it to where I had found it, or hand it in to the police.

Whatever method I chose, I didn't have long. Instead of hurriedly trying to read through the diary, I decided I would photocopy it in the university reprographics suite, *ridiculously posh name for photocopying room*, then I would have a backup copy to read at my leisure.

Time was rolling on. My adventures had taken me into the late afternoon, and activity on the campus was dying down. I was overjoyed to find that there was nobody in reprographics when I got there. No doubt the rest of the Grantstone students had better things to do late on a Tuesday afternoon!

It took me a long time to photocopy the whole thing from end to end, and I'd had to put an extra three pounds on my photocopy card, which ordinarily would have made me hyperventilate.

More than once I was tempted to scan through the book and see if there was anything attributable to Hannah. However, time was of the essence and my nerves were jangling like windchimes. I just got on with it, turning the pages, closing the lid, pressing the green copy button. *Repeat until fade*.

By the time I got home, it was after eight o'clock and I was exhausted. I wanted to look through the diary desperately, but knew I wouldn't take anything in until I'd eaten something and had a little rest.

Pleased that there was still no sign of my mum or Snatcher Harris anywhere, I shot upstairs and began to run a bath. Whilst the water was running, I took my rucksack into my room and emptied out the little diary and the chunky copy I had made. I stowed the photocopy in my desk drawer and laid the diary on top of the desk.

I didn't want it to come into too much contact with my own things, although I knew deep down there must be some traces of me on it somewhere. I felt a little bit nauseous as the realisation dawned that I would probably have to actually *take* the book into the police, rather than leave it where I had found it.

If there was any tiny trace of me on it, I could never find a way to explain. Still, I would worry about that when I had eaten and rested. My head was too mashed for any more thoughts.

With the bath run, I shot back downstairs to boil the kettle and make myself a tasty and nutritious pot of Euro-Saver instant noodles to eat in the bath. *Yummy.*

I laid in the bath until after ten o'clock. The water was almost cold by the time I rose up out of it like a big, wrinkled raisin.

Once I was dried and pyjama clad, I let my hair dry naturally. I decided I would go downstairs and make myself a cup of tea, then drink it in bed whilst I read through the photocopied book.

As I began to make my way out of the room, my eyes flew to my desk. It was empty. The little diary had gone. My heart suddenly began to thump. I looked on the floor all around the desk, hoping that it had somehow just fallen. Still, I knew that just *wasn't* possible; I had left the diary on the middle of the desk.

It would have had to come to life and leap off the desk of its own accord. Pointlessly, I turned and turned again, looking all around my room for any sign of it. I knew it was ridiculous.

As my hands began to sweat, I reached for the desk drawer, praying that the photocopied version was still inside. It was. So, I was left wondering where the hell the diary had gone. I was exhausted, and I was having a bit of trouble thinking in a straight line. Then there came a noise from downstairs.

It sounded like a tread on the creaky bottom step. My heart nearly stopped there and then. Was someone going down, or was someone coming up? Suddenly all fatigue fell away, and I was as sharp and aware as a frightened meerkat. I strained to listen for any further sounds over the ragged whistle of my own breathing.

After several seconds of vigilant listening, not another sound came. It was, quite literally, silent. And yet, I had the awful, creeping sensation that I was not alone in the house. Suddenly I thought of my mum and nearly laughed out loud at my own stupidity.

She'd probably just come back from Snatcher's place. It would not be unlike her to take something from my room, even a diary. I thought there might be a very good chance she was downstairs right then reading through the book in a fog of confusion. And yet….I had never known my mum to do anything quietly.

If she *had* walked back into the house, the television would already be blaring, she would be shouting up the stairs to me and there would be all sorts of other disruption going on all around her. I knew it couldn't be her. I felt suddenly so scared that I was rooted to the spot.

If it wasn't my mum, then who was it? If someone had broken in, why just take the diary, unless…..? I couldn't even finish that thought. Surely it was a huge, overly imaginative leap to think that the person who may well have taken Hannah against her will was *actually* in my house.

I felt sick and sweaty. I wanted to call the police, but what would I say? *I think Hannah's kidnapper came into my house and stole the diary I pinched from under the very noses of the Grantstone Constabulary!* Perhaps I could just say there was an intruder? But it all felt too complicated.

It wasn't a big policing area and whoever turned up would no doubt realise my connection to Liam. Maybe I would make things even worse for him somehow?

I wondered where Liam was. I silently pulled my phone out of my rucksack and checked for messages. There was nothing there, so I had to assume he was still at the police station. Nonetheless, I sent him a hastily typed text.

"Liam, are you out yet? Can you come to mine?"

I knelt on the floor clutching the phone as I waited for a response. I turned the phone on to silent, just in case a noisy beep would alert the intruder to my presence. But, of course, the intruder, if indeed there had been one, would have known I was here. I had been sploshing about in the bath and there were lights on throughout the upstairs.

After five minutes of silent kneeling, I got no response from Liam. I thought about Dale Webb, but if I called his mobile, he would probably call the job in to the police station and I would be back at the start of my internal debate.

Then I remembered Rich Richard, before realising that he probably lived miles away. Anyhow, a smart young lad wandering about on the Moss Park estate was likely to be spotted with the same keenness employed by sharks scenting blood. He would be easy meat in my world.

In the end, I decided I would act for myself. Feeling suddenly more alone than I had ever done in my life, I looked about for a weapon. Finding only the hefty *An Introduction to Thermodynamics*, I picked it up. It would have to do. I then dialled 999 on my phone, but didn't press the call button. I planned to creep downstairs and, if I found someone there, I would *quite literally* throw the book at him, then press the call button on my phone and start yelling for help.

As I silently crept down the stairs, the book sliding about in my sweaty hand and my thumb hovering over the call button on my phone, I though *what would Betty do?* One thing was for sure, Betty wouldn't be shaking like a leaf. Betty would have just charged down the stairs and rugby-tackled the intruder to the floor. Ok, maybe I wasn't ready for the big leagues just then. I would have to work at trying to be Betty another day.

Once I reached the bottom of the stairs, I stopped to listen. Nothing. I crept through the kitchen and into the living room.

Again, nothing. I forced myself to silently tip-toe to the sofa and peep along the space at the back where it leaned against the wall. Ok, the intruder would have needed to be pretty skinny, but I wanted to be really, *really* sure.

Once I had checked behind the long door curtain which hung in the tiny entrance porch, I felt more comfortable. Instead of proceeding by the dim light provided by the streetlamps, I finally started to switch lights on everywhere.

Putting *An Introduction to Thermodynamics* down, I kept hold of the phone, and began to open every cupboard in the house, even tiny kitchen cupboards, as if my intruder was one of the Borrowers.

Once I was certain I was alone in the house, I started to look for how this person had got in. I was able to think again and knew, *really knew*, that there *must* have been an intruder whilst I was in the bath, and it had been *that* intruder who had taken the diary.

The very fact that I had heard them on the creaky bottom step, *presumably leaving*, meant that they must surely have been upstairs with me when I had gone into my bedroom and discovered the diary gone. I reasoned that, whoever it was, had heard me getting ready to come out of the bathroom and had maybe ducked into my mum's bedroom out of the way. If I had come out of the bathroom any sooner, I would probably have found them in my room. We'd have come face to face.

That realisation hit me like a brick, and I found I was suddenly so shocked that I could hardly breath. I started to take in huge breaths, each of which ripped at my dry throat and made awful shrieking noises. In the end, my head felt full and numb all at once, and I could feel my eyesight dimming. Quickly, I dropped purposefully to my knees. There was just no way I was going to faint. No way!

After about five minutes of this, I began to return to normal. Well, *physically* normal anyway. I very much doubted my troubled mind would ever be the same again.

Once I was back on my feet, I checked the front door. It was locked tight, just the way I had left it when I came in from uni hours earlier. The back door in the kitchen was a different story. Whilst it was firmly closed, it was *not* locked.

I quickly found the key on the kitchen counter and locked myself in. I hadn't used that door for weeks. Had me or my mum left it unlocked? Mum tended to use the back door and, being rarely sober, she didn't always lock it. Had I been in the house alone for nearly two weeks with a totally unlocked back door? My brain was aching as it whirled with a full-house of possibilities.

In the end, I made myself a cup of tea. I propped chairs in front of both doors, not realistically to keep someone out, but so that the clatter as they fell would provide me with some kind of early warning system. If whoever it was came back, then I would be calling for the police immediately and to hell with the explanations.

As I climbed into bed with my tea, I noted that it was half past eleven. I had spent almost an hour and a half on red-alert. My body ached and my head throbbed, yet I knew I would get no sleep. I thought about reading through the photocopy, but my poor shredded nerves just couldn't stand it.

That would be a daylight-hours job, and one which I would do in the university library the next day, in the complete privacy of one of the single booths in the silent study area.

In the end I did, amazingly, manage to get some sleep. I woke up at seven and plodded about my room, trying to get the events of the previous evening straight in my tired brain. Despite the two-hour bath, I had done so much sweating and shaking in the hours which followed that I thought a shower would put me to rights. If nothing else, it would sharpen me up a bit.

I laid out my clothes on my bed and headed to the bathroom.

I stood under the shower for twenty minutes, partly to wake me up and partly because it just trickles out and it takes that long to get a proper soaking.

When I finally emerged, the room was full of steam. I opened the bathroom window onto the cold January morning and hoped I wouldn't get pneumonia. Seriously, a lack of sleep always makes me negative and fatalistic.

As the steam began to clear, I was finally able to see again, and deemed it safe to close the window. On my way out of the bathroom, I caught sight of the mirrored front of the elderly wall cabinet. Once again, I was almost floored by fear.

As the steam in the bathroom had condensed on the mirror, the words *"I'm Watching You"* appeared with horrible clarity.

Chapter Four

By the time I'd made it onto the first bus I was pretty much a gibbering wreck. *I'm Watching You…..* It was like something from a horror movie. As sayings go, it's right up there with *You're Next…*

I'd cantered out of the house as soon as I was dressed and had stuffed the photocopy into my rucksack. No flask, no sandwiches, no Euro-Saver crisps; I would have to buy or starve, simple as that.

Once I'd got off bus number two outside the university, I felt safe. There was just something about the campus that felt like home. Real home. What a great shame they wouldn't let me have a bed there.

Anyway, I went straight into the canteen and bought, *yes bought*, a cup of tea and some toast. It was only just nine o'clock, and I was their first customer of the day. The lady on the till looked me up and down with a certain amount of curiosity. She recognised me, of course, as *that* girl who always sat so close to the counter but never actually bought anything. You know the one, *her with the flask…*

I tore through the toast in no time at all; fear had really given me an appetite. As my tea was cooling down to red-hot-magma levels – you've got to love polystyrene – I decided to call Dale Webb and find out what the hell Grantstone Constabulary had done with my best friend. I'm pretty sure that people don't *help police with their enquiries* overnight.

"Hello."

"Dale, sorry to bother you, It's Josie."

"Hi Josie. You Ok?"

"Yes, I'm good thanks." *Apart from a thieving intruder leaving threatening messages on my bathroom mirror, everything's tickety-boo.*

"How's Liam doing?"

"That's what I was going to ask you. When are they going to let him out?"

"They already did, Josie. He left the nick about tea-time yesterday."

"Are you sure?"

"Uh, yeah Josie."

"Thanks Dale."

"Look, don't be too hard on him. I'm guessing he was maybe not in the mood to talk last night. He looked kind of knackered when I saw him."

"Ok, I'll be gentle. Look, thanks for that and sorry to have bothered you."

"Anytime Josie, I told you. And you're not bothering me."

"Thanks Dale. See you later."

"See you Josie."

I risked a swig of tea and found the temperature to be almost bearable. So, Liam had been released about the same time as I was photocopying the little book. And Dale had said he looked exhausted, so I guessed he must have been asleep when I'd sent him my SOS message, live from the scene of the unfolding drama at my place.

It was no use. However much I tried to be Miss Magnanimity, I found myself falling flat. I couldn't help but feel just a little bit hurt. I mean, I know I hadn't put *come quick, there's an intruder and I think he's gonna kill me*, but still my text had a certain air of urgency about it.

Not to mention the fact that I'd asked him to call me as soon as he got out. Don't get me wrong, Liam's a free man and he can wander about at will without checking in with me, but on *this* occasion, I'd been *seriously* worried about him. Not only that, but I'd taken liberties with a police radio, snooped around at a police search, and stole what very well might turn out to be evidence.

All in all, I thought my hurt little feelings had every right to be parading about somewhere between my solar plexus and chest cavity. At that moment, my mobile rang.

"Morning Dude." Liam's sleepy voice was unmistakable.

"Oh, good morning. How's the breakfast in police custody this morning?"

"The sausage is kind of rubbery but the scrambled eggs are better than I get at home."

"Uh-huh."

"I'm sorry Dude. I got home last night and just laid down on my bed for five minutes. Anyway, next thing I knew it was, well, *now*. I'm still in yesterday's clothes."

"Oh, you crusty git."

"I just saw your text. What's so important?"

"I don't know where to start. I've got loads to tell you. What time are you coming in?"

"Coming in where?"

"Uni, you plumb."

"Oh, Dude. There's no way. I just can't face all that crap, I had enough *insinuation* to last me a lifetime yesterday in the police station."

"Liam, you've got every right to be here."

"But I'm not up to the fight today, Josie. I had a really bad day yesterday."

"Ok, I'm sorry my friend. Look, somebody broke into my house last night and stole something I, well, *nicked* from outside Hannah's place."

"What? What did you nick?"

"I found a notebook, well, a diary, on the canal path at the back of Hannah's. It looked like it had been tossed there. Anyway, I took off with it and last night someone broke in and took it while I was in the bath."

"Jesus! Are you alright Dude?"

"Not exactly. They left me a threatening message on the bathroom mirror."

"Whoa!"

"Liam, don't sound *impressed*, you fool. I was scared witless."

"Sorry Dude, lost myself there a bit. I'm back now. What was the message?"

"I'm watching you."

"Whoa…. Sorry. Look, where are you?"

"I'm in the canteen. I'm heading to the library."

"Well, come around to mine when you're finished. You can stay if you want, like, if you're too scared to go home and stuff."

"Thanks Liam."

"Are you alright, Dude?"

"Yeah, I'm fine."

"I'm going to go back to sleep for a bit. Just come around when you're done, Ok? And keep your eyes open. Well, you know, just be careful Dude."

"Yeah, Ok. I'll see you later."

"See you later."

As I hung up, I realised that I hadn't told Liam about the photocopy. I had been about to call him back when I thought better of it. Liam really had sounded rough, and I could certainly look through the papers on my own.

My hurt little feelings had climbed back into their box and I was ready for a bit of detective work. *Betty* wouldn't let oversensitive feelings stand in her way, and neither would I.

So, I hurriedly finished my tea, resisting the urge to eat the polystyrene cup just to get my money's worth, and set off for the library.

I'd established myself in one of the single booths at the very far end of the silent study area. For the most part, the silent study area tended to be sparsely populated; only people like me who were far too serious to talk ever used them.

Most of the other students preferred to be in a part of the library where all that was required were hushed tones. Not *my* end of the library where even noisy breathing was punishable by death.

I was pleased to find that there was only me and one other in the silent study area, and the other person was at the opposite end, on the cusp of being allowed to talk. So, I more or less had the place to myself.

I don't really know why I was so keen to hide away. It's not like I would look out of place studying papers in a university library, after all. Still, the feeling of my own *wrongness* was still with me, and I wanted to stay way below the radar.

I took the great wad of paper out of my rucksack, along with my own notepad, in case there was anything worth scribbling down. As soon as I looked closely at the first page, I knew it was Hannah's.

The handwriting was pretty unique. It was chubby and arty, and looked so neat that you could be fooled into thinking you could read it with ease. That was actually *not* the case. It was *so* arty that it kind of took a bit of work. On that first page was written the same thing over and over, which kind of creeped me out a bit. The word *Rebellion* was everywhere, in all different sizes and styles.

The larger ones were written in a kind of elaborate 3D, and filled in with hand-drawn stripes and dots. It was a genuine worddoodle, and I wondered if the whole Rebellion thing was something to do with an art project.

As I moved to the next sheet, I realised that nothing was dated. It was a diary notebook rather than a traditional diary. I resisted the urge to skip ahead to see if Hannah had actually dated anything herself later on in the book; I wanted to be as methodical as possible. If I skipped ahead, I'd no doubt get side-tracked reading another bit, then I could easily miss something. See, *real* detective work.

Page two looked like a shopping list of art supplies. There were brushes and paints, pads and what-not. Then there was a list of art history text books. I chewed my pencil for a bit; this looked like the list I had made of things I would need before starting university. I mean, obviously not the *same* stuff, but text books and sundries. So, the diary must have been started before Hannah even arrived at Grantstone University.

The next few pages were more helpful; there were going-out plans with names and dates. *Fliss and Amelia cinema 4th Aug. Fliss clothes shopping 9th Aug.* All pretty standard stuff. *Fliss and Amelia at spa 12th Aug (Richie).*

Not quite sure about that one. Did Hannah go with Fliss and Amelia to the spa? Or was that just when *they* were going? And where did Richard fit in? Assuming that's who *Richie* was. All in all, I couldn't see how this stuff was helping me in my quest.

It went on in this vein for many pages. Family birthdays, meals out, aerobics classes; I was starting to wonder if this book was such a gem of a find after all.

I looked at my watch. Already it was nearly eleven o'clock, and I had a fluid mechanics lecture at one. I really didn't want to miss it, even though I had my new-found responsibility of finding Hannah.

If I started missing lectures, well, put it this way, the stuff I was studying wasn't so easy to catch up on, and I dreaded to think what would happen if I began to get behind. I know that's geeky, but there it is.

If Liam was going to start missing lectures, then I would need a good job at the end of it all to help subsidise his wage at the hamburger drive-thru.

Add *overactive imagination* to geekiness.

Finally, I reached a page with more bite to it. There was the usual run of things-to-do and dates, but scrawled at the top of the page was an e-mail address. It was upside-down, so I guessed that it was done in a hurry and not necessarily on the same day that the rest of the stuff had been written. It was that kind of writing you do when you need to make a quick note of something and you scrawl it down just about anywhere. *Trixie1234@hotmail.com*. Trixie? Maybe that was one of Hannah's friends. And yet, somehow, I couldn't quite imagine Hannah having a friend called *Trixie*.

After all, they had once been talking about middle names in the canteen, and when I said I didn't have one, Fliss said "Are you sure? It's not *Chardonnay*, is it?" Fliss had let out a superbitch snigger, which Hannah quietly echoed.

Once again, I was having to swallow it down. However much I despised Hannah and Co, she was still out there somewhere, and probably far from safe and happy. Still, I've got to be brutally honest, it wasn't *easy*.

So anyway, I jotted down the e-mail address on my notepad. If this was a friend of Hannah's, I thought that maybe I could contact her.

The next page took my mind right off e-mail addresses. The writing had turned from chubby and cute into angry and haphazard.

How am I supposed to deal with this? Everything I thought was real is a lie!

As Liam would say, *Whoa!* Whatever it was supposed to mean, it seemed like it was kind of heart-felt. But was it anger? Was it despair? Whatever mood it had been written in, it had been *meant*.

The handwriting was clearly Hannah's, but the emotion had turned it into something much more hasty and far less arty. The hastiness had made it so much more legible. I wondered what had happened in Hannah's life that made everything she had previously known a lie. I very quickly realised that staring into space would not help me. The answer just wasn't there.

I scribbled it down verbatim in my notebook. Already I was thinking about just highlighting it on the photocopy, but then wondered if I might end up having to hand it in to the Police after all. I shuddered. I really didn't want to think about that and the great pile of crap I'd be in. But, if it came to it and I found something obvious, I wouldn't have a choice.

Fighting a mental image of myself in a stripy uniform breaking rocks along a dusty highway whilst chained to my nearest inmate, I ploughed on. The next couple of pages were nothing to get excited about.

Hannah had drawn out her timetable for her first semester at Grantstone University. It was neat and pretty; a perfectly straight table strewn with pencil drawn flowers and bumble bees.

I looked closely at the detail of the little sketches and realised how talented Hannah really was. Personally, any bumble bee of mine would be a vague baked-bean shape with makeshift wings. I was not artistic by any stretch of the imagination.

I had my own talents, but I was well aware how I could sometimes see the things I was learning and achieving as *real* and of much more importance. Looking at the tiny sketches, I was forced to re-think.

As I squinted at the little bees, I could see the fine lines which created that furry look that bees have. The nearer I pressed my nose to it, the more life-like it became. There was something odd about that moment; the realisation of the time and effort that must have gone into the perfect little bees and the thought that their artist might never sketch again brought unexpected tears to my eyes.

Nobody was more shocked than me, I can tell you. I squashed the tears with my fists before they had a chance to roll down my face. It was time to get on with it; crying and staring at bumble bees wasn't going to help in any real way.

The next page was a revised version of the beautiful timetable. There had obviously been a couple of changes in the first few weeks. I'd experienced the same thing myself. This new timetable was neat, but without any of the artistic flourishes of the first, which was good; I didn't want my emotions to be further provoked.

Written underneath the timetable was a single sentence, again in the not-so-neat handwriting. *Maybe it's time for a rebellion of my own!* What? I wished I could have made sense of it. The fervency of these declarations made me feel that they were of great importance. If only I could find something that would tell me what had happened in Hannah's life to bring on the cryptic phrases.

Anyway, I scribbled it down in my notebook. Time was getting on and I needed to find something which might help me get to the bottom of it.

For the next few pages, life seemed to have returned to normal for Hannah. The usual run of social engagements was back, each one neatly listed. These were dated throughout October and November, so around the time we were all settling into our first semester.

At the end of the third page was an entry which made my stomach lurch. Not because of its evidential value by any stretch of the imagination. No, the reaction was just a gut-thing. *30th Nov First date with bad-boy Liam!*

I can't explain why it was that I hated to see his name in Hannah's diary, but let me re-iterate it's not a jealousy thing! Just friends, remember? I think it was because it somehow marked the day when things in my world started to shift uncomfortably. It wasn't just the date with Hannah that had prodded at me, but what that date represented to me.

Change. The end of the old order. And *bad-boy?* Seriously? Liam? That got my hackles back up again. Who was she calling a bad-boy? Liam had never done a bad thing in his life.

As I pondered the possibility that Hannah had confused *bad* with *poor*, I knew I was losing my focus. How was I going to figure this out if I was forever trying to work with a giant chip on my shoulder?

I wrote it down. There had clearly been something *big* going on with the whole idea of *rebellion* in Hannah's world. Was badboy Liam nothing more than an expression of that? I wrote that down too, not because I had thought it overly important, but because it was the only conclusion I had drawn so far and I thought it warranted a mention.

The next page almost had my eyes popping out. The handwriting had returned to normal, but the content was just about the last thing I had expected. *Emjay is so funny! He acts like the sight of naked flesh is some kind of spiritual experience! So, so amusing to watch him trying to be normal with me in front of everyone else. He's just so awkward.*

Whoa! Whoa! Whoa! What the hell? Who was Emjay? I didn't need to rack my brains; I already knew there wasn't an Emjay that I knew of. It was an unusual name, that was for sure. I wrote it down, all the while wondering about the timing.

If this diary was written in any sort of chronological order, then this *Emjay* character, and the whole business of nakedness, was something which ran kind of concurrently with Liam.

Whichever way I looked at it, I couldn't see how it *didn't* mean sex. I mean, sure, it could have been something else, but *seriously*, what? I began to feel a sense of outrage that my friend had been cheated on already.

They had only been together five weeks, for Heaven's sake. That seems like an awfully short time for boredom to set in. I wondered if Liam had any idea. But, of course he wouldn't, *would he?*

Already breaking my sworn method of detection, I flipped the pages quickly, scanning for any other sign of the Emjay. After several minutes, I found nothing. Still, I knew that I would have to go back over it meticulously, I might well have missed something.

I went back to the Emjay page and stared at it. There was something about this diary. Things were *said* but not said. Events were *hinted at* but not described. It was almost as if these were just reminders, and that Hannah could look back over it and, from her few scattered phrases, conjure up the events of her life in detail.

This book was not meant for anybody else's eyes. I mean, most diaries weren't, this much I knew. But this was written in a way that almost seemed like code. If it fell into the wrong hands, it couldn't be entirely made out. You know, like if the Bletchley Code Breakers had found it laying in the bushes, and not an engineering student without the first idea about detection.

I looked at my watch; it was nearly twenty past twelve. Not long before I would need to pack up and head off across campus for my fluid mechanics lecture. I neatly stacked the photocopied pages and put them back in my rucksack.

I kept my notebook out and had a last glance at everything I had found so far. I had an e-mail address, the use of which I wasn't yet sure, the hint of some catastrophic life event, and the whiff of infidelity. I had a feeling about this Emjay which I couldn't shake. Perhaps he might have something to do with Hannah's disappearance.

It was getting to that time where I would have to make myself accountable to the Grantstone Constabulary and throw myself upon their mercy. *Mercy?* Yeah right! Because Liam had been treated *so* well.

I wondered what the police would make of the Emjay thing. I couldn't help but suspect that they would assume that Liam had found out about an affair and had done something terrible in a jealous rage. If I handed them the photocopy, perhaps I would be setting Liam up further. I wondered for a moment if Liam actually *had* known.

Still, I couldn't see it; Liam was like an open book to me and I would have felt his disappointment. Anyway, Liam would have told me. I had been treated to every other trial and tribulation of his life; some big, some *unbelievably* tiny. My point is, the guy misses nothing out. He's open more often than our local EuroSaver.

I put the notebook away too, and rose to leave. As I was putting my duffle coat on, something caught my eye. It was such a quick and tiny movement that I didn't actually see what it was. I had seen *movement itself*, rather than anything tangible. Suddenly, my heart was pounding again.

Amidst my studies, I had more or less forgotten about the message on the mirror. With one arm in my duffle coat and my mouth dangling open most unattractively, I scanned the room. The movement had been a tiny and fleeting thing, over by the natural history shelves.

I stared hard, but nothing was out of the ordinary. Students and staff were quietly going about their business, with no sign of the cloaked and fanged creature who had left me the warning.

I did up the toggles on my coat without taking my eyes off the natural history section. I moved from the silent study area with uncharacteristic grace, and made my move. As I rounded the corner of the shelf in question, I felt sweaty and unpleasantly tingly. For reasons best known to my fight-or-flight system, I was holding my breath as I darted around the shelf to see who was there.

Nobody! There was nobody there. I must have imagined it. My nerves were probably on red-alert, so a bit of paranoia was to be expected. *Wasn't it?*

Chapter Five

The whole fluid mechanics lecture was painful. I kept on top of it and made even more *copious* notes than usual. Fearing that I wasn't entirely taking it all in, I knew I'd have to have some pretty thorough notes to look back on. When it was finally over, I decided to make my way to the canteen to get a cup of tea. Yes, *another one.*

With my tea and a packet of posh crisps, I sat down at the table we tended to sit at, my head whirring with all sorts of thoughts and fears. I felt kind of lonely sitting there without Liam, and vaguely looked about the canteen for the first time since I had walked in. Immediately, I was aware of being stared at.

Well, not stared at exactly, but *glared* at. Several tables away sat Fliss and Amelia, with three other girls, none of whom I'd ever seen before. So, I could presume that they *wouldn't* be continuing to join me for lunch the way they had when Hannah was there. When Fliss saw me looking back, she huffed loudly enough for me to actually hear it across the room, and tossed her head so wildly in the opposite direction that it *had* to have hurt.

Once Fliss had performed her little theatre piece, naturally Amelia did exactly the same. Seriously, I hoped that every muscle in their necks had twanged like knicker elastic, and that neither one of them would be able to turn their silly heads without pain for the rest of the year.

The rest of their table seemed to follow suit, albeit with a little more decorum. So, the new group of girls were all over the *poor Fliss has lost her best friend* riff. Wow! What a way to attract new and interesting people into your stratosphere.

I was torn really as to what I should do next. There was a part of me that seriously considered walking over to their table and up-ending Fliss' chair without either warning or explanation; but the larger part couldn't give a damn about the silly girl's antics, and was secretly relieved not to have to spend valuable life hours in the vacuous damsel's company anymore.

The larger part won; I just looked casually away and nonchalantly melted away my lips on my scalding hot tea.

"Hi, Josie. How are you doing? How's Liam?" My eyes nearly popped out. It was Rich Richard. He was talking his coat off and hanging it on the back of one of the many, *many* vacant chairs at my table in Myra Hindley corner.

"Erm…isn't it like, *illegal* or something, for you to sit with me here whilst your girlfriend is trying to burn holes in me using the power of thought alone?"

"Ha, Josie, you're so funny." Rich Richard was actually laughing. *Ok*….

"Richard, I'm serious. I mean, you seem like a nice bloke, so I'm only concerned for your safety. You'll be ostracised by your own pack and left in the wilderness to fend for yourself. Think about it, old bean, before you *actually* park your bum-cheeks on that chair."

"My bum-cheeks will be fine." Richard was laughing loudly enough to draw stares from the table of hatred.

"Richard, your *girlfriend* is over there and she's not looking too pleased with you."

"I'm none too pleased with her either, if I'm entirely honest, Josie." Well, he'd done it; he'd parked up and made it official. "I saw what was going on as I walked into the canteen. Do you really think I would join a group of people who were behaving so childishly?"

"Honestly? If you'd asked me, *like*, three minutes ago, I'd probably have said yes. But in fairness to me, I really don't know you very well."

"Well, I'm here now. I'm just going to get a drink." He rose again. He was like some kind of giant Jack-in-the-box. "No flask?" Richard looked at the polystyrene cup and I felt rather bemused by the interest of the general populous in my refreshment habits.

"No, not today." I shrugged.

"It's a very sensible idea, actually. I wish I was as organised as you. Honestly, you could buy a *whole box* of tea bags for the price of a cup of tea in here." Ok, I was reeling a bit. I *knew* I had been right all along, and now an *economist* was agreeing with me.

"Which is alright if you can afford it, I suppose."

"No, it isn't really. I mean, it's kind of wasteful, isn't it? I'm studying economics, I should know better." Richard pulled a handful of change out of his pocket and looked down at it thoughtfully.

"Well, your secret is safe with me. Anyway, I'm not sure you'll be ejected from the economics degree even if they *do* find out about your crazy and irresponsible spending habits."

Richard wandered away to the counter, laughing all the way. I was left with the feeling that he was nice, but odd. Very, *very* odd.

No sooner had he wandered off than I was suddenly joined by two more guests. Well, not *joined by* so much as *flanked by*. I immediately recognised one of the CID officers who had carted Liam away the day before. He pulled out a chair and sat down right next to me. As the chair on the other side of me scraped back, I spun around to see another, older guy, presumably also a police officer.

"*Do* sit down." I said quietly.

One look at their faces told me that my sarcasm was misdirected; they'd totally missed it. I was vaguely aware of Richard hovering a few feet away, clearly not knowing if he should come back to the table.

"Miss Cloverfield. I'm Detective Inspector Malcolm Thorn, and I've got a few questions for you."

"*Here?*" I said, hoping that they would one day see how very *wrong* their behaviour was.

"Yes." The Detective Inspector looked at me in a somewhat confused way.

"So that *all* of the people here think I've committed a crime, the way that they *now* think Liam Attwood has?"

"Excuse me?"

Your methods are heavy handed. You treat potential witnesses as actual *suspects*, and you do it very publicly. There is a very good chance that you have ruined the university career of a young man who has actually done nothing wrong, simply because your officers insisted on making a performance of dragging him out of *this very canteen* in front of everyone." I was more furious than I could ever have realised.

"Now look here. A young woman is missing and we have *very* good reason to suspect your friend has something to do with it. You need to tell me what you know about all this, or it will be all the worse for you." Thorn threw the comment at me like a petulant child would have, and I just *knew* he hadn't thought it though.

"What? Just run that by me again?"

"You heard me."

"Are you accusing me of something?"

"Well… I… erm, no, of course not."

"You just said that you have reason to *believe* that Liam Attwood has *something to do with it* and I should tell you what I know or I will be in trouble. Implying that I either have knowledge of, or was complicit in, a crime."

"Don't get smart with me."

"I wouldn't dream of it; it would clearly be a waste of time. So, what *exactly* is your question?"

"Well, has Liam told you anything of what's happened?"

"No. As far as we are *both* aware, Hannah is missing. That is it."

"Oh really!"

"Meaning?... Look, you cannot just stride into a public place and abuse an innocent member of the public."

"Oh, is *that* what you are? Tell me, are you the *same* Josie Cloverfield who lives on the Moss Park estate?"

"How very foolish. If you thought I was guilty of something, then you would *not* be talking to me here. You would have arrested me. Instead, you have chosen to come here and assume that my knowledge of my own rights is *so poor* that I would be humbled by a few choice insults and threats. And yes, *I am* the same Josie Cloverfield who lives on the Moss Park estate. The *same* Josie Cloverfield who has never been in trouble of any kind in her *entire* life, unless living on a council estate is officially a crime these days. What, *specifically*, is your question? And what is it that Liam has done that you can so *openly* declare that you have reason to believe he is guilty of something?" I could not believe that it was me who was speaking.

Not only speaking, but speaking so very loudly. There was not even the clank of a plate to be heard throughout the entire canteen.

"Well, I didn't actually *say* he was guilty of anything…." I could have done a victory lap. He'd been lying, and I'd caught him out!

"Actually, you did. If I can just rewind for you, you said *a young woman is missing and we have reason to believe that Liam Attwood has something to do with it*. You went on to threaten me that if I didn't tell you what I knew, it would be *all the worse for me*." Ok, I have a really chunky IQ, not to mention a fab memory for great swathes of text and conversation.

And I was showing off a bit, if I'm honest.

"Look, don't push your luck. You could be in big trouble if you don't co-operate."

"I already *have* co-operated. I've already told police officers what I know, which is exactly *nothing!* Despite your appalling behaviour, if I *did* have something to tell, I *would* tell it. I have told you that I don't because that is the truth. Yet you have chosen to come here and insult and threaten me. You have chosen to taunt me about a poor upbringing I can do nothing about, as if my home address should immediately make me a suspect."

"No listen, we only wanted….."

"Stop. I am refusing to speak to you any further, except to tell you that I will be making a formal complaint to your Professional Standards Department and the IPCC." I reached for my tea, dismissing him with a flick of the head, Fliss Hardcastle style.

The IPCC?" Thorn was in a bit of a state. He was a mixture of furious and dismayed. No doubt his heavy-handed tactics usually went by without being challenged.

"Yes, it stands for the Independent Police Complaints Commission."

"I know what it stands for!"

"Obviously, I will start with Grantstone Constabulary's Professional Standards Department, but if I'm not impressed, I'll escalate my complaint."

"Look, there's no need for that. We're just trying to find a missing woman." His voice was suddenly very much gentler, and his tone had turned into something you might coax a cat from behind the sofa with.

"Oh, I think there's every need." He should not have messed with a woman who had studied the police at such close quarters and for so many years.

"Well, I think you'll find you'll have to *prove it*, Miss Cloverfield." He hissed, clearly surprised that his mini charmoffensive hadn't struck gold.

"Well, I daresay witness testimony counts as evidence. I heard every word of that, Detective Inspector Thorn." I had never been so relieved to hear such stridently posh tones in all my life.

As far as heroes went, Rich Richard was suddenly neck and neck with PC Betty Butler. "Richard Allencourt, by the way." He nodded a curt introduction.

"Oh, *are* you indeed?"

"*Yes*." Richard said, really slowly, and I almost laughed at the simple brilliance of his reply.

"So, since Josie is unable to tell you anything, perhaps this meeting is at a close?" Richard went on.

"For now." Detective Inspector Thorn just couldn't help himself.

His parting shot sounded utterly pathetic. Clearly, he could not walk away from anything without the feeling that *he* had won the fight. Even if he was just digging himself in deeper. However, finally he and his minion marched out of the canteen, and the chattering began once more.

"Oh my God, Josie! You were amazing!" Richard was, I must tell you, wide-eyed!

"Well, you did a pretty good job yourself. Thanks for coming in as a witness. Nobody else in here would have done that."

"I wouldn't have had the guts if you hadn't already pummelled that Thorn character into submission." He was beaming from ear to ear, and just a little bit wiggly, like a puppy.

"Well, I've seen a fair few police officers in my time. I'm glad to say that most are not like that."

"Yeah, that was pretty crappy what he said, you know, about where you live and what-have-you. You should definitely complain."

I have to admit, Richard was growing on me. Not because of his tall-blond-handsomeness, but just his way of doing things. I mean, even the last statement came out kind of level, you know, not *pitying the pauper.*

He seemed like a *right-is-right* kind of a bloke. He wasn't taking me on as a cause, he just didn't think the treatment I was getting from either his girlfriend or the police was fair, and he acted accordingly.

As a matter of fact, Richard, or people like him, were exactly what I had been hoping university life would be all about. A kind of *moving on*, where the stuff that had mattered right through school finally meant nothing at all. If I'd met more people like Richard, it might have changed me for the better too. I might not have been on-point all the time, waiting for insults.

"Yes, I definitely will be complaining."

Suddenly, I wondered how much Richard knew about Hannah's life. Since we seemed to have become kind of unusual buddies, I thought I might just as well ask him a few questions.

After all, hell would freeze over before I handed the photocopy of the diary over to that utter moron of a Detective Inspector. There was no way I would give him ammunition to wrongly accuse Liam with.

Right, I'm going to get a fresh cup of tea. Do you want one?" I threw Richard my very most winning smile.

"I have to say, I don't really know Hannah all that well. How long have you known her?" I really had to work on my technique, I felt totally blunt and awkward just asking Richard outright.

To make things seem more natural, I dunked my Kit-Kat into my tea. I don't know why I thought that would make me seem like less of a snooper, I just did. As I dunked, I reflected that if I bought any more stuff in the canteen, I would have to see if I could do a double shift in the dry-cleaners on Saturday. Perish the thought.

"I've known her right through high school and sixth form. I mean, I didn't always hang out with her and the others. That really only came about when I started dating Fliss."

I cast a look over at Fliss; she was scowling in a way her skin might never recover from. Richard was sitting with his back to her too, which seemed to be making her even more incandescent with rage. I totally had to fight the urge to throw her a sneaky smirk. I'd have loved to, though.

"Oh?"

"Yeah, I guess I started seeing Fliss about a year ago. We were in the last year of sixth form. Before that, I'd kind of known the girls, but not so well." Richard reached out and snapped off one of my Kit-Kat fingers.

As he popped it into his mouth, I smiled, all the while noting that Liam would never have got that far. "Then, all my friends went to universities out of town. They all wanted to go away to far flung places and have exotic experiences."

"And you didn't?" I laughed at the idea of exotic experiences just because you were in another county.

Richard was no so much funny as he was an unintentional comedian.

"No, not particularly. I just want to get my degree and get on with it. I kind of knew that if I followed my friends, I might not concentrate as well as I tend to need to. I'm not naturally gifted, you see. I have to put the hours in."

"Yeah, I put a fair few hours in myself."

"But not because you have to."

"Huh?"

"You're genuinely brainy, Josie. You have the kind of brain that universities were invented for. A couple of the guys on your course told me that you're like Euclid or what-not when it comes to maths."

Ok, so I suppose it's not too many girls who would be flattered to be compared to the ancient Greek *Father of Geometry*, but I have to admit, I felt a little glow forming in my belly-area. Still, the thrill of pride notwithstanding, this was getting me nowhere in my investigations.

I was starting to wonder if I might actually just tell Richard what I'd done, vis-à-vis stealing the diary. It gave me horrible palpitations just thinking about it, but I really couldn't see how I could introduce the subject of Emjay, as well as all the rest of it.

"Richard, look. I'm going to tell you something, but I really need you to keep it to yourself."

"Ok." He said so matter-of-factly that I almost didn't know how to proceed.

In the end, I just did it. I told him all about my rage at the way Liam was dragged away and how I'd overheard about the police search on Dale's radio and gone along to snoop.

I kept looking around me, making sure there were no witnesses to the conversation, and I was whispering so quietly that Richard and I were almost nose-to-nose by the end of it.

"So what? You didn't steal it, Josie. You found it. Big difference. You were out on a walk and you found it."

"But on the day of the police search!"

"So? How on earth would you find out about the time and date of a police search? They have no way of knowing you overheard the police radio. And anyway, the diary didn't have Hannah's name in it, so how would you be expected to know it belonged to her? I think you're worrying over nothing."

"Wowsers, you're totally Mr Nonchalant, aren't you?" I had to admit that I'd judged Richard so differently.

The guy he really was bore no relationship to the guy I'd assumed him to be for the five long excruciating weeks of the Hannah-Liam romance. There, you see, that's the trouble with being judgemental. It didn't matter which way you were aiming it, there was never really a way to excuse it. Even if it's me doing it….

"Well, I think you've got deniability on your side. And anyway, if that Thorn guy is the lead investigator, I doubt he could make much use of the notes in it, other than to trump up even more painfully inadequate insinuations."

"I feel oddly better about myself."

"You should do. You're pretty cool. I wouldn't have had the nerve or the noggin to work it all out."

"So, did you see any changes in Hannah in the Summer?"

"Well, I didn't see her much, but, yeah, I guess there was something."

"What?"

"Nothing major, just a bit of odd behaviour. Odd for Hannah, I mean. It sounds lame, I suppose, but she got drunk a couple of times in the Summer. Like two weeks in a row or something. I guess that sounds like a stupid thing to highlight, what with her being old enough to drink and getting ready to go to uni, but still it was kind of out of character."

"And she didn't say why?"

"No, but then I didn't ask."

"Would she have told Fliss or Amelia?"

"Trust me, if she'd told Fliss, I would have known about it. Fliss doesn't keep confidences, and she doesn't have any real loyalties either."

"Just a quick segue, Richard, but why *are* you dating her?" I knew I was being rude, but it had flown out before I had a chance to stop it.

However, Richard didn't appear to see anything intrusive in my question.

"I just sort of fell into a relationship with her. Although I think it's fair to say that I'm no longer in it." He smiled in a comical kind of a *whoops-a-daisy* fashion which made me give a little involuntary snort of laughter. "Is she still scowling?" He winced at me.

"Oh yeah, *hard*. She's going to need Botox if she doesn't call it a day."

"Ha! You crack me up, Josie."

"Oh, in the diary Hannah referred to some guy called Emjay. It would have been written around the time she was here at uni I think." I chose not to mention *exactly* what Hannah had written. It felt kind of unfair, you know?

"I don't know anyone by those initials I don't think."

"Huh?"

"I don't think I know anyone by the initials MJ. I'll have to have a think about that. If I come up with any, I'll text you."

"No, not M and J. Emjay, spelt E-m-j-a-y."

"Really? Is that even a name?"

"I thought it maybe sounded foreign? Like a foreign student here?"

"I don't know that Hannah really hung out with any of the foreign students to be honest. Liam would know better, being on the same course and what-have-you." "Yes, good point." My heart sank.

If I asked Liam, I would also have to tell him about the possibility that Hannah had cheated on him. The thought gave me a horrible feeling. Liam and I always tried to protect one another from life's hurts; now I was going to be the one bringing it right to his door.

"Are you alright, Josie?"

"Yeah, sorry, I was miles away. I just thought of another name in the diary. I don't suppose Hannah knew anybody called Trixie?"

"Trixie? That sounds like something an old lady would call her Pomeranian." Richard looked thoughtfully into the distance as I stifled a laugh. He really did have no idea that he was funny. "No, I never heard of a Trixie. I'm not actually a lot of help, am I?"

"Actually, you have been. If I didn't soon tell someone about taking that diary, I would have evaporated from pure guilt. You've made me feel better, if nothing else."

"Glad to have been of service." Richard looked at his watch and suddenly

had the air of a man who should really be somewhere else. "If you need anything, just call me. I think it's great that you're trying to find Hannah and help Liam, you know.
I'd like to help if I can."

"Thanks, that's really kind of you."

"I've got to go. Are you going to the vigil tonight?"

"The what-now?" I was so far on the back foot I didn't know how to get back.

"Oh, you haven't heard. Fliss has arranged a candlelight vigil on the campus quad tonight. She'll be handing out missing persons' flyers and what-have-you. Her new friends seem keen to be involved, but...." He tailed off.

"But what?"

"Look, I think flyers are a great idea. I daresay she's even got the press interested. But there's just something kind of, well, *icky* about her motives. I mean, I know this is going to make me sound cynical, but I think Fliss is enjoying this a bit. I think she's playing a part and it's making me a bit sick."

"Richard, I'm already there. Don't beat yourself up. There is such a thing as healthy cynicism, you know." I smiled at him.

Poor old Richard. He definitely needed to re-think his Christmas card list; his current friends were utterly crap.

"Are you going?" I looked up at him as he put his coat on.

"No, I think I'll give it a miss. I want to keep out of Fliss' way, in any case."

"I totally understand."

As I watched him leave, I thought about the vigil. I knew I would have to go, of course. If the telly was to be believed, the person responsible might very well turn up there. You know, like arsonists watching firemen put out the very blaze they had started. Ok, it was on the lame side, but I had to follow it.

Chapter Six

"A vigil? You've got to be kidding. I can't go to that, Dude. Everyone really *will* think I've done something to Hannah if I show up there!" Liam was sitting on his bed with a big open pizza box next to him.

"I wasn't expecting you to go, Liam, I was just keeping you in the loop, my friend. Anyway, I'm going to go. I want to get a good look at who turns up and what sort of performance they put on." I'd been perched on the bed telling Liam about my exploits with the police search, the diary, the terrifying intruder, Emjay, and the visit from DI Thorn.

I hadn't quite got to the whole business of the *nakedness* which I'd seen in Hannah's own handwriting. I just couldn't find the right moment.

"Are you sure about this whole detective thing, Dude? I mean, you could get yourself into real trouble. That Thorn bloke probably hates you."

"Well, I suppose he's not too keen on me." I laughed.

"No, Dude. He *hates* you. I've met him. That guy's *harsh*."

"Oh, give over, Liam." Liam was on one of his silly segues and I wanted to hold his concentration.

"You gave him one of your big, *pompous* dressing-downs. And now he *hates* you. Hates your *guts*." Liam lifted another big, greasy slice of pizza out of the box.

"Oh Liam! Shut up will you!" I kicked off my plimsolls and tucked my feet underneath me on the bed. "Those pizzas are ridiculously expensive. You'd be much better off buying your own and cooking it. You could get, like, *four* pizzas for the price of that one."

"Or *you* could get about *twenty-five* from the Euro-Saver. Yum-yum." Liam pulled a daft face and started licking his lips like a dog.

Seriously, even when there's trouble all around him, the sixyear-old Liam I met all those years ago is never really far from the surface. "Want some?"

"Yes please." I leaned over and lifted out one of the smaller slices.

"Total hypocrite, Dude."

"No, I'm not." I mumbled, trying to keep the copious amount of sweetcorn from dropping out as I spoke.

"Totally! You were just telling me about what a waste of money it was!"

"To you, *yes*. To me, this is simply a *free* slice of pizza. Even the Euro-Saver doesn't have those!" I laughed, savouring the true magnificence of the ready-made take-away pizza. Dee-licious!

"So, what *are* you going to do with this diary? Or photocopy, at any rate?" Liam's sudden seriousness kind of caught me off guard.

"You know, I don't think I'm going to hand it over to DI Thorn."

"Because he'll have you hung by you heels from a lamppost outside the magistrate's court?"

"No, it's not that." The time was coming to be completely honest with Liam.

"Well, why then?" Liam pointed at the last slice of pizza and raised his eyes in a *you want it?* way.

I knew better. If I'd reached for that last slice, Liam would have shut the pizza box lid down on my fingers and called me a cheeky git.

"No thanks." I shook my head. My stomach had started doing a kind of flippy thing anyway, so another slice wouldn't have gone down too well. "Liam, there was something else in that diary that I haven't told you about yet." I had never, ever been nervous with Liam before in my life. Once again, I found myself wishing that Hannah Davenport had never come into our lives.

"Come on, Dude. Just out with it, ok? You've been weird since you got here and you're starting to freak me out a bit."

"Have I?"

"Yeah, seriously, poker would *not* be your game. Stop dithering about and just tell me."

"Liam, there was more to the Emjay thing than just the name. Hannah had written something about this person which kind of makes it look as if she might have cheated on you. But that's just my interpretation. I mean, it could be anything really, but I'm not sure. And I didn't know whether or not I should tell you but also
I didn't want to……."

"Steady on, Dude. Take a breath."

"Ok. I've said it now. I'm sorry." My hands felt kind of shaky and I was horrified to feel tears in my eyes.

Sometimes, tears can be blinked away, like without anyone knowing. Then there's other times where the tears are just too fat and you daren't even *blink* because you'll displace them and they'll just fly right down your face.

Well, in this instance, the latter applied. As a result, I sat with my eyes wide open like a Madame Tussaude's wax work.

"Hey, Dude. *Dude?*" Liam closed the pizza box and reached out to slide it on top of the chest of drawers.

He shuffled down the bed just at the very moment I was forced to blink and the two big whoppers rolled down my cheeks.

"Dude, don't cry. It's alright." Liam parked up right next to me and gave me a really big hug.

I'll openly admit to a little bit of sobbing. Well, mini-sobbing, really. I think it was the relief that Liam hadn't dissolved when I told him about the Emjay thing.

"Is it really alright? I mean, it's not the best thing to find out after only five weeks." I dried my eyes on my sleeve.

It would be truly pointless to ask Liam if he had any tissues.

"Well, yeah, I guess I'm fine, really. I mean, after five years, maybe it would sting a bit, but, you know, I didn't….well….I didn't….." Liam was totally stuck for words.

"What?"

"Dude, I could not say this to anyone but you. I mean, I don't even know what you're gonna think of me, but, well, I wasn't exactly that *into* Hannah. I mean, she was *alright*, and I'm really, really worried about her. But only in the way I'd be worried about anyone I knew who'd gone missing. If I'm really honest, I'm probably more worried about myself. If she doesn't show up soon, I think I'll end up in prison or something. I know how bad that makes me sound. And I really *am* worried about her. It totally makes me feel sick to think of her out there, especially if she's been hurt. I mean, I can't even think about it. But whether she did or didn't cheat on me, well, I won't lose any sleep over that, Dude."

"Liam, nobody's expecting you to be head over heels in love after five weeks."

"Yeah, but I wouldn't have been head over heels in love after five months.

Or *ever*, really. And I think it was the same for Hannah. We were never built to last. It was just a *thing*. So, do you think I'm a complete *tool* now?"

"No, I don't. Just don't be *that* honest when you're talking to the cops."

"Too late, I'm afraid." Liam spread his arms wide, kind of *oops* fashion.

"I take it back. You *are* a total tool."

"I know that now. DI Thorn said that it made sense for me to try to distance myself from Hannah. You know, make it seem as if there was nothing serious between us, especially if I was looking to deny any crimes of passion."

"Oh my God. That man is such an idiot."

"Well, with me he was kind of in good company I suppose."

"Well, that's true."

"Oi, Dude!" Liam punched my arm and laughed.

"So, you see why I can't hand in that photocopy, can't you? The moment he saw the whole Emjay business, he'd really think you'd committed a crime of passion."

"Yeah, I do see." Liam set off for his own end of the bed again, leaning into his pillows and making himself comfortable. "And thanks, Dude. I mean, you're pretty much risking your own neck for me."

"You'd do the same for me."

"I *have* done. Many times. *Many, many* times!" Liam was smiling, despite the fact that he was rubbing his temples like he had a big, serious headache coming.

"Oh please! There's a limit to how many times you can use the colouring book story, my friend."

"No there isn't. That story's got a bit of everything! Bravery, poignancy, six-year-old kid covered in snot saves the day. It's a winner every time, and you know it is."

"God, you're such a fool."

"So, what's your next move, Detective Dude?"

"The vigil. I'm going to go along to that tonight and see what I can see. After that, I'm going to have to do some kind of research to find someone named Emjay."

"Well, I can do some googling and Facebook searches and stuff, if that helps?"

"Yes, that *would* help, actually." Another thought struck me as I sat staring into space and chewing my bottom lip. "Actually, can you look through Hannah's Facebook page and make a list of all of her friends. Just separate them into people you know and people you don't."

"Oh, shrewd move Dude."

"Oh please, Liam, you're slipping into verse now."

"Just shut up while I'm trying to be impressed with you."

"Well, I'd better get cracking. I'm just going to go straight back to uni, this vigil will be starting soon." I got up off the bed and put my duffle coat back on. "No doubt Queen Fliss will be all done up like a sherry trifle for the cameras."

"Ha, I'll bet." Liam got up too. "Look, I'll grab some crisps and biscuits and stuff from the kitchen on the way out for your rucksack."

"Thanks Pal."

Chapter Seven

With my rucksack full of the kind of tasty treats which could easily render a person a type-two diabetic overnight, I headed out of Moss Park and back towards the University. Stepping onto the first of two busses, I thanked God for my bus pass.

It was nearly six o'clock and, as the bus trundled slowly along through the evening traffic, I wondered what time the vigil was due to start. Pulling my phone from my bag, I performed a few rather obvious searches on Facebook to see if anything had been posted. Not entirely to my surprise there was *not only* a post or two about Hannah's disappearance and the upcoming vigil, but an entire *page* had been set up, rather mawkishly titled *Hannah Come Home*.

I winced when I saw it; it sounded like the title of some Godawful musical. It certainly had a certain ring of artistic selfindulgence to it. It had clearly been dreamt up by someone who couldn't see that their smart-arse creation rather made it sound as if Hannah had trotted off of her own accord, leaving those who remained at home with nothing else to do but call whimsically after her, before bursting into song for the final number.

I checked through the page set-up and could see that Felicity Hardcastle was clearly the administrator. Already it was packed with photos of Hannah, most of which seemed, rather fortuitously, to have Fliss in them too.

Even more fortuitous was the fact that every shot of Fliss was truly picture-perfect! Not a blemish anywhere, not a hair out of place, and definitely no embarrassing nostril-shots. The same could not be said for Hannah Davenport who, whilst very obviously pretty in most of the photos, was less so in others.

Of course, had Hannah herself been able to choose, she most certainly would have left some of them out, however pouty and adorable her alleged best-friend looked in them.

I scanned through all the relevant data with the nimble fingers of a seasoned social media pro. It was odd, really, that I was so good at that stuff, especially since my list of Facebook *"friends"* was exactly seven.

It included Liam, two of his jail-bird brothers, and four really odd guys off my engineering course, three of whom had never actually spoken to me, and one of whom really struggled with English and tried to communicate via mathematical formulae, which he was actually very good at. The problem is, I have that same dreadful responsibility towards politeness as most of the inhabitants of the British Isles....

You have a friend request from David Montgomery!

Who the hell is David Montgomery?

Accept or decline?

David Montgomery..... Oh, is he the guy with the perpetually runny nose who sits seven rows behind me in fluid mechanics and has never even looked my way, never mind spoken to me?

Accept or decline?

Oh Lordy, I'd better accept, or I'll hurt his feelings and, if he ever had actually spoken to me, he sure as hell would stop if I decline his friend request.

Congratulations! You and David Montgomery are now friends!

Yippee! Followed by a quick shifty look at his profile to discover that David Montgomery has somewhere in the region of seven-million friends, all of whom he picked at random, *just like he did you, Josie Cloverfield....*

Ok, I'm exaggerating, but you get the picture.

Anyway, whilst I might not be the friendliest person in the world, I'm not above a bit of nosy-parker behaviour. Judge me by all means, I *know* you do it too.

To be honest, I'd scanned through the lot; Hannah, Fliss, Amelia, and *even* Rich Richard. Still, that had been in the early days when I had thought it best to *know thine enemy*. All I'd actually discovered was that Hannah was a rather spoiled princess, Fliss was a narcissist who would probably need some kind of physical therapy for repetitive strain injury from taking two-thousand selfies too many, Amelia was a notably nondescript disciple of Fliss, and Rich Richard was an odd ball who re-posted curious-humour stuff such as the hunt for a missing giant ball of edam cheese.... I'm being serious.

So, my scan through the relevant data gave me a start time of seven o'clock, and that the event was definitely going to be held on the pristine lawns of the Grantstone University Quad.

I looked at my watch; it was twenty past six already, and I still had one more bus to go. However, I guessed I would probably make it in plenty of time to see the start of things at the vigil.

With any luck, there would be enough time for me to hot-foot it to my rented locker. Yes, rented locker! I realise that this seems like an extravagance, but I tended to only take home the books I needed for the evening.

I had many library books and other text books which I had paid for out of the meagre earnings from my job at the drycleaners, and did not want to find that any of them had been sold, stolen, burnt for warmth, or simply destroyed for the hell of it by either my mum, or one of her unsavoury acquaintances.

Anyway, I wanted to stow away the photocopy of Hannah's diary. I had been carrying it all day and it was starting to feel as if it was getting heavier and heavier; I could feel myself developing some kind of a stoop.

The charity shop duffle coat was bad enough. I didn't need to add a Quasimodo-style walk to my already questionable sense of style.

Bus number two was bang on time and the driver wasn't one of the kind who gives way *ever*, or waits for old ladies to finish crossing the road before he roars towards them. At any other time, despicable; at *that* moment, much appreciated.

I leapt off the bus outside the uni with twenty minutes to spare and made my way quickly over to the locker room.

Once the photocopy had been offloaded, I felt like a whole new woman. I'd also found the woollen scarf I had been looking for since the temperatures had dropped to ear-freezing levels, which was a total bonus as far as I was concerned.

Wrapping the scarf about my neck, I headed for the Quad. At only ten minutes to seven, Fliss was already there directing operations. The problem was that, at that time, there were very few others in attendance, so I could not feasibly watch what was going on without being seen.

For me to brazenly walk over and offer my new-found enemy some kind of assistance would look truly suspicious, so I plumped for finding a decent hiding place from which to spy.

It didn't take a lot of thinking about; I simply darted in through the nearest door and walked the through the university corridors which effectively corralled the outdoor Quad in a neat square.

After two complete circuits, I finally found myself alone in the east corridor. Although the corridors were lined with windows, I was able to tuck myself behind one of the great stone mullions, surveillance style.

Not that Fliss would have been looking at the windows. A solo journalist and a photographer had arrived on the scene and Fliss was suddenly busy. She approached them with a fixed smile and, judging by the way she kept surreptitiously looking off into the distance behind the pair, I rather thought that she was expecting more than just an appearance by the Grantstone Echo, Visitor, or Herald; whichever they were from.

Her fixed smile notwithstanding, Fliss had really gone to a lot of trouble with her appearance. Even on a bad day, she dressed like an off-duty model. However, at the vigil, Fliss had applied even more make-up than ever. I could clearly make out her eyelashes from several yards away.

They were so heavily caked that any kind of rapid blinking would cause the sort of backdraft that would take the rather skinny photographer right off her pins.

My eye was suddenly drawn to the sight of Amelia struggling across the Quad with a heavy-looking bin bag.

She looked over at Fliss with a *where shall I put this?* shrug, only to be treated to vigorous bout of pointing which aimed her in the direction of a massive photo of Hannah on a tripod stand.

Amelia seemed to take Fliss' crap in her stride, and dutifully set off across the lawn with her heavy burden.

Had I been in her shoes, I would probably have tipped the contents out onto the grass and used the empty bag to suffocate Fliss with.

I watched as Amelia began to take an inordinate amount of chunky cream coloured candles out of the bag. So many, in fact, that it was a true wonder that the bag had not split long before she'd had a chance to set it down. She set them all around the base of the tripod and began to light them. I could not help but feel relieved for Amelia that it was a pretty still evening and her candle-lighting was not in vain.

I stared at the photograph of Hannah. It was a head and shoulders shot of a smiling and extremely pretty woman in her late teens, with glossy brown wavy hair and flawless skin. The press would love it.

Still, as I continued to stare, I wondered where that teenager was now, and if she would ever smile again. Once more I was knocked sideways by a sudden belt of emotion and had to blink hard for a moment or two.

If I'm honest, it wasn't Hannah as such whom I was getting emotional about; it was the girl in the photo who was young and carefree and who should have been at home studying, or out eating pizza with her bad-boy goon of a boyfriend. It seemed suddenly sickening that a human could be reduced to a giant photo and more candles than you see in a church. Nobody should be the centre-piece of a candlelight vigil, even if that someone was no more my cup of tea than I was hers.

Fortunately, the vigil attendees began to arrive in dribs and drabs before I could be swept away any further by my truly unhelpful bout of melancholia. I instantly spotted the girls I'd seen earlier with Fliss, who seemed to constitute her new set. They smiled broadly as they approached Fliss, and seemed to be rather inappropriately congratulating her on her organisation of the event. The journo and photographer had wandered away, seemingly looking for some good shots, and Fliss greeted her new besties with a certain amount of self-satisfied gusto.

Finally, the photographer called Fliss, who bounded over to her like an excited puppy. As I watched Fliss pose for a photograph at the side of the big picture of Hannah, I felt my stomach churn with distaste.

Fliss, who had been smiling and almost twinkling with excitement, was suddenly transformed into the sad and forlorn beauty whose best friend had disappeared leaving her broken hearted. I wanted to climb out of the window, fly across the lawn, and rugby-tackle the heartless little beast to the ground.

Whilst I'd had the very same suspicions as Rich Richard about Fliss' motives for the vigil, to actually see the evidence of it with my own eyes left a very bad taste in my mouth. In that moment, I felt rather sorry for Hannah.

Being missing without a trace aside, I wondered how Hannah would have felt to see her best friend totally capitalising on whatever it was the poor woman might be going through at that very moment.

My stomach tightened at the thought and I knew I would have to get a grip. Sadness, anger, revulsion, guilt; these emotions were going to have to be swallowed down for the time being.

There simply wasn't room for them all; they would have to be addressed and dealt with a later time. I needed to start looking on the scene before me with the eyes of a detective, and not with the eyes of a girl who could not keep her thoughts and feelings in check.

As the vigil began to get underway, I decided that it was probably best if I just stayed where I was and continued as a spy, rather than an attendee.

Since all the action was happening outside, the Quad corridors were totally deserted, and I was able to move about them to get good views of the whole proceedings.

I recognised lots of the students on the Quad as being people to whom Liam either nodded, or spoke to outright; mainly other art students doing the same classes as him. No doubt many of them either knew Hannah, or knew her by sight, and felt that there was something to be achieved in attending.

In truth, most of them looked truly concerned, and in some cases, disturbed by it all. Maybe attending a vigil such as this one was the only course of action available. Maybe it was the only thing which made the gathered students feel as if they were doing something to help.

People seemed to be wandering past Hannah's giant likeness, almost procession-like. Most of Amelia's candles were still burning, although the breeze had obviously picked up a little and a handful were either guttering, or extinguished completely.

Suddenly, the art lecturer, Matty Jameson, was crouched down at the foot of Hannah's photo. It startled me a little, since I hadn't even seen him approach, and with his long coat and scarf, and the general appearance of being a total parody-come-throwback, he was not really an easy man to miss.

Matty was fumbling about in the pocket of his long, shabby coat, and I wondered what an earth he was doing. I squinted hard, as if this would somehow magnify my target.

He had evidently pulled a lighter from his pocket, and was attempting to re-light the candles which had gone out.

Several of his students looked on sadly, and even the photographer was touched enough to hurry over and snap a few shots of him. For a few terrible moments, I classed him right alongside Fliss, assuming that his actions were nothing more than attention seeking mixed with a dreadful, cheesy kind of pathos.

I was actually beginning to shake my head and tut in annoyance before something in his manner made me stop. As he rose to stand and look at Hannah's picture, his shoulders seemed to hunch slightly.

It wasn't a big shift in his stance, and clearly wasn't contrived, or else it would have been so much bigger. It was just a slight rounding forward, almost as if he had sagged just a little.

I stopped tutting and felt a little awkward, kind of in the way you do when you make a really stupid comment in public. I felt as if I'd misjudged what I was seeing, and that Matty Jameson's actions were far from the act I had judged them to be.

Just as I was mentally castigating myself for letting judgement get in the way once more, I had the creeping feeling that I was not alone. It was the same inexplicable feeling I'd had in the library which had caused me to think a simple movement had been somehow significant.

The sudden feeling of fear made my scalp tingle and the tiny hairs on the back of my neck stand up. I was hoping that I was just being overly sensitive and hyper-vigilant. After all, I hadn't heard footsteps approaching.

"You total nosey parker!" I squealed like a pig and spun around so fast I almost fell over.

"God Almighty!" I said, clutching my chest and gasping for breath.

"No, it's just me." PC Dale Webb grinned like a fool, completely loving the fact that he had almost hastened my departure from this world.

"What did you do that for, you clown?"

You know when you've had a shock and you kind of have that angry stage? Well, that's just about where I was at that moment. Not only could Dale Webb see it, but he was thoroughly enjoying it.

"Did I startle you?" His shoulders were bobbing in that *I'm about to burst out laughing* way.

"No. I'm pretty much squealing for kicks these days." I said, sarcastically. "Anyway, what are you doing here and why the hell are you creeping about frightening innocent members of the public out of their wits?"

"Same as you, I suppose. I wanted to see who turned up at the vigil without actually attending the vigil." Dale looked really different in his own clothes; by which I mean he was not in uniform.

He looked more like someone who might hang out with me and Liam. Well, a bit older, I guess, but he would more or less pass in our demographic.

I've seen off duty officers in the past and, I'm going to unapologetically generalise here, they mostly look a bit dorky and uncomfortable out of uniform. Something about the cop outfit makes them look a bit cool and riddled with authority, yet something about the weirdly-cut jeans teamed with the too-clean trainers or lace-up shoes they wear in the real world makes them look like they are going to have tea with their great Aunt Augusta.

You see, so many of the police officers who roam the Moss Park Estate looking for miscreants are totally recognisable to me; after all, most of them have been in my house at one time or another. So, when I see one of them out there in his or her natural habitat, say out shopping or what-not, I am always kind of floored by how odd they look.

Anyway, the point I am about to make is that PC Dale Webb was by no means a fashion disaster away from the combat trousers and body armour. He was pretty cool, it has to be said. Not quite Liam's grungy-cool, or Rich Richard's fancy-pants cool, but maybe somewhere between the two.

Determining to stop giving the once-over to the cop who'd seen way too much of my embarrassing home life, I grinned and shook my head, finally letting the shock-anger subside.

"I did want to attend." I began with a bare-faced lie. "But I didn't think I'd be welcome." And followed it up with a sympathy fish.

"Yeah, right." Dale laughed and kind of threw his head back. It was odd because it wasn't something I saw too often. I suppose when he was all policed up to the eyeballs, unguarded laughter was not exactly encouraged.

Anyway, for the first time I noticed that he had some pretty nifty straight teeth. Not PC Betty Butler teeth, all gleaming and stuff, but nice nonetheless. Yep, he definitely looked more like one of us when he laughed.

"It's all true, Dale." I spread my arms wide in some sort of comical supplication. "And, anyway, why don't you want to go out there and mingle?"

"I was going to, until I saw that Felicity Hardcastle woman prancing about. I dunno, it made me feel a bit….well….a bit…" "Like throwing up?"

I supplied, helpfully.

"*Uncomfortable* was the word I was searching for."

"Same diff, old bean." I sniffed, and turned to look back out of the window.

Once again, my eyes were drawn to Matty Jameson. He was standing alone and looking down at the flyer he was holding. As I scanned the Quad I could see Fliss handing them round with an air of importance.

"There she goes again, huh?" Dale was suddenly at my side.

"She sure does." My beak was so close to the window that my breath fogged up the cold glass.

I stepped back a little and rubbed the condensation away with the back of my hand and carried on peering, much to Dale's amusement. "Poor Hannah." I said, hearing the sadness in my voice and hoping that I wasn't coming off as pathos-ridden as Fliss.

"I know. I suppose she never realised how little her pal thought of her. Maybe that's a good thing." Dale was pretty perceptive.

I don't know why I was so surprised that he'd picked up on my meaning without me saying a word. After all, he'd had years of doing just that, and never once been found lacking.

"Maybe." I said, a bit day-dreamy.

I was looking at Matty Jameson again; for some reason, my eyes were drawn his way once more, without any real reason. Perhaps it was the feeling of sadness that I got from him, I don't know. He just seemed a little more forlorn than you would expect him to be. I mean, he was Hannah's art lecturer; I get that.

But he would have taught her maybe once a week over the four months since we had started our first semester, so it was unlikely he knew her well enough to be personally affected by her disappearance.

I chewed at my bottom lip in a truly thoughtful way as I wondered if it was me just placing sanctions on what people should or shouldn't do, say or feel. Perhaps he was just a great lecturer who hadn't just wandered into the profession as a means of making a living out of an arts degree, but was following a vocation and truly had the best interests of his students at heart. Who knew? Well, not me, and that was a fact. If I was going to get anywhere with my own detective lark, I would have to try to understand other humans a lot better than I did. I was making comparisons that probably didn't work in the real world.

I was thinking that I probably knew Hannah a lot better than Matty Jameson, having spent so many precious break-times in her company, and I wasn't wandering around like I'd lost someone close the way he was.

Even though I didn't care for Hannah's personality, I did care about what had happened to her. And yet, I was sure that I didn't feel what Matty Jameson was feeling, if his demeanour was to be trusted.

"Who's the guy in the big coat and the silly scarf?" Dale's interruption mercifully ripped me right out of the confusing vortex of human psychology.

"He's Matty Jameson, one of the lecturers here."

"Arty stuff?"

"Yeah." I said with a laugh. "How'd you guess?"

"Just call it a hunch. I'm a copper, after all." We both had a little chuckle at that one. Nothing irreverent; just a breaking up of the strangeness of it all.

"Are any of the other lecturer's out there?" He asked, scanning the crowd.

"Yeah, there's quite a few." I spent several seconds happily pointing them out.

"I don't know if it's the outfit, but that Jamie Matheson stands out a bit."

"Jamie Matheson?" I laughed at Dale's near-spoonerism. "It's Matty Jameson." Something about the accidental transposition was prodding at my left cerebrum. "Great listening skills, Dale."

"I could have sworn it started with a J." Dale chuckled good humouredly at his mistake.

"Nope, it starts with an……M."

"You don't sound like you're too sure yourself, Brain of Britain." As Dale amused himself with a bit of low-level sarcasm, I tried my hardest to act casual and not yell *A-ha!* like some sort of bizarre female Columbo.

Matty Jameson. M.J. That's what Rich Richard had thought earlier when I had asked him if he'd ever met someone called Emjay. *I don't know anyone by those initials.* That's what he had said.

Still, Hannah's diary clearly stated Emjay as her, well, special friend, right? Some smarty-pants thought I'd had in the library about Bletchley code-breakers was coming back to me. I'd thought that Hannah's diary was kind of code-like in parts, like it was written in a way that would take some figuring out to someone else reading it. Someone like me, for instance.

Surely, I was reaching a bit with this, but Emjay never really did sound like a name, foreign or otherwise.

Suddenly I wanted PC Dale Webb to clear off so that I could make my next move, whatever that was.

"What time is this going on 'till?" Dale cut in, obviously not noticing the sudden mental activity that was warming my brain up.

"I think it said nine on Facebook." I said, somewhat distractedly.

"Facebook?"

"Yeah, Fliss has set up a page for Hannah. It's got lots of photos and stuff and appeals for information; you know the sort of thing."

"Oh, right. What's the page called? It might be an idea if the Police can keep an eye on it, just in case anything of interest or use gets posted to it." Dale was suddenly a police officer again.

"Hannah Come Home." I said, surprised that it still had the capacity to make me wince.

"Right." Dale said. He was all business, but I was gratified to see that he winced a little bit too.

Maybe I wasn't such a cynical swine after all, or if I *was*, I wasn't the only one.

Dale seemed as if he was getting restless; maybe he wanted to go off and scour the new Facebook page for any responses to Fliss' heartfelt appeal for information. I didn't blame him at all, I'd probably be doing something similar myself later.

"I'm going to get moving, Josie."

"Yeah, sure." I said with a smile. "Don't go creeping up on anyone though."

"I'll take that on board." Dale winked as he turned to saunter away down the corridor. "Take care, Josie."

"Yeah, you too."

So, there I was, totally police-free and with a genuine hunch to follow up on. I looked out across the Quad once more and, seeing Matty Jameson still out there, I wondered if I really had the stones to canter away to his office and have a poke around.

Chapter Eight

Since I was still seemingly alone in the building, I sprinted off in the direction of the Art Faculty. It was right on the other side of the campus and, by the time I arrived, I was red faced, panting, and totally sweaty.

I didn't know where Matty Jameson's office was exactly, so I had to do a fair bit of roaming around. *Ten minutes' worth* of roaming around, as it happens, before I finally turned down a long, narrow corridor and happened upon a door with the art lecturer's name on it. Success.

However, once my jubilation at simply finding the room had subsided, I stood there for what felt like a couple of minutes, trying to overcome nerves. Not just any old nerves, but big, shameful, jelly-belly nerves.

I tried to build myself up with all the recent images which had served to make my blood boil; Liam being led away by the CID officers, snooty Fliss looking at me like I was some kind of grimy accomplice. Detective Inspector Malcolm Thorn sneering at me, my best friend, and my alleged crime of poverty.

It took a few seconds to work, but by the time I'd got to DI Thorn, I was almost snorting with rage and could have kicked the door of the office down with ease. However, I tried the handle first and was gratified to find it unlocked. Taking a deep breath, I lurched into the room and closed the door behind me. I leaned against the wall of the office and listened to my terrified breathing for a few seconds.

It was pitch dark in Matty Jameson's office, and I felt along the wall for a light switch. Almost fearing to switch it on, I was rather glad that I'd finally summoned up the courage.

There was nobody in there waiting to pounce on me for trespassing. Also, there were no windows at all. I was torn between feeling sorry for Matty Jameson and his obvious *lowerend-of-the-scale-lecturer* status, and relief that I would not be observed from the outside as I carried out my clandestine activities.

The problem was, although I had been full of investigative zeal on my canter from the Quad, I had absolutely no idea what I should be looking for. There was another door, presumably leading to another room of Matty's, at the back of his office. It certainly wouldn't lead back into the corridor I had just tip-toed through.

But first things first.

I hurried to stand behind Matty's desk and wiggled the computer mouse enthusiastically until the whirring of the fan and the flickering of the monitor told me that, like all other campus computers, Matty's would spring to life somewhere in the next five minutes.

As the standard Grantstone University screen saver came into view, I felt a little pang of disappointment. It wasn't that I expected to see a happy-couple photo of Hannah and Matty suddenly come to life, but rather that I didn't expect a long coated, stripy scarf wearing, big haired guy like Matty Jameson to have such a run-of-the-mill conformist screen saver.

Suddenly thinking of fingerprints, just in case my hunch actually came to anything, I dug my gloves out of my duffle coat pocket. I say gloves when what I actually mean is mittens.

I know; not great for performing a detailed yet hurried search, just a giant clump of wool and an opposable thumb. Before putting them on, I used one of them like a cloth and rubbed the door handle, light switch, and computer mouse thoroughly. God alone knows why, but it certainly made me feel better.

I went back to the computer and stared uselessly at the password box. Never in a million years was I going to be able to guess at a password for Matty Jameson. It always kind of makes me laugh when you see a TV show and the hero cop, or whomever, has three or four really inspired attempts before finally hitting the jackpot.

I knew right away that I was not about to emulate any of my telly heroes that night, so I didn't bother to try. Plus, how many smart TV cops wear mittens whilst trying to type on a keyboard?

I'll tell you exactly how many; none.

Instead I sat down in Matty's chair and tried each of the two desk drawers. In the first was a rather broad array of over-thecounter nose un-blockers; sprays, vapour rubs, that type of thing. Poor dude must be one of the chronically bunged up types. The collection was vast and, judging by the faded colours on some of the dated packaging, had been carefully built over a number of years.

Drawer two was no better; It was all pens and pencils, not to mention pencil shavings. Seriously, why do that? Why open a drawer and sharpen a pencil over it, allowing the skimpy wooden spirals to simply land inside? Why not just reach a little further and do it over the bin?

So, apart from finding out that Matty had sinus issues and was clearly too lazy to reach for the bin, I basically had nothing.

I scanned the room for anything else of use. There was no filing cabinet or anything else with drawers I could snoop through. There were a couple of old comfy chairs covered in brown corduroy, slightly facing each other. It reminded me either of a talk show interview set up, or a psychiatrist's office.

Matty probably held his one-on-ones with his students right there. I nurtured a mental image of Matty sitting in one chair, his floppy curls dangling over his eyes like a cockapoo puppy, and Hannah in the other chair, her shoes on the floor and her legs tucked under her totally unselfconsciously as they talked about her progress on the arts degree course.

I checked my watch; it was almost half past eight. Only half an hour of the vigil to go. Still, to assume that Matty would stay for the whole thing might be a mistake. After all, he might have been trundling his way over to his office at that very moment. Or he might not even return to his office until the following day. Whichever was the case, I needed to get on with it.

Judging there to be nothing else of interest in the first room, I hurried over to the second door. I was hardly able to believe that it was locked. Matty's main office was left wide open for anyone to stride into, day or night, yet his back room was locked. Well, that got my spider-senses tingling, I can tell you.

With no other detective expertise to rely on, I had seized upon the *locked door means something to hide* theory. Rather stupidly, I tried the handle of the door again, as if it would somehow have become miraculously unlocked in the few moments in which I had stared at it. Almost forgetting my earlier fear and need to hurry, I looked about the room for some way of making my way in.

The ceiling was made up of those big grey tiles which sat suspended in a flimsy aluminium framework. You know the ones; you're sitting in a lecture, bored, and suddenly you're looking up at tiles of all different ages, judging by the yellowing of some, and wondering at the watery stains and holes which look like a rodent has been up there nibbling.

I wondered if there was any way I could go in through the ceiling, like Jack Bauer or something.

I pulled one of the brown chairs over and placed it next to the big old cast iron radiator. It was floor mounted, so I was sure it would take my weight. As I stood on the chair and put my foot on the radiator, I wondered at the total stupidity of what I was doing.

Then I thought of PC Betty Butler. If I was Betty, I'd already be in that back room, expertly rooting through Matty Jameson's secrets.

I climbed up onto the radiator and wobbled about as I pushed up one of the ceiling tiles and slid it away into the ceiling space. I squinted as dusty bits showered down from above, then stifled a sneeze. My sneezes are always pretty epic and I knew that if I gave into it, the sneeze might very well rocket me clean off my precarious perch.

I looked up again and could see that the wall between the two rooms was good old-fashion brick. I could pull myself up onto it without risking pulling the whole wall down on top of me.

I would love to be able to say that I hopped up onto said wall in a graceful ninja style, but that was very much *not* the case. I gripped the wall and scrambled, puffing and panting, in a most undignified manner until I was perched on top of it.

I then leaned over into the ceiling space in the back room and pulled another tile out of the way. I leaned in a little, looking around in the room.

There was a line of top-light windows, you know, the sort that you have to open with a hook on a stick. Anyway, there was a good bit of campus lighting shining in through them, so I could see that the room was a jumble of all manner of stuff.

I hadn't really thought through the details of how I would get down into the back room. I looked down and felt a bit foolish. It would be ridiculous to get this far and have to turn back.

With that in mind, I turned around and, holding on to the top of the brick wall I was sitting on, I kind of slid down. When I got to the point where I was at arm's length and my poor little hands were supporting my entire body, I just let go. And not *willingly*,

I just fell.

I landed on my feet, then fell over backwards, in the most painful sit-down I'd ever done. My backside was going to be bruised, I had no doubt about that. Getting quickly to my feet, I scanned the room and realised that I would probably need to put the light on.

I didn't want to alert anyone to my presence but, at the same time, the windows were so high up that nobody would actually be able to look in on me anyway.

With the light on, I could see that the room mostly contained paintings on canvas, all over the place, stacked several deep against the walls. There was an easel in the middle of the room, and a big basket full of brushes on an old paint-splattered table. The table was the flat kind, with no drawers for me to rummage through.

With a big sigh, I suddenly realised that I had crawled through the ceiling like Spiderman only to land in a room of Matty's paintings. Well, I assumed they were Matty Jameson's.

I decided to have a quick shuffle through the canvases before I made my perilous journey back into the ceiling, through Narnia, and down into the first room.

It's fair to say that I don't know a great deal about art, but I thought that Matty Jameson's paintings were really good. There were a few landscapes, but not the normal kind. They had been purposefully painted in the wrong colours; grass was not green, but orange, skies were not blue but purple, and so on. They seemed to have been skilfully painted and I couldn't help but like the topsy-turviness of his colouring.

As I trawled through, I could see that Matty's real area of expertise was portraits; he'd painted loads of them.

I was once again struck by my previous dismissal of art and its value. Just as with the fine detail of Hannah's little bumble bees, Matty's portraits held the sort of detail I'd never bothered to notice before.

I looked at a portrait of an elderly man and was mesmerised by a tiny, *tiny* stroke of light-coloured paint on the eye. It was an almost non-existent fleck of paint which had been applied to the faded blue iris, but it's effect was amazing. It gave an *age* to the eye, a kind of vaguely watery appearance that was totally lifelike.

There was something about that tiny fleck of paint, that minute attention to detail, which left me with the feeling that I was looking right into the real face of the man who had sat for the portrait.

I might have been a superb mathematician, but in many other respects I realised that I was a totally single-minded philistine. Still, there wasn't time to work on my somewhat flawed personality at that moment, and I hurriedly pulled the painting forward to look at the one behind it.

I had taken at quick squint at most of the paintings and was starting to feel that my intuition settings were obviously broken, when I *finally* hit pay-dirt. And, wowsers, what pay-dirt indeed!

As I'd leafed through the last stack of canvases I suddenly came face to face with none other than Hannah Davenport. Not in the flesh, but in oils on canvas.

Hannah seemed to be looking right at me, her face a picture of pure melancholy. It was absolutely and unmistakably Hannah;
Matty had employed the very same high standard of attention to detail, and the portrait was not *off* in any way. It was entirely, *exactly*, like Hannah. It was a perfect likeness.

I had never seen Hannah wearing that kind of expression before, and something about it made me feel so very sad. Actually, kind of gutted. There was something there in those oilpaint eyes which spoke of pain and, if she had really felt anywhere near as sad as she looked, then I could feel only pity for her.

What the hell had happened to her to give her such a look? Surely it hadn't been contrived for the painting? Or maybe it was all from Matty's imagination? Maybe Hannah hadn't actually sat for the painting at all.

In many ways, I rather hoped that she hadn't because, much apart from looking so deeply unhappy, Hannah was also entirely naked.

I was pretty shocked, but not in the way you'd imagine. I was shocked that Matty had painted one of his students naked, but I wasn't shocked by the nakedness itself. It wasn't a kind of lascivious nakedness, if you will.

Hannah was simply sitting on a chair with her head tilted slightly to one side and that heart-wrenching look on her face. Oddly, the nakedness seemed almost secondary to the whole piece, almost as if she had sat down and had forgotten she wasn't dressed yet. From my perspective of knowing next-to-nothing about art, I'm kind of hoping that makes sense.

One thing I was certain of; Emjay was MJ was Matty Jameson. *Emjay is so funny! He acts like the sight of naked flesh is some kind of spiritual experience!* There was no other explanation for it.

And what were the chances of there being another person called Emjay with whom Hannah had been naked in the last few weeks? I shrugged off my new-found art appreciation jacket and stepped back into my cloak of logic; *balance of probabilities...* I'm just saying.

As I knelt on the floor congratulating clever old me, there came that scratchy noise of someone putting a key into a lock. I nearly expired there and then. I had nowhere to go and no time to switch off the light and hide behind a tiny canvas.

And anyway, there was a chair up against the radiator and a ceiling tile out in the other room; it wouldn't have taken Sherlock to know what was going on. I was pretty much busted and I knew it.

I realised with a sort of horrible clarity that my predicament might well go beyond the obvious nightmare of being busted. I was in a deserted part of a huge university campus at night, and probably about to be in the company of a man who may or may not know more than he was saying about the disappearance of one of his students.

Not only that, but he'd painted her naked. There was a connection here and I'd more or less made it; and that much was about to become abundantly clear to the man who was now opening the door and about to discover me.

Matty Jameson entered the room cautiously, his eyes darting furtively to and fro like some kind of hunted animal. To my horror, he was holding a weapon high above his head as he inched his way into the room, although perhaps I would be one of the few who would have recognised it as such.

    It was a heavy-looking art text book. Respect to the ninja.

"What the hell are you doing in here?" He lowered the book when he saw me crouched on the floor amongst his paintings. I didn't know whether to be relieved that he wasn't going to kill me on the spot, or insulted that the lowering of the book suggested I was no threat whatsoever to him.

Instead of answering, I continued to crouch as my mouth opened and closed goldfish style. I just couldn't come up with a thing to explain my presence in his room.

"You're a student, presumably! Which course?" He demanded, all strident snottiness.

"Mechanical Engineering." I croaked dryly.

"Well, we'll see about that!" He was one of those people who spat a bit when they spoke in anger, and I was tempted to use one of his canvases as a shield.

"What?" I was just getting a hold of his threat.

The mop-headed naked-student-painter was threatening to get me thrown off the degree, I felt sure of it.

"You heard me. The University most certainly does not take breaking into a lecturer's rooms lightly." He threw his head back, somewhat diva-like.

His little threat had tipped me over from scared and busted to insanely angry.

"And tell me, Mr Jameson, how lightly do the University take the notion of a lecturer painting one of his first-year students naked?" My anger notwithstanding, I wondered at the ambiguity of my question. "I meant that *she* was naked, not that *you* were naked whilst you painted her. Well, I don't think you were. Oh God, you weren't, were you?"

Despite the entirely un-cool manner in which I was conducting my investigative interview, somehow, I now had the upper hand and it was Matty Jameson's turn to let his mouth open and close wordlessly.

My fear had departed altogether. Something about this man and his bumbling attempt at a threat had left me doubting that Matty was dangerous. I didn't drop my guard altogether in that respect, I just felt a hell of a lot calmer.

"You're not supposed to be in here." His tone had changed into something far less strident and his obvious comment seemed to be all that he could summon in his defence.

"And you're not supposed to be painting naked teenagers!" As soon as I'd said it, I knew I had behaved in absolutely the very worst Daily Mail way possible.

I had chucked the word *teenager* in to set the seal on my victory; I was making it absolute and entirely unequivocal. And I felt like a complete git, because that's exactly how I'd behaved.

I'd used the word to suggest something I didn't even suspect him of, and I'd always, *always* hated people who do and say anything to win; the kind of people who spuriously throw child and animal welfare into arguments because they feel sure that nobody would dare challenge it.

Yes, Hannah was a teenager, but she was nineteen, almost twenty, not thirteen, just finished being twelve. Like me, Hannah was a grown woman.

"Hey look, I didn't mean that how it came out. I should have said student, not teenager." My cheeks were flaming, and so were Matty Jameson's. This interview was turning into a disaster. "What do you say we start again, without threatening each other, huh?" I tried to sound like the adult I was not *entirely* sure I could claim to be at that moment in time.

"Yeah, ok." Matty's shoulders dropped.

I rose from my crouch and, feeling the bruising on my backside with every step, was almost relieved to have been caught so that I wouldn't have to climb back through the ceiling.

As he sauntered out of the back room and into the office, I followed him, glad for a couple of second's worth of unobserved bum-rubbing.

Matty sat down in one of the brown corduroy chairs, and I dragged over the one I had left as my stepping-stool next to the radiator. We sat opposite each other, and I was reminded of the talk-show interview image.

"It's really not what you think." Matty spoke first whilst I was still making myself comfortable.

"Look, I don't really have any conclusions, to be honest, but I'd still like to know. You see, my best friend has been hauled in by the Police and treated really very badly."

"Oh, you're Liam's friend."

"Yes."

"Josie, isn't it?"

"Yes, Josie Cloverfield." I was somewhat on the back foot.

Either he knew my name because I was the subject of gossip amongst the lecturers as well as the students, or Hannah had spoken of me previously. Either way, I would wait until I had wrestled some of the more important facts out of him before I satisfied my curiosity in that regard.

"Can I just start by telling you that I don't know where Hannah is or why she went missing. Whatever has happened has nothing to do with my painting her portrait."

"Were you sleeping with Hannah?" I said in as flat a tone as possible. I didn't want to seem to be judging him.

"No, I wasn't." Matty said without any of the agitation I might have expected the question to illicit.

"Did you try to?" I said, as gently as possible.

I'd seen his look of desolation out on the Quad when he'd had no idea he was being observed.

"Well, no, I didn't. I don't think Hannah was particularly interested in me. I mean, she liked me, I guess, but not in the same….."

"Not in the same way as you liked her?" I finished for him.

"That's right." Matty looked suddenly defeated, as if he might just as well tell the truth of it all.

"Did she know you liked her?"

"Yes, I'm sure of it. I think she liked the idea of being adored by someone she had very little regard for."

"Mmm." I said, absently thinking of Liam.

But Liam hadn't really adored her, had he? At least, that's what he'd said.

"As much as I thought of Hannah, she could be quite cruel."

"Yes, I know." I was still speaking absently and my lack of investigative professionalism made me suddenly concentrate. "I mean, was she?"

"Yes, she was. Hannah was silently mocking me and I knew it. I knew it, and I didn't care. I would have done anything to have been around her. Just in her company, you know?"

"Yes, I know." I lied. I had never particularly wanted to be in Hannah's scratchy company and could not understand the sentiment at all. "So, did you and Hannah spend much time together?"

"No, not really. It was mostly just while she sat for the portrait. I suppose just a couple of hours a week for three weeks."

"Not long then." I said, more to myself than to Matty.

"No, not long. At first, I'd really thought that she liked me, but I soon realised that she would be off as soon as the painting was finished."

"Really?" I straightened in my chair, as if to somehow comprehend all the better. "So, Hannah was keen to be painted, then?"

"Yes. She asked me, not the other way around."

"Oh."

"Yes, I know that sounds odd, but it's true. It would be totally stupid for me to approach a student with the suggestion of a nude project. Hannah had come to me and asked…. well, demanded, actually, to have her portrait painted."

"Demanded?"

"Yes, she could be quite forceful."

"But surely a student is not in a position to *demand* that her lecturer of just a few weeks paint her in the nude?" I was incredulous. There was more to this than he was saying. As I studied him, his cheeks flushed again and his eyes darted away from mine. "What aren't you telling me, Mr Jameson?"

"Well, Hannah was rather holding something over my head."

"What?"

"Well, let's just say that it was something that the administration here would certainly frown upon. Maybe even find a way to get rid of me."

"Let's just say more than that, shall we? Let's just say exactly what it was Hannah was holding over your head." I couldn't believe how firm my voice sounded.

Betty would have been so proud.

"Oh, I might as well tell you. After all, you've got more on me than Hannah ever had." Matty spoke more to himself. He sighed with a sort of purpose, ready to tell me it all. "Hannah had seen me in a strip club. Well, not a strip club exactly, but more of a rundown, dirty old pub in town where they have a stripper on every Sunday afternoon. The Duchess of Devonshire."

"Oh, right." I said flatly, hiding the most terrible and inappropriate urge to laugh. At first, you see, I thought he was suggesting that the Duchess of Devonshire *was* the stripper.

"It's not what you think. I only go in there to study the female form."

I bit my tongue, all the while thinking that his reason was probably the same as that of every other saddo punter in the place.

"I mean, for paintings. It helps in my nude paintings, because I very rarely work one to one with live nude models, unless it's in an open live model class."

"Oh."

"Because in open group classes or sessions with live models, you cannot pose them yourself. You simply get to sketch or paint whatever tableau the art tutor decides upon. It's rarely anything inspiring." Matty finished on kind of an elitist, almost snobby note.

I wondered if he meant that the models were rarely inspiring, or if the poses were. Maybe it was both.

Judging it not to particularly matter to either me or my investigation, I more or less let it go. I say more or less, because I had a sudden image of poor Matty trying to paint an elderly nude dude.

After all, live classes, as Liam had previously told me, rarely contained the sort of stunning models you might imagine. Liam said that you had to learn to draw and paint *reality*, and reality included wrinkles, chubby bits and all sorts.

"So, you went to this pub to watch the Sunday stripper for artistic inspiration?" I made my question sound like a statement. I really didn't want to seem like I was mocking him. In truth, I sort of felt for the guy.

"Yes, that's right."

"But I can't imagine that the Sunday afternoon stripper would draw too many female patrons to that pub, surely."

I was trying to place Hannah there in some seamy spit-andsawdust pub watching a stripper with the smell of roast potatoes and cabbage cooking in the background, assuming the Duchess of Devonshire did Sunday lunches.

In my head, I was imagining the Dalton Arms, where my total role-model of a parent spent a good deal of her time and benefit money. It always smelled of school dinner type food and a general sour fustiness.

I would have laid odds that this rundown, dirty old pub which Matty had been to smelled exactly the same. Wowsers, imagine stripping somewhere like that!

"No, none at all. I suppose it's not surprising, really. Most women would feel rather uncomfortable with it all, I daresay." Matty seemed to be thoughtfully mulling it over.

"But Hannah wasn't uncomfortable?"

"No, not a bit." Matty seemed oddly surprised by my question. "So, who had she gone into the pub with?"

"Gone into the….. oh, no, no, Hannah wasn't a patron." Matty rolled his eyes in a kind of *oops, silly me* way, which felt totally surreal. "Sorry, I forgot to say! Hannah wasn't drinking in the

pub and watching the stripper; Hannah *was* the stripper!"

Chapter Nine

By the time I had once again traversed the old town of Grantstone, I was starting to feel exhausted. The last couple of days had seemed to fly by in a whirlwind of shock, anger, fear, frayed nerves, and lines crossed, all of which had rather taken it out of me.

As the second bus rumbled on towards the edge of the Moss Park Estate, I contemplated the fact that I was detecting my heart out on very little sleep.

In just two days I had snooped about at a Police search, stolen evidence, had *that* evidence stolen from me by an intruder, slept fitfully, discovered a warning on the bathroom mirror, discovered the possible betrayal of my best friend, discovered the identity of the instrument of betrayal, and then discovered it wasn't betrayal at all. Well, not the bog-standard type of betrayal I had thought it to be.

All in all, I was knackered.

I let my head rest against the glass of the bus window without once considering who might have lolled there last. Ordinarily, I was a bit twitchy, and was one of those people who tries to back out of a public toilet without touching the door handle.

As my head bounced lightly off the glass, the mild thumping sensation was curiously soporific, and I had to guard against closing my eyes for fear of waking up at the bus station in town an hour later.

As I stepped down off the bus and started the twenty-minute walk through the estate, I looked at my watch; it was nearly ten o'clock. I was so glad that tomorrow was a Friday. I had no lectures to attend at all.

Ordinarily, I would have spent the day at uni anyway, working away in the silent study area of the library. I loved it there, and I loved the fact that I finally had a place to study which wasn't in my bedroom with some sort of dreadful goings-on in the house all around me. Once I was in that silent and solitary little booth, the world felt like it was totally mine.

However, Friday would not exactly run to my routine; I would need to get a decent sleep of some sort before I made my next investigative move. I knew I had to work my shift at the dry cleaners on Saturday, so my investigation would be necessarily halted whilst I put in six hours of smiling politely in order to rebuild my tattered coffers. The flask was definitely coming back into play, as were the Euro-Saver crisps.

So, a good lay in followed by a day of chasing leads. Decision made.

As I neared home, I decided to take a detour and go to Liam's. I hadn't really thought about the intruder too much, since my day had been so full to bursting that I hadn't had time to dwell on it.

The idea of going home and trying to sleep with chairs against the doors did not exactly appeal. Of course, my mum might have returned home in the meantime but, honestly, the idea was not more much more appealing than sharing house space with a crazed intruder.

As I took a detour away from my home, I pulled my phone out of my bag and sent Liam a text. I knew he would still be wide awake and, as for the rest of his family, some of them would only just be getting up.

In short, there was no-one who would take offence at the lateness of my arrival.

"Just around the corner. Can I come round to your place?" I kept walking, totally sure of finding myself welcome.

"Sure Dude. Back door open, just come straight up."

I did as instructed, and let myself in through the back door into the kitchen. The layout of Liam's house was exactly the same as the one me and mum lived in. The Attwood place seemed smaller, somehow, but I reckoned it was because it was always full. Full of things and full of people.

I smiled at Mrs Attwood as I opened the door and peeked in.

"Hiya Josie, love. He's upstairs." Mrs Attwood always seemed to speak on an outward sigh, as if life was way too hard and speech was a mere afterthought.

Thanks Mrs Attwood." I smiled as I closed the door up behind me and stepped around a great pile of boxes.

Well, boxes of brand new toasters, to be precise. In fact, boxes of brand new *stolen* toasters, to be truly thorough in my description of the scene. Mrs Attwood, as always, showed no hint of even noticing the boxes were there. It was as if the activities of her sons were none of her business.

For the most part, I wasn't sure I could blame her. With a husband in prison, and three of her sons constantly stealing, fighting, and evading the law, I could quite see why she had decided to look without seeing.

But she applied the very same ethos to Liam; Liam, the son who had fought for the great armload of GCSEs he had achieved, not to mention the A-levels, and now a place at university. All without a single word of encouragement.

As much as I pitied Mrs Attwood at times, I was still almost overwhelmed by an urge to take hold of the back of her neck and ram her forehead into the nearest hard surface; table, wall, whatever. I knew this urge well; I had the very same one concerning my own mother.

In their own ways, both women had definitely had hard lives; no arguments from me. But instead of encouraging their own children on to better things they either *ignored* effort, in the case of Mrs Attwood, or actively *denigrated* effort, in the case of my own mum.

Instead of belting her head on the table, I shot past Mrs Attwood with a grin and ran off upstairs to find my mate.

"Well, I was trying to work, anyway." I could hear Liam's angry tone as I was half-way up the stairs.

"On what, you swatty little geek?"

"Why do you care? Just get out, Jack."

"What if I say *no?*" Jack was not blessed with brains or any kind, and had certainly not evolved one iota in the last ten years or so. He'd just got bigger.

"Mind out of the way, Jack." I said sharply as I made for Liam's room.

Jack turned to look at me but moved aside, as he always did. Jack had never really known how to deal with me and, whilst we had never connected on any level, he afforded me a certain amount of grudging respect.

"Move back a bit, I want to shut the door." I said as soon as I made it into the room.

Once again, Jack did as he was told, and I was able to gently close the door in his face. I stood for a moment or two, waiting for some kind of objection. When it didn't come, I wasn't particularly surprised.

"How was the vigil?" Liam said, putting down his art history textbook and moving his other books off the bed to make room for me to sit down.

Liam's room was even more Spartan than my own. He had a bed and a chest of drawers, and that was it. He used to have a little portable telly; you know the really old ones with the round wire aerial and the tuning dial?

But either his dad or one of his brothers had pinched it from him a couple of years back, presumably to sell. In these days of digital everything and HDMI cables everywhere, I wondered who *exactly* had bought the old antique of a set, and how much they had paid whichever Attwood had stolen it.

Anyway, Liam hadn't bothered to replace it; what would be the point? Instead, he, like me, had invested hard-earned money in a smart phone. It might seem like a luxury but, to us, they were lifelines.

They were communication, internet, books and TV all in one, and neither one of us ever carelessly let these valuable commodities out of our sight for a moment. I never went to the bathroom without taking my smart phone with me.

My mum, or some Snatcher Harris type of a character, would have no qualms whatsoever about stealing mine and selling it. "The vigil was kind of cheesy." I said, plopping down onto his bed.

"What, a bit cheesy, or the sort of cheesy that gives you bellyache?"

The bellyache one." I said, with a tired little laugh. "Well, no, that's not fair, really. There were lots of people there who really did seem to be genuinely concerned."

"But?"

"But Fliss wasn't one of them. She was lapping up every drop of attention she could get out of it. And she'd had this big photo of Hannah set on a tripod. I don't know, it kind of felt like…..well, like a wake or something."

"Jeez. Poor Hannah." Liam looked down at his hands.

I felt sorry for him; Liam didn't have the connection to Hannah that I'd assumed he'd had, and I was getting the impression that he was feeling guilty about it. Either that, or he was wishing he'd never told me about his feelings, or lack thereof.

"Yeah. I honestly wonder if she had one real friend in all the world." I said, and meant it.

"I know." Liam looked up from his hands. "I guess we're luckier than we realise sometimes, huh, Dude?"

"Yeah, we are." I smiled at his sad little mush before scooting across the bed to give him a hug.

It seemed to take forever to tell him all the evening's events, especially the Matty Jameson stuff. Liam, as was his custom, kept interrupting; either to ask questions, or to take the mickey out of me and me and my new self-appointed detective status.

"You did what? You crawled through the ceiling?" Liam was holding his belly whilst he laughed hard. "Like some kind of spy, Dude! MI6 or something!" He was wiping his eyes now. "Dude – Ace of Spies!"

"Yep. That's me." I gave him a few moments to thoroughly enjoy himself with it. "Until I slid down the wall on the other side and landed on my butt!"

"Smooth, Dude! Very smooth."

I told Liam about all the paintings, trying to gauge his reaction to my discovery of Hannah's naked oil-on-canvas. Liam seemed really shocked by it, but not hurt. I guessed it was more or less the same as earlier that day when I told him that Hannah had maybe cheated on him.

"I just can't imagine it. I don't know, it just doesn't seem like something Hannah would do."

"But I guess you didn't know her too well, Liam. Neither of us did, did we?"

"No, I suppose not." Liam sat up straighter, something else had clearly occurred to him. "Dude, we need to tell the Police about this."

"Wait a minute...."

"No, listen, Dude. He's a suspect now. He has to be, surely." Liam seemed a little more relieved than I was comfortable with.

"Why?" I said cautiously, waiting for the chunky eyebrow of doom to race up his forehead and totally chastise me.

"What do you mean, why?" *Hello Mr Eyebrow, what took you so long?*

"Liam, just wait for the rest, ok."

"There's more?"

"There's more." I hurriedly cantered through the rest of the tale.

"*A stripper?* Are you serious?" The eyebrow had forgotten itself and had slid back into neutral.

"Yes, but just on a Sunday afternoon." I really have no idea why I said that.

"Oh well, if it was just *Sunday's*, Dude!" Liam spread his hands wide and his tone was sarcastic.

"Oi! Can it, Attwood!" The feeling of walking on eggshells was starting to grate on my nerves. I was completely exhausted and needed his sarcasm like I needed another night without solid sleep.

"Sorry, Dude." Liam reached out and patted my knee, but we were still on shaky ground, and I could swear I felt it moving.

"Anyway, I'm going to go over to this pub at the weekend and….."

Take in a show?"

"I've had enough now, Liam." Something about his obstructive anger had hurt my feelings and I could feel a kind of thickness in my throat which was about to start affecting my speech noticeably. I began to get to my feet.

"Dude, don't go. I'm really, really sorry." Liam grabbed my arm and tugged me back down onto the bed. "Pleeease…"

"Ok." It was all I could say whilst I tried to swallow down the emotion.

"So, I wonder why Hannah decided to become a stripper. It can't have been for the money." Liam was trying hard, and I appreciated his effort.

"Well, no, I guess not." My voice was back properly and I felt safe to continue. "I keep thinking about that diary of hers, though. It had *Rebellion* written all over it. There was, like, a whole sheet of it. *Rebellion, rebellion, rebellion*…. In fancy writing, like 3D and stuff. There was even a line which said *maybe it's time to have a rebellion of my own?* Could that be what this was? The stripping, I mean."

"Sounds pretty likely. But what was she rebelling against? I mean, you can't have a rebellion without a reason."

"True, Liam. But God knows what it was. Did she ever say if anything kind of big and troubling had happened to her at any point?"

"Dude, we just weren't that close, I guess." Liam shrugged apologetically. "So, do you think she was having an affair with Matty Jameson?"

"No, I really don't. I think she kind of strung him along a bit, but it seems like she just wanted her portrait painted. Maybe just another part of the rebellion."

"But then, he would say that, wouldn't he? It makes sense for him to try to distance himself from her." Liam said, chewing his bottom lip in thought.

"Wow, Liam! That's just what DI Thorn said about you!"

"Well, it might be right in this case."

"And it might be wrong."

"He might have been strung along and been so angry that he killed her."

"Killed her?" I was open mouthed. "Liam, for God's sake! You weren't so keen on having false accusations chucked at you, so why do the same to someone else?"

"Really, Dude? *Really?*" Liam's voice had suddenly raised in a way that made my eyes fly open. "So, you're happy to see me as the number one suspect, whilst you do all you can to protect some perv of a university lecturer who had more reason to do something to Hannah than I did!" Liam was actually shouting at this point.

We'd had our rows over the years, the way people who are totally comfortable with each other can; but nothing like this. We'd never been this angry with one another.

I was so furious with Liam that I began to get to my feet once more. This time, he let me pull my duffle coat back on without trying to stop me.

"You have it so wrong, Liam." I began, as soon as I was ready to go.

"Oh yeah?"

"Yes. You see, if the Police became aware that Matty Jameson painted your girlfriend in the nude, they would *still* suspect you. That painting alone doesn't give Matty Jameson motive. It gives *you* motive, you idiot!"

"What?" Liam's jaw dropped.

"Your girlfriend went behind your back to become a stripper and have her naked frame painted by another man." I paused long enough to watch Liam process the whole thing. "For the same reasons that I am reluctant to hand them Hannah's diary, I am also reluctant to tell them what I discovered tonight. Not because I'm doing all I can to protect some perv of a university lecturer, as you call him, but to protect some ungrateful little git of a best friend who doesn't deserve me risking all sorts of trouble to clear his name!" Now I was the one who was shouting, and Liam was looking worried. God, I was furious with him.

I strode out of the room, with Liam calling out after me.

"Dude? Josie? wait."

"Go to hell!" I flew down the stairs and out through the kitchen door before the first of the angry tears had even begun to sting my eyes.

I flew down Liam's street, not wanting him to catch up with me and knowing that, because he's a really good guy at heart, he would certainly give it a go.

It wasn't that I was being a prima donna who wants the drama of being chased, all tear-stained and vulnerable, through the streets. It was simply that I had more or less had enough and really did not want to go over it all any more.

I was exhausted and I wanted to go to bed. And, well, ok….. I didn't want to have to forgive Liam right there and then. You see, I'm very much of the mind that a genuine apology for something that's not, like, murder or something awful, is usually something that must be accepted. If Liam had caught up with me and apologised, just as I felt sure he wanted to, then I would have accepted it.

But, you see, after all the ducking and diving, the intruder in my house, lying to the police, and all the rest of it, I just wasn't ready to shrug my shoulders and politely accept unreasonable crap being thrown at me, even if the crap-thrower was my very stressed and very scared best friend in the world.

I slowed down a little once I had developed a sweaty top lip from my exertions, and realised that I was panting like an aged Labrador on a hot day. When I was just a couple of streets from my own house, I started to think about whomever it was who had broken into my house just the night before.

Now that they had Hannah's diary, would they even need to come back? After all, I'd clearly been in the house at the time and the intruder hadn't done anything to me. But what if they'd read the diary and thought I might actually *know* something I shouldn't, which I probably did if I could but work it all out?

What if they had decided that I needed to be silenced?

After all, surely the only person who would come looking for Hannah's diary would be the same person who must surely have something to do with her disappearance. It seemed less and less likely that Hannah had gone of her own accord. *Or did it?* The whole thing was so confusing. Had she run away? Had she met someone who then *stopped* her going home? Had she simply been abducted by someone, a stranger perhaps?

As I slowed down to my normal saunter, I realised that these questions must be the very same which absolutely tormented the families of the missing time and time again. Hannah's family must have been suffering a living nightmare. The pure helplessness of not knowing must be truly appalling.

Then there was the diary and the intruder; whomever had broken into my house the night before must surely have known that I had the little book. Which meant that they must have seen me take it.

Just as I was wondering how on earth someone could have seen me on that deserted canal footpath, I heard the light pattering of footsteps somewhere behind me. They weren't big, noisy, purposeful steps; rather they were the sort of footsteps that were produced by someone actually *trying* to be quiet. I realise how that sounds, but I was on red alert and I know what I heard!

My scalp was positively tingling with fear and I was torn between simply breaking into a sprint, or my version of the same, or turning around and surprising my stalker with a sweeping blow from my swinging rucksack.

I was suddenly dismayed at the thought that the only book not in my locker was actually tucked away under my mattress at home. I didn't even have the weight of the photocopy of Hannah's diary to rely on, although, in the circumstances, that was probably a good thing.

At least I would still have that piece of evidence. Some comfort that would be when I was in a total body cast in hospital, drinking every meal through a straw as I recovered from the dreadful injuries inflicted by my attacker.

That final thought was enough to make me do something other than meekly mooch along waiting for someone to put a sack over my head. I spun around so suddenly that I actually surprised myself.

"Whoa, whoa! Hey, don't shoot, ok? It's only me, Josie."

I blinked in confusion for a few seconds, trying to work out what on earth Rich Richard was doing there. Of all the people I would have expected to see wandering around on the Moss Park estate at half past ten on a Thursday night, Rich Richard most certainly wasn't chief among them.

I had slid my rucksack off my shoulder and had been swinging it around by the straps, ready to strike. In all honesty, the pencil case, scientific calculator, and solitary Golden Delicious apple were unlikely to have been weighty enough to have made any sort of impact upon a would-be attacker, even if you allowed for the pure shock of it all.

"What the hell are you doing here?" My voice was so aggressively bad-ass that it totally sounded like someone else was speaking.

"Looking for you." Rich Richard had backed up a couple of steps and was eyeing my almost-empty rucksack with undisguised curiosity. "What's with the bag swinging? Are you planning on trying out for the University hammer throwing team, or auditioning for the Christmas Panto?"

As much as I wanted to laugh, my heart was still cantering along and I was still recovering from sweaty-top-lip number one when number two followed hot on its heels. I slung my bag back over my shoulder and slayed the sweat moustache with the back of my rough wool mitten which I had pulled out of my pocket.

"Richard." I said in a low and pretty exhausted way. "Why are you looking for me?"

In my mind, Rich Richard came from the good part of town; the very good part of town. By my way of reckoning, he was at least two, if not three, bus rides away from home, and wandering around on one of the county's roughest council estates late at night. That was not normal behaviour. I mean, not normal for someone like Rich Richard.

In truth, the estate never scared me. Why would it? I had grown up here and I knew it like the back of my hand. And, like most of the lifelong residents, I had a general air of belonging.

I'm not saying that in a cynical social-engineering way, although I could go on and on about *that* subject until the cows come home, but in a very practical sense.

As weird as many of the folk on the estate found me, they still accepted me as someone who lives there; someone who belongs; one of their own. Rich Richard stood out horribly, in a kind of easy meat way; a *please do mug me, it'll so be worth the effort* way.

When I added that to the ever-so-quiet footsteps, I started to feel a little bit unnerved by his presence. My spider senses were tingling again!

"I really need to speak to you, Josie." He said, smiling happily as if we were sharing a Kit-Kat in the canteen.

"Here? In the middle of the night?" The suspicion in my voice was evident.

"It's barely half-ten, Josie." Rich Richard looked at his watch, then turned big, confused eyes on me.

"You know what, Richard? That wide-eyed sort of innocence only works when it's puppies running through the house with toilet rolls on the telly."

"Christ, Josie, you're *suspicious!*"

"Too right I am! You are so unbelievably out of place here, not to mention the fact that you have my mobile number and you could have called to speak to me, rather than skulk about in a dark street."

"Look, I'm sorry if I startled you; I really didn't mean to. And yes, I could have called you, but this is kind of…. well, delicate, I guess."

"What is?"

"Well, there is something I think I need to tell someone. I don't think it has a bearing on things… well, Hannah's disappearance. Anyway, I don't think it really makes a difference, and I don't really want to tell the Police my private business, especially seeing the way they treated you and Liam. But, at the same time, I just wanted to tell someone, and since you're kind of, well, investigating it all, I thought you'd maybe hear me out." Richard spread his hands wide, palms up, kind of plaintiff fashion.

I searched his face, although I honestly could not tell you what I was looking for. You see, I really didn't know Rich Richard well enough to know if he was lying or not.

I tried instead to think of reasons why he *would* lie. Chief among them was that he was the person who had broken into my house and swiped the original diary; the same person who had been lurking, or possibly lurking, in the library as I had gone through the photocopy, and had been creeping up on me to…. what? What could he possibly have hoped to do?

When I thought about it sensibly, stalking someone through the streets of a housing estate is not the smartest plan ever; you see, there's usually someone milling about, whatever the hour, and also the streets are so narrow that, the minute a scream is heard, about sixty faces appear at assorted windows.

In truth, the same sixty faces might very well refuse to give statements to the police but, out of them all, *someone* would come flying out if they saw a man attacking a woman. Still, his motive might not have been to clock me over the head in the street.

He might simply have been following me home, ready to break in when I was safely inside. Again, my scenario failed to stand up to scrutiny; if Rich Richard had broken into my house the night before, he already knew where I lived and had no need to follow me.

I was so tired that I could hardly think anymore.

"So, what is it that you want to tell me?" I said, my voice riding the surf of a really deep sigh.

"Here?" Richard looked furtively about him, as if for a witness of some sort. "I mean, can't we go to your place or something?"

I looked at him incredulously. I supposed, in Rich Richardland, a household was ever-ready for sudden and unexpected guests. In Josie-land, however, there really never was a good time for such a thing.

Even if I could be assured that my mum was still absent, somewhere out in the dark dank world at Snatcher Harris' side, I still did not want to invite Richard in. Not because of the issue of my vaguely suspecting him of having something to do with Hannah's disappearance, but rather it was something worse; well, worse to me in that moment.

Richard was not one of us; he was one of them.

I'd have felt no more comfortable inviting him into my shabby and impoverished abode than I would have if he was actually Fliss Hardcastle, or someone very similar.

"That's not such a good idea, Richard." I said, hearing the utter flatness in my voice.

"Why not?" The very fact that he couldn't simply sense my discomfort and misgivings and simply move on had kind of made me angry.

Seriously, how could he not look about him and take a wild guess at why I wouldn't want to invite someone from the good part of town into my home?

"Because my mum might be there."

"So?"

"Alright, Richard." I started, my annoyance rising exponentially. "Because my mum, if she is there, is more than likely going to be as drunk as a skunk. If she's as drunk as a skunk, there's a good chance she'll be yelling like a banshee." I was giving him the works, and I knew it. I was so needled by what I saw as a casual lack of insight into my world that I could feel myself warming up horribly under my duffle coat. My breath felt hot, like I could breathe fire right out of my flaring nostrils if I put my mind to it. "If she's yelling like a banshee, there's a good chance the cops will arrive and lock her up for a Breach of the Peace." Richard's eyes were getting wider by the second. "And even if she's fairly lucid, there's a very good chance that she won't be alone. There's a strong likelihood that she will be in company with Snatcher Harris, a one-toothed heroin addict who smells like an open drain on a hot day! And, trust me, your lovely mummy and daddy will not be at all pleased if they found out you had spent quality time with Snatcher Harris! Does that answer your question?"

"Yes, thank you." Richard said quietly.

Then, as I rapidly blinked to disperse hot and angry little tears before they fell, I could hear a rumbling sort of a noise coming from Richard. Well, from his chest, to be precise. At first, I thought it must be some kind of truly spectacular bout of indigestion or something similar. It took a few more seconds before I realised that it was suppressed laughter that refused to be denied and was doing all it could to make its way out of him.

"Erm... are you, like, actually laughing?" I asked in a voice which tended to suggest that his life might depend upon his answer.

"Yeah. Sorry... it's just...Snatcher Harris? Seriously, that's a name?" Richard finally gave in and the laughter just boomed right out.

"Yes, Snatcher Harris. That's my mum's current boyfriend." As I watched him holding his belly and laughing hard, I began to see the funny side and felt pretty bad about how harsh I'd been. "Hey look, I'm sorry, ok? It's just that a lifetime of being looked down on can make you pretty touchy, you know?"

"Yeah, it's ok, I get it." Richard was still laughing, although it was in its final stages. "Look, shall we just go and sit in my car instead?"

"Ok. Where is it?"

"I parked it on Dunmore Street." Richard said, squinting a little, as if he wasn't sure he'd got the name right. "That's where I was when I saw you. I wasn't so sure it was you, so I thought I'd better not drive alongside you, in case it wasn't you and I got reported to the Police or something."

"Ok." I laughed. "If it's still there, we'll sit in your car."

The idea that Richard had spotted me and simply got out of his car to approach me on foot seemed pretty feasible and had made me feel secure enough to sit in his car with him.

As we rounded the corner of Dunmore Street, Richard silently pointed to a battered old Peugeot parked under the bright light of a street lamp. The council had been experimenting with some kind of *designing-out-crime* type of a deal, and had installed the sort of high wattage lighting that made the Moss Park estate as brightly lit as a football stadium. It was almost like perpetual daytime on some streets, like that place in Lapland, and I sometimes wondered if Moss Park could now be seen from the Moon.

"That's your car?" I said, the surprise in my voice totally undisguised.

"Yes, why?"

"It looks kind of…"

"Old and knackered?"

"Well, yes. Sorry. That's totally rude coming from an eternal bus-pass holder."

"Don't worry about it. It is a bit of a heap, but it's all I could afford."

"Really?" Voice totally incredulous. Such double standards!

"Yes, really. Look, I know I come from a family who are well off, but that doesn't mean I'm spoiled, ok?"

"Yeah, sure. I'm sorry." And I really was.

"You don't have to be sorry, Josie. I come from a well-off family and you don't. That's not something either one of us had a say in, is it? I mean, it just is as it is. But does it have to mean that we can't be friends?"

"No, it doesn't." I said, my head a bit on the droopy and ashamed side as I tried to open the door of the old heap.

"See, that's the kind of thing that just doesn't matter to me. It matters to

Fliss and Amelia and people like that, but I'm not one of them. People are all different, Josie, and it wouldn't hurt you to give me a chance." Richard was thoroughly enjoying the moral high-ground and, as I struggled in vain with the door of the Peugeot, I could not find any way of taking back my selfrighteous indignation.

"Yes, you're right." I said, wishing he would just let it go already.

"I mean, I bet you have very little in common with Snatcher Harris! I wouldn't judge you to be the same as him just because you come from the same place."

"Alright! I get it! Social prejudice is no more justified for being aimed upwards!" I said, completely frustrated by being wrong, being tired, and being completely unable to get into the car. "How the hell does this door open?"

"Oh, you have to kind of lift it up a bit as you pull it towards you. I think the hinges have dropped a bit or something."

I did as instructed, with a certain amount of gusto, and very nearly ended up on my already bruised backside.

"You're pretty smooth, aren't you?" Richard said, once again holding back the laughter.

"So I've been told." I said, smiling; well, at least he seemed to have forgiven me for my bout of class intolerance.

Once I'd successfully negotiated my way into the old Peugeot and slammed the knackered door shut, I was further surprised to find that the interior of Rich Richard's car was even worse than the exterior. The seat I was on had a hole in it big enough for me to hide in.

"Keep your comments to yourself." Richard said, but with a lovely, jokey tone. I really had been forgiven.

"Roger wilco." I said, a tired little laugh escaping. "So, what did you want to tell me, Richard?"

"Well, I don't know how to say this in a way that won't make you look at me differently." He began, suddenly all bumbly and nervous.

"Richard, we hardly know each other." I said, wondering why he gave a damn what I thought of him. "I mean, what I know of you, I like. And you've been there as an ally whenever something ugly happens in the canteen……"

I stopped for a moment. "Actually, the fact that you *are* always there when someone takes a verbal swing at me or stares me down might *actually* qualify you more for the role of jinx than ally."

I was cold, tired and extremely hungry. Apart from the single slice of pizza and the sugary treats, all donated by Liam, I had eaten very little that day.

The fact that the day seemed to have grown to about ten metres long was not lost on me either. It was like the longest day ever. I opened my rucksack and took out the battered Golden Delicious apple.

"Thanks." Richard said, rather genuinely.

"For what?" I said, taking a huge bite of the apple whilst I wondered what the hell he was thanking me for.

"For putting me at my ease. You know, making me laugh and stuff. You're pretty cool."

"I actually meant the part about you being a jinx." I said, through a mouthful of well-passed-its-best appley goodness.

Richard just laughed, presumably assuming that I was still joking. *Ok, if that makes you happy....*

"Anyway, I suppose I'd better just come right out with it." Richard began with a rueful smile.

As I took the second bite, I was so done-in that I couldn't summon up a single suspenseful emotion. In fact, all I had left in me was the notion that, if this thing was not as worth hearing as it promised to be, I would wrench off the knackered old car door and use it to beat Rich Richard to within an inch of his life.

"I slept with Hannah." He said, in the same way a person might say *pass the salt*. Totally flat and what-not. So much so that it took a second or two for that little gem to sink in. When it did, I kind of shrieked, but I inhaled quite a sizeable chunk of apple at the same time.

"Josie? Are you ok?" Richard leaned forward in his seat and turned to look at me.

I was coughing so hard that my eyes streamed and my hands were full of chewed apple bits. Sadly, not the errant apple-bit that was causing all the problems.

"Josie? Are you choking?" He looked just the right amount of serious now and, without any further ado, Richard shoved me forward and hit me really hard on the back. And, voila! One huge piece of apple hit the dashboard with the intensity of a bullet.

It took me a few minutes to get my breath back and sort out the whole horrible mess of chewed apple, and Richard just waited patiently. Finally, red faced and damp eyed from the strain of it all, I turned to look at him.

"You slept with Hannah?" I said, my voice a tiny squeak emanating from a severely sore throat.

"Yeah." Richard said, somewhat shame-faced. "And sorry about the apple and stuff. I thought I was playing it down, you know?"

"Yeah, I know." I said, smiling at him regardless of my neardeath experience. "When?"

"It was before Liam, if that's what you were worrying about." He said, keen to let me know he hadn't done my best friend a wrong'un.

"I hadn't really thought of that." I said, truthfully.

After all, it was beginning to look like Liam wouldn't have been too bothered about that anyway, if his reaction to all the other revelations was anything to go by.

"But I was seeing Fliss at the time. It only happened the once…" He began, spreading his hands wide as if he somehow needed my forgiveness. "But it was kind of…. planned. It wasn't like a spur of the moment thing, you know? I can't just say it *just happened* or it was *just one of those things*."

My brain was back up and running, despite the fact that the rest of me was just about ready to pass out from pure fatigue.

"When Fliss and Amelia were at the spa?"

"Jeez! How did you know that?" Richard's eyes were wider than saucers.

I have to admit to a little bit of self-satisfaction at this point. I've got a wicked memory for things I've read.

"Hannah's diary." I said, simply.

"She put it in her diary?" Suddenly, Richard looked totally alarmed.

"Not in so many words, no. There was just a note in there that Fliss and Amelia were going to the spa on 12th August, but it wasn't clear if Hannah was going with them. Anyhow, at the end of the entry was *Richie* in parenthesis."

"In what?"

"Brackets, you numpty."

"Seriously? And you just made that connection from that?"

"Uh-huh." I said, trying to be nonchalant, but beaming like the Cheshire Cat.

"No way!" I have to say that he certainly seemed impressed; so much so that he lost the panicked look.

"Oh God, you haven't told the Police about the diary yet, have you?" And the panicked look came back.

"Well, no. I don't really know what to do about that. I mean, I don't want to hide stuff from the Police, you know? But at the same time, I haven't read it all the way through yet and I'm not keen to give them something that might be misconstrued by them and used against anyone who is actually innocent." I knew my explanation was clumsy, to say the least.

"So, it says something about Liam?"

"Actually, no. Well, not so far, anyway." I kind of lied a little bit, but not much.

It didn't really say much about Liam, but rather spoke volumes about a possible motive. Still, I didn't really think Rich Richard needed to know it all just yet. After all, could I really trust him?

"And does it say anything else about me?" Richard asked so openly that I didn't know if I should be suspicious or not.

"No, just your name in paren… brackets. That's all."

"I'm just worried that if the cops knew I had a fling with Hannah, then they might think I have something to do with her disappearance. After all, look at the way they are treating Liam."

"Yeah, true enough." I said, knowing that he had a point. "Look, I wasn't planning to go to the Police with it yet. Maybe not even at all."

"But you're going to keep investigating?"

"Well, I guess so. If you can call it that. Mostly it just feels like I'm stumbling around in the dark and banging into wardrobes and stuff." I said with the sort of sigh that should have told anybody that I was exhausted.

"Good, well… if you need my help with any of it. You know; just call me, ok?"

"Thanks Richard." I said with a smile, getting ready to take my leave. Sadly, my brain was still having its own little private disco, and another thought occurred to me. "Hey, Richard, did Fliss know that you and Hannah….?"

"Jeez, no! I wouldn't be sitting here now if she did." Richard said, his expression somewhere between comical exaggeration and the awful truth.

"Really?"

"Well, yes, really. Fliss has a nasty temper when provoked, and my cheating on her would definitely have provoked it." "Nasty like, violent nasty?" I said, my interest piqued once more.

"Yes." He said, quietly. I was really hoping I wasn't about to get some horrible tale of teen domestic violence. He looked kind of tortured at that moment, and my fears were all heading in the same direction.

"You mean….. you?" I really didn't know how else to say it. I was almost wishing I had totally choked on the apple.

"No, not me. Amelia."

In that moment, I hated myself for being relieved.

"Oh, I see. How, though? I mean, she, like, hits Amelia?"

"Yeah, from time to time. I saw her fly at Amelia once for buying a pair of shoes that Fliss had her eye on. She scratched her face. It was nasty, actually. Kind of deep scratching. It was a couple of weeks before we started uni, and Amelia was still wearing thick make-up at the start of the semester."

"Oh no." I said, with gusto. Obviously, Richard didn't know how crappy I was feeling about my relief.

It wasn't that I thought it was ok for Fliss to hurt Amelia; I was just glad she hadn't hurt Richard. I hope that makes sense.

"And was it a regular thing?" I went on, my disco brain now dancing like Napoleon Dynamite.

"It was the only time I saw it, but… I don't know…. Amelia didn't seem outraged, or even surprised by it. I guess I just came to the conclusion that it wasn't the first time." Richard said, looking a little ashamed of himself. "But

I did tackle her, Josie. I said I couldn't believe she went off like that over something as stupid as shoes."

"What happened then?"

"She turned as if she was going to run at me too, you know, for interfering or something. Anyway, I just held a hand up to her and told her that she was out of order. I guess I shouted. Anyway, next thing Fliss was in floods of tears and Amelia was all over her, comforting her. Suddenly *I* was the bad guy." Richard seemed so unsure of himself and was looking at me, waiting for my reaction.

"Good for you Richard. Bullies need standing up to. I can tell you that from experience. And Amelia standing up for her abuser? Textbook!" I said with a knowledgeable flourish. "It means that she can forget about her own humiliation for a while." I was glad to see the relief on his face. "You let Amelia know that you were on her side. Just because she chose to ignore that doesn't make it your fault." I sighed. "Still, poor Amelia. I don't like the girl, but nobody deserves that."

"No, they don't."

"Hey, did Fliss ever get violent with Hannah?" I blurted, showing every card in my detective pack right there.

"No way. Hannah was too strong for that. She used to put Fliss in her place now and then. Fliss is the stereotypical bully, you know? Only picking on people she thinks won't fight back. I suppose she put me into that category for a while."

"Until you shouted at her." I said with a broad smile.

I really despised Felicity Hardcastle and was shocked, but not entirely surprised, by her behaviour. And it still gave me pause for thought, however strong Rich Richard thought Hannah might be.

If someone can turn violent over shoes, what else might they turn violent over? And how sure could Richard be that Fliss was totally in the dark about his little transgression?

I smiled to myself, but only a little bit. I didn't want Rich Richard to become aware of my silent *a-ha* moment. I mean, it's not that I seriously thought Fliss had something to do with Hannah's disappearance, it was simply that I could safely put her on my list of suspects.

As I stared out into the brightly lit Dunmore Street, I wondered exactly who else was actually on my list of suspects. In truth, I didn't really think I had a list, and I was just too tired to make one there and then.

"Richard? I'm shattered." I said, the sound of my tired little voice making me feel even worse.

"I'll give you a lift home."

As Richard started the car up, I had to quite literally bite my tongue to stop me from protesting. See, I had learned a lesson!

"So, do you need to tell anyone about my fling with Hannah?" Richard asked as I directed him through Moss Park with nothing more than vague pointing.

"No, I don't think so." I said, wondering if that was the right thing to do.

With my brain turning the lights off in the disco, I was struggling a bit, but I gathered that Richard really hadn't needed to tell me anything; he'd volunteered the information.

It wasn't like he was already a suspect. At least, not with the Police. I wasn't quite sure if he was a suspect on my not-yet-upand-running list, but I would ponder that one a bit later.

"Oh, blue lights." Richard said, somewhat vaguely.

"What?" Straining to get my brain back into focus, I looked into the distance. We had turned onto my street and I had a horrible, gut-twisting feeling. "Richard, stop!" I said, rather vehemently.

"Ok." He pulled over and turned to look at me.

"Alright, Richard. Looks like Mum's home after all. Good thing I didn't invite you round, huh?" I tried to sound amusing, but felt pretty tragic.

And, forgive me if you will, but in that very moment, I *hated* my mother.

"Are you sure it's your place?" He said, trying to be helpful.

"Yes." I said, all my fight totally gone.

"Hey, I can come with you if you'd like? Or go away if you'd like? Or you could just stay at my place? All totally up to you." He added the last like a man who was expecting a repeat of my former bad manners and hyper-sensitivity.

"Oh, that *is* nice of you, Richard." And I really, honestly, meant it. "But

I'd better go and have a look. If there's any problems, I'll just dart over to Liam's place. It's kind of what we….. well, it's just what we've always done."

"Understood, Josie. Look. I could wait here and if you're not back in ten I'll go, but I could hover to see if you need a lift?"

"It's ok. It only takes me a few minutes to get to Liam's. But listen, I really appreciate the thought."

"No problem." He smiled. "What time are you in uni tomorrow?"

"I'm not. I don't have anything on Fridays. I mean, I usually go in, but I thought I'd get a good lay in and maybe see what I should do next, you know?"

"Yeah, sure."

"I might be there, I might not."

"Well, if you are, ring me and I'll meet you in the canteen or something."

"I will do, Richard. And thanks again for the lift." I smiled and scooped up my bag.

I pulled the door handle, only to discover that getting out was even more of a problem than getting in was. Without a word, Richard shot out of the car and pulled the passenger door open for me.

"Night, Josie." He said, before getting back in and getting ready to set off.

"Night, Richard." I said, before slowly dragging my tired and aching body up the street to see what sort of hell was being unleashed at my house.

Chapter Ten

Richard pulled away, tactfully doing a three-point turn and heading back the way he had come, rather than sailing slowly past my house for an eyeful. As I reluctantly made my way up the street, I felt my shoulders sag.

Well, not just my shoulders, but my whole body. I'd had enough already and I wasn't in the mood for my mum and her latest antics. I realise that there is a sort of *innocent until proven guilty* line of reasoning that I could have followed but, to be honest, I'd given up on that one years ago.

Not with respect to everyone, don't get me wrong; just my mum.

As I got to within a hundred yards I could see two things clearly. One, my mum was waving her arms in a most aggressive manner at PC Betty Butler and two, by doing so she was, without a doubt, going to get herself arrested.

Especially since she seemed to be holding a vodka bottle that she intermittently swigged from. Well, the sooner they took her away, the better, I was ready for bed.

"Ah, there she is!" My mum shrieked when I came into view.

"Hi Mum." I said, dripping sarcasm.

"Honestly! You do your best for them." My mum began, slurring horribly and swaying as she fixed PC Betty with a look designed to gain the woman's sympathy. "And this is how they repay you. God knows where she's been and what she's been up to, but does she care about me? Does she care that I'm here night after night worrying about her? And what with some young girl getting kidnapped too." She took another swig, then looked pained and confused when she realised the bottle was empty.

"Mum, be honest. I have hardly seen you since you took up with Snatcher Harris. For the last few weeks I've been here alone, so I'm not sure how you've managed to get so much worrying done." I said in a flat tone.

Betty peered over at me and gave me a huge and warm smile. "Hey, how are you doing, Josie?" She said, keen to let my mum know that she probably saw more of me than my drunken parent.

"Tired really. And so worried about Liam and Hannah and everything. But thank you for asking." I smiled back. I loved Betty.

"Oh yeah. Poor little Liam. Trust me, he wouldn't hurt a hair on that girl's head. He adored her." My mum added, speaking with drunken authority on a subject about which she knew absolutely nothing.

Still, I stopped myself from correcting her and saying out loud that Liam did not, in fact, adore Hannah Davenport.

"So, what's happening?" I said, torn between not wanting to know and, well, *seriously* not wanting to know.

"It appears that your TV has gone missing, Josie." Betty said with an apologetic shrug, almost as if she herself had stolen it.

"Not missing, darlin'; stolen! By that no-good piece of……" She began, kind of rounding on Betty as if my mum's dubious taste in men was entirely the fault of the Grantstone Constabulary. "I'm telling you, Snatcher Harris took it. Now get over to his place and lock him up." My mum finished, with a wave of her hand which made her seem like she was dismissing a servant.

"First things first, Mrs Cloverfield." Betty began, coolly. "I need to get some evidence together before I go locking anybody up."

"I just *told* you he did it!"

"That is not evidence. I need a statement, then I need to get the CSI unit down to get fingerprints. The doors haven't been forced, so I need to know if he had a key. I also need to know if you saw him take it. Those things are evidence."

"I ain't giving no statement to the Police!" My mum said, very much on her dignity as if Betty had just asked her to strip on national television.

"Oh? Why is that?" Betty said, still keeping her voice low and her temper so very level.

By this stage in the proceedings, my mother has usually irritated the attending officer beyond repair. Betty was just cut from different cloth.

"'Cos cops are all liars! I wouldn't be seen dead giving a statement to the Police!"

"And I wouldn't be seen dead arresting somebody without evidence." Betty retorted. I almost cheered. "So, I'll say goodnight, Mrs Cloverfield. You obviously don't need my help." "Do something, Josie!" My mum screamed at me.

"Look, mum, can't we do this inside for a change? Why do we always have to do everything in such a humiliatingly public way?"

"Oh, get her!" Once again, my mum had turned to Betty as some sort of ally. The wonders of alcohol! "Five minutes at university and she thinks she's clever."

"I *am* clever, Mum. I was clever *before* I went to university."

"Well more fool you. Where do you think it's all going to get you?" Mum was now standing, with one hand on her hip, her head wobbling from side to side quite vigorously, very much in the style of some poor devil on the Jeremy Kyle show who thinks they've delivered the final and definitive statement, truly declaring their own victory.

I am, of course, referring to Jeremy himself.

"Well, it will most likely ensure that I am never screaming drunkenly in the street because my one-toothed drug-addict of a boyfriend has stolen my telly! I'll probably be too busy with a job and what-have-you!"

Betty grinned. She liked me, and I liked that she liked me. I still wanted Betty to be my mum.

"You little….." And then mum ran at me, her just-empty bottle of Euro-Saver vodka raised high above her head.

In the very second before my own mother rendered me unconscious in the street with a bottle, PC Betty Butler, faster than a speeding bullet, had her arm up her back and one handcuff already on.

In the time it took Betty to do all of that, I was still standing with my mouth open. I've got to tell you, it had been a while since my mum had gone for me in a drunken outrage, but that was the first time she'd come at me with a weapon!

"Lorraine Cloverfield, I'm arresting you for Affray. You do not have to say anything, but it may harm your defence if you do not mention, when questioned, something which you later rely on in court, and anything you do say may be given in evidence."

"Affray?" My mum screamed at the top of her lungs. "What the hell is affray?" She sounded very much on the back foot.

My mum was used to being locked up to Prevent a Breach of the Peace and released scot-free the following morning. Affray had a big, stinky whiff of court about it, and even my drinkaddled parent could smell it a mile off.

"Thank you, Betty." I said, genuinely.

"Look, I'll get her in the van then come back inside to speak to you, ok?"

"Don't you dare give them a statement, baby." My mum squealed, as if her very life rested in my hands.

Funny, one minute I'm being threatened with a bottle and the next I'm my mum's baby. Who knew?

"Oh, and I *will* be giving you a statement, Betty. And I can fill in the DV forms with my eyes shut." I really wanted to hurt my mum.

I needed to take some sort of action that would stop me crying in the street at the final horror of it all. As hardened as I was and as much as I keep telling you all that I hated her, I was still truly gutted that my mum had been prepared to hit me with a bottle.

"What are DV forms?" Mum was asking, suddenly all sweetness and light as if we were having some sort of discussion over afternoon tea, best china and everything.

"Domestic Violence forms, Mum. I have been filling them in since I was old enough to write."

"Domestic violence?" She said, incredulously. "But you have to be married for that! Don't be silly, Jose!" She began to laugh, clearly indicating just how stupid she thought I was.

"I'll be inside, Betty." I said, unable to keep it together a moment longer.

As Betty forcibly folded my mum neatly into the back of the Police van, I scooted into the house. No sooner had I got in through the door than I was sobbing.

I was exhausted and sorely wishing that I had taken Rich Richard up on his offer of a place to stay for the night, or that I had never stormed out of Liam's place. I needed Liam right then, and there was no way I could call him.

I'd pushed Rich Richard away and put Liam in his place and, as a result, had successfully isolated myself. Taking my multipurpose woollen mitten out of my pocket once more, I dragged it across my face in an attempt to stem the tide running down my soggy red chops. I hoped Betty wouldn't be back for a good few minutes.

"Hey, Josie!" The voice came from behind me and I almost screamed. I had thought I was alone in the house.

"Dale! For God's sake! I thought you were off-duty! And why the hell are you creeping up on me again?" I was nearly, but not quite, shouting.

"I'm on nights. I started at ten. This is my first shout." He said, apologetically. "I'll make sure I let you know my work schedule next time I see you." He was clearly trying to cheer me up, but then fully took in my appearance. "Oh God, sorry! What's happened?"

"Mum just tried to hit me with her vodka bottle outside." I sniffed. "Betty has locked her up for affray."

"Affray? Well, it *is* an affray, but I'll dial it down to Breach of the Peace, if you would prefer it. Anything you want. But it really is an affray. Just tell me what you want."

"Affray it is." I said, quietly defiant. For an odd moment, I thought of Amelia Ledbetter. "If Betty hadn't stopped her, she would have hit me with the bottle. Right on the head, actually."

"Oh, I'm so sorry, Josie." Dale was with me in one big stride, and he scooped me into his arms.

For the second time in two days, I balled all down the front of his immaculate body armour.

"Look, Jose. This time it will end up in court." It was a statement of fact.

I'd heard all sorts in the past from other officers hoping and praying I'd just accept the whole Breach of the Peace thing without making their workload any bigger. *I'm afraid it'll end up in court, love. And you'll have to give evidence, and they won't go easy on you....but with a Breach of the Peace...* But that wasn't what I was hearing from Dale, and I knew it. "And I'll be right there with you, ok? You're doing the right thing. She's gone way too far this time, and if you let it go, it'll become her new big thing; her new M.O."

"I know, Dale." I murmured into the heavy zip of his body armour. "And I *will* go through with it." I was so tired that I was actually leaning on him.

Seriously, if PC Dale Webb had stepped back, I'd have fallen face down onto the balding carpet, without even bending in the middle or putting my hands out to break my fall.

"Good for you, Josie. We'll need the statement tonight. Are you up to it?"

"Yeah, just about." I said, straightening myself up. "And give me one of the DV forms, I'll start filling it in while you sort your paperwork out."

"Oh, Josie. You know way too much about all this." Dale said sadly, putting his arms around me again.

I hugged him back this time. He was such a nice bloke.

"Ok, let's get started. I'm just knackered." I smiled up into his handsome and familiar face.

I was so glad that it was him and Betty there, and not some other Grantstone bobby with a superior attitude and a penchant for dealing with working class domestic violence by way of a simple Breach of the Peace, as if the victims didn't bloody matter.

"I wish Betty was my mum." I said, as if from nowhere. "She was ace."

"I wish Betty was my mum too." Dale laughed, and I was glad he didn't mock me for my silliness. "Even if she does scare me a little bit."

The whole business of statement taking and form filling was over surprisingly quickly. Betty, despite being right there at the scene, asked me to tell her it all in my own words, and wrote a thorough statement which was entirely faithful to what I had told her. And she did it in record time. Betty really was amazing.

As they left, Dale assured me that, should my mum get bail, she would be bailed to a different address with conditions not to approach me, which meant not to approach the house either. That was just fine by me.

When I finally fell into bed, I could think no more. My mum, Hannah, Liam, Rich Richard, Fliss and Amelia, the diary…. It would all have to wait until I'd slept off the preceding twentyfour hours. And as for the intruder? Let him come in, if he thought he was hard enough!

Chapter Eleven

After sleeping like a corpse for several hours, I woke up at around seven the following morning. It was still dark and it took longer than normal for me to figure out if it was a school day, so to speak.

Remembering that it was Friday and that I had promised myself a nice lay in, I had that lovely *I'm going back to sleep* feeling commonly associated with Saturdays. That was until my brain began to let the rest of my memories filter through.

I have to be honest that the serious upset I'd felt the night before seemed to have diminished with sleep. The idea that my mum would have bail conditions not to return to the house gave me a curious lightness of being.

I'm not fickle in my emotions, they've just been stretched to breaking point over the years and the whole thing is much too complicated to try to explain.

Then, of course, I thought about Liam. That he had totally deserved my wrath, well, mini-wrath, was without question. However, that did not stop me missing him.

So, feeling rested enough that I knew I didn't really need to return to the dark world under the duvet, I took my smart phone out from inside my pillowcase. I know my mum was detained in the Grantstone Custody suite at the time, but old habits die hard.

Anyway, I was missing my good buddy and I was going to have to do something about that. I checked my text messages and was totally dismayed to see I had none. I had been kind of hoping to find some sheepish missive from Liam, and felt like I'd swallowed a rock when it didn't appear.

Sighing, I opened my emails. Lo and behold, at the top of the list, Liam Attwood! Phew!

"Alright Dude.

I know you told me to go to hell, but I thought I'd do that Facebook research you asked me to do before I pack my things and leave. (What does one wear to Satan's fiery abode?) Anyway, it's thorough but boring. Two lists. Just the sort of thing that appeals to a totally unimaginative left-brainer like you. Most of the people in the list of Hannah's "friends" that I know, are known to you also, so no surprises there. The rest of them are a mystery to me. All female, and all a bit fancy looking. High fashion and way too many of those wide-eyed and pouting selfie profile pictures. I seriously don't know any of them, and I don't think Hannah did particularly either, because there's never anything on her wall from any of them. I've even gone back through my own wall and can only see things from Rich, Fliss and Amelia which Hannah has liked and shared and what-not. Anyway, here's the two lists for you to do your detecting with. That is, if you're still detecting and not throwing the towel in and leaving me to my fate.

Ring me later, like about lunchtime. This has taken me until four in the morning and I need my beauty sleep.

I'm sorry, Dude, by the way. I was a git and I know I was. Please say you'll still be my Dude because I love ya… and you know you love me too. How could you not? If all else fails, remember the colouring book.

See you later (hopefully)

Liam x"

There followed two lists; one really short, and one really long. How sad that the longest list of so-called friends were really just vague acquaintances. Still, there was no time for that sort of wondering; I had work to do. So, I shot off downstairs to make myself a cup of tea and a bowl of Euro-Saver honey clusters. Let me tell you, if there's any real honey in them, then I'm a bumble bee.

With my clusters eaten and the beginnings of a sugar rush starting up, I sat up in bed with my tea on the cabinet, my phone in my hand, and my notebook and pen at the ready.

Just as I was about to open my emails again and scribble down Liam's list of un-knowns, my phone bleeped. I had a text message. At just half past seven in the morning, it surely wasn't Liam. No, indeed, it was Dale.

"Sorry for early text. I'm just off duty and going to bed. Just wanted to check you are ok. If you need anything, or to talk about your mum, just ring me. I don't mind if you wake me up. Dale."

I couldn't help but smile. Now *there* was an officer who could teach most of Grantstone Constabulary a thing or two about community policing!

"Thanks old bean. I'm doing much better now I've slept. Still determined to go ahead with the affray thing. I should be ok, so I'll try not to rocket you *awake with a call! Thanks again, Dale. You and Betty were ace!"*

Wow. I'd crawled into bed the night before feeling isolated and totally crestfallen. By half seven in the morning, I'd got my best friend back and had a pastoral care message from
Grantstone's finest. That'll do for me.

I hastily copied the list of unknowns into my notebook whilst my tea was cooling. There were forty-seven of them. It could have been a lot worse. Some people have, like, thousands of Facebook friends. I silently thanked Hannah for her discernment, even if she didn't really know too many of the forty-seven.

I noted down each name and left a good chunk of writing space to note down whatever I found of interest in each of their profiles. I then opened Facebook on my phone and clicked onto Hannah's profile.

Fortunately, she was one of the many who didn't bother with any sort of security measures, and I had instant access to her list of friends.

By the time I'd reached number seven in the list, I was already bored. They seemed, so far, to be an assortment of girls Hannah had been at school with, most of whom seemed to have plumped for universities elsewhere. Either they had never really been close in the first place, or the distance and new way of life they had now had made them all rather careless about old friends.

Regardless, I had found nothing which made me spill my tea all over the duvet. In truth, I don't really know what I had been expecting. This was like grunt work. I was doing it for the sake of doing it, without any kind of aim or intuitive reasoning. Still, that was probably what a lot of police work was all about.

But I wasn't a police officer, I was an unpaid and unofficial private detective! I could veer away from the methodical if I wanted, surely.

If I was honest, the very idea of that went totally against the Josie Cloverfield grain; but Lordy I was bored.

Flipping back through my notebook, I scanned the brief notes that I'd made from Hannah's diary. As I sat up in bed, I sorely wished I had kept the heavy photocopy with me; it would probably have been much more productive from an investigatory viewpoint.

I looked at the Emjay stuff for a while; somehow it seemed like old news.

But was it?

Was Matty Jameson as clueless about Hannah's disappearance as he claimed to be? I scanned through Hannah's friend list, just in case Liam had missed one.

Of course, he hadn't, and of course Matty Jameson wouldn't be there on her list of friends for all the world to see.

As I continued to wonder about the woolly-haired lecturer, my eye was drawn to the e-mail address I had written down. Trixie1234@hotmail.com. I read through Liam's list of unknowns, finally trusting that he had made a thorough job of it all. I knew there were no Trixies in there. I'd have made the connection immediately.

Rich Richard had said there was no Trixie in Hannah's circle of friends that he knew of. In fact, he'd said that it sounded like something an elderly lady would call her Pomeranian. I chuckled as I took a swig of me tea. I thought of Rich Richard. He actually was a pretty decent sort of a guy and I had a sudden urge to send him a thank you text for trying to offer me some assistance the previous night.

I checked my watch; it was only just coming up to eight o'clock. Maybe it was a bit early yet, even for heartfelt gratitude. I fully determined to be nicer to Rich Richard from that point onwards; after all, he'd shown me nothing but kindness and respect from the moment I had met him, even when it meant being turned on by his own pack. I knew I had repaid him with wary cynicism, and he'd done nothing to deserve it.

If my Facebook research came to nothing, I would go into uni and spend a few hours on the photocopy. And if I did that, I would give Rich Richard a call and see if he wanted a cup of tea before I got started. Anyway, that was for later. I needed to knuckle down. Something about Trixie and the Pomeranian was picking at me, and I didn't know why.

Trixie did kind of sound like a name for a pet. In truth, it also sounded like the name of a stripper. *A stripper!* Like a Sunday afternoon stripper in a grotty little pub?

I sat up straighter, like you do when you think you're onto something. Thankfully the tea was all finished, or it might well have ended up all over the duvet.

I opened my emails again on my phone. I stared for a moment, wondering what the point of sending an email to Trixie1234@hotmail.com actually was. If it was a secret email address for Hannah, would she even see an email from me? Even if I sent her a desperate plea to return home. *Hannah Come Home.*

I was being ridiculous. If the Police ever got wind of this Trixie email address, if they hadn't already, then an email from yours truly would look so suspicious. What I really needed was a peek inside the Trixie inbox; see who she had been in contact with, or was even *still* in contact with.

I closed the email and opened my browser. Once I was on the Hotmail login screen, I already knew what my one and only attempt at a password would be. Rebellion. It just had to be. I mean, *I* used the same thing over and over again for my passwords and my locker combination. Just about anything I had that needed a password had the same one. Mine was my postcode. Not very imaginative, I know, but usually acceptable as a strong-ish password on most applications. But so many other people had passwords that meant something to them. Liam, for instance, used Montecristo for everything.

He just loved the Count. I could break into Liam's email accounts and stuff easy-peasy. I never did, though.

Not once. Not even a little bit. I ordinarily know how to respect other people's privacy. But would Hannah have really minded in this instance? Probably she would, because she didn't like me one little bit. However, there was just too much else at stake for me to be so floored by my own conscience.

It had to be Rebellion. If it wasn't, I had nowhere else to go.

And so it was, with slightly sweaty palms, I began to type it all in. I knew there would be some issue or other with upper and lower case letters, so I wrote down each attempt, so as not to foolishly repeat myself and get locked-out unnecessarily.

My first attempt was all lower case. Nope. My second attempt was all upper case. Nope again. My third attempt was a capital R with everything else in lower case. Bingo.

As the inbox opened, I kind of gasped a little bit.

My heart was thundering away like the hooves of a cantering stallion.

However, as inboxes went, it was kind of scant. There were no friends or even sales emails. Every one of the six emails were Facebook notifications.

I began to groan, feeling like I had enjoyed a great big *a-ha* moment, only to end up right back where I started. But then I stopped, mid-groan. It wasn't for Hannah Davenport's Facebook account. The title of the very first of the emails made me sit up again. *Trixie Sunday, you have three new notifications.*

Trixie Sunday! Oh my word! So, not only did Hannah have a spare email address, but she also had a spare Facebook account.

Ok, if it *was* Hannah. At that stage, Trixie could still have been anybody. But with the whole Rebellion thing and the Sunday thing! *Trixie Sunday!*

Anyway, I sat there for a few moments wondering what I could do next without getting into serious trouble. The emails were all unopened, so I had a very strong feeling that I should not open them.

If the Police looked at this lot later, maybe they would see that someone had opened them. But would they know who? And also, the same probably applied to the Facebook account. And anyway, I would need to open one of the emails to get the link to Trixie's page on Facebook. Unless I wanted to start searching randomly.

In the end, I just kind of came to a conclusion. I had already kept back the diary and was most likely to be in enormous trouble if the Police ever found out, so what the hell. I just clicked open the first of the emails. I clicked on the link to open her Facebook page.

When the page sprang to life, asking me for a password, I just smiled at it.

"You can't thwart me with a little password." I whispered, all cocky as I typed Rebellion in again.

Well, Trixie Sunday's Facebook page was not exactly a hive of activity. Her profile picture was a kind of cheesy silhouette stock photo from a web store or something. There were no photographs at all on her profile, and no posts or likes or anything.

There were the usual stock things from Facebook; sponsored posts and what-not. The stuff you generally ignore. Still, there was nothing personal.

Just as I was about to wonder what the point of the page actually was, I realised that Trixie had one friend. Just one friend. Finally, my twenty-first century Miss Marple-ing had come to fruition. I was no longer hiding behind lamp posts and spying pointlessly on Police searches. I was really doing the investigation thing; no turning back now.

I clicked on the friends list, and there he was. *Dirty Harry*.

"Oh, for God's sake!" I wheezed at the total lack of imagination. So, anyway, I opened his profile.

Once again, there was a barely-there profile. The profile picture consisted of nothing more than a silhouette of a smoking gun. Seriously, what was with all the silhouette stuff? It seemed a bit eighties to me.

Again, no posts or likes or shares. Nothing. And Dirty Harry had just one friend. Trixie Sunday.

I don't know why, but something about the two profiles kind of gave me the creeps. I felt like I'd stepped into a place I was not qualified to be in, and had the horrible notion that this was definitely Police territory.

I sat for a little while and wondered at the purpose of two such empty profiles. Even as a means of secret communication, they seemed unused. No posts to each other or anything.

Then I slapped myself hard on the head. Messages! PMs, of course. In a furious rush, which totally superseded all my Policerelated misgivings, I returned to Trixie's page. Having no password for Dirty Harry, I could not access his messages, but I had full control over the Trixie Sunday Facebook page.

When I finally got there, I knew I had come close to mastering my new craft. There was a small message stream between the pair, and I read it greedily.

Trixie: So, did you like the show?

Dirty Harry: Of course (winking emoji).

Trixie: So, you wanna get together? (red-cheeked, embarrassed little emoji).

Dirty Harry: Of course I do. Anything to help you in your little rebellion.

This little stream was all on Sunday evening; the day before Hannah went missing. The hair on the back of my neck stood up. I read the next stream.

Dirty Harry: So, are you busy tonight? (again with the winking emoji – yuk, right?).

Trixie: Not yet! (laughing emoji).

Dirty Harry: Good.

Trixie: So, where and when? (embarrassed emoji again).

Dirty Harry: There's an old disused building just a few hundred yards back from the bus-stop on Weatherby Lane. It's fenced off, but there's a gap in the wire. You'll need to poke about in the bushes a bit, but the gap is there.

Trixie: Seriously? Sounds a bit manky??

Dirty Harry: Not manky, just totally secret.

Trixie: Oh, right.

Dirty Harry: Come on! Are you rebelling or not? Make your mind up, little girl.

Trixie: Oh, I'll be there!

Dirty Harry: Good, I'm really glad. (smiling emoji – like he wasn't a creep!).

Trixie: What time?

Dirty Harry: Say about half six? It'll be dark by then, so you can slip in through the fence without being seen.

Trixie: Cool. See you there. (smiling emoji).

And there the conversation ended. At three o'clock in the afternoon on Monday; the very day Hannah disappeared. At three o'clock in the afternoon, she would have been at uni, checking her phone every few seconds for another message from Dirty Harry. Then she had cancelled her date with Liam.

And yet, despite it all, I couldn't find the old fighting spirit with which to hate her. I had a horrible feeling that somehow Hannah had got more than she bargained for with Dirty Harry, and I felt sick to my stomach about it.

Chapter Twelve

After much internal wrangling, I finally decided to go to the bus-stop on Weatherby Road and sneak through the hole in the fence, if there really was one. I knew Weatherby Road in a vague sort of a way.

It was half-way along my second bus route on the way to uni. It was not a place I ever got out and walked around, but I knew the bus-stop well enough.

And yet, despite knowing the stop, I could barely bring the surrounding area to mind. Was it a bit leafy and overgrown? I really couldn't remember.

Anyway, by the time I'd taken a hasty shower and dressed, I had thought the whole thing through.

My original instinct was to simply tell the police what I had found out. I thought I could ring Dale and hope that he and Betty would tell CID on my behalf. Even as I started to think about that one, I knew it would never pan out the way I wanted.

Dale and Betty would have to call it in, and I would be wheeled before the appalling Detective Inspector Malcolm Thorn in no time at all.

I played the whole sorry interview through in my mind. Thorn would want to know how I had come to find the Trixie email address, then the Facebook account, not to mention the Rebellion password.

As I had stood in the shower, wondering how long I would need to be under the trickle of water before I could declare myself washed, I realised that there would only be one explanation for all of the above. Hannah's diary.

The diary I had picked up on the canal side. The diary that was stolen from me just hours later. The diary I had photocopied and kept from the Police. The *same* diary which had led me to Matty Jameson and the nude painting and the whole stripper thing. Everything, in fact, which would give Thorn a mind-boggling array of motives with which to saddle Liam Attwood.

If it were anyone other than DI Malcolm Thorn I would be dealing with, I would have totally caved in that moment, called the Police, and handed it all over, throwing myself upon their mercy. I'd even be hoping that they would find my involvement naïve yet helpful. Of course, that was not going to happen with Malcolm Thorn.

He'd already made his feelings about me very plain, even before I had tied him in knots and publicly handed him his ass on a platter. Malcolm Thorn had suspected Liam immediately, and he seemed determined to make whatever evidence came his way fit my friend like a glove.

Not only that, but he had decided I was either an accomplice or had full knowledge of Liam's supposed crimes, even before he had met me.

So, I decided to go over to Weatherby Road and have a look. I don't know what I thought I would find, although it's fair to say that my imagination was running riot. My rationale, in the moment I made that decision, was that if I went there and found nothing, I would reassess my investigative activities and come to some kind of conclusion *then* regarding speaking to the Police.

But I really had to go before I decided. If I simply called DI Thorn and told him everything I had without going to Weatherby Road to see for myself, there might very well be nothing of note to find, and I would be putting Liam at risk for no good reason.

Once downstairs, I made myself a final cup of tea before setting off. I considered another bowl of Euro-Saver clusters, but felt way too fragile for that.

If I stopped to contemplate for too long, I actually felt pretty scared about my little mission. I really didn't want to go alone, and was desperate to call Liam and wake him from his beauty sleep.

However, I could think of no-end of ways in which taking Liam with me might eventually incriminate him in some way.

Rich Richard also popped into my brain, only to be dismissed again. As much as I liked Richard, my sensible self told me that I couldn't quite rule him out as a suspect. I hated myself for it, but I had to be pragmatic.

Richard was in the diary; he'd had a fling with Hannah, albeit a very short one. And he'd seemed horrified at the idea of his name being found in the pages of Hannah's diary. Still, that was probably quite natural. Who really wanted to be dragged up as a suspect? Whatever way I looked at it, I knew I had to just go it alone, and the very thought of it was making me queasy again.

There was, of course, another part of me shouting as loud as it could, trying to make itself heard. It was the part of me which was urging me to do nothing. Stay at home, stay in bed, stay under the duvet. Nobody had to know what I had found out about the email address and the Facebook account.

Nobody had to know about the messages I had read. The Police would get there on their own, sooner or later, without my interference.

I've got to be honest; it was tempting. As I sat on the first bus, gently rumbling my way into town, I knew that I could just turn right around and go home again at any point. I was fighting nothing and nobody. Not Liam, not Richard, not DI Thorn. Nobody knew except my own conscience; the one thing I couldn't hide from.

Hannah was out there somewhere, by choice or otherwise. If it was by choice, I needed to find her for Liam's sake. If it was not by choice, then Hannah needed to be found, plain and simple. I tried to imagine myself in her place.

What if some dopey girl on a bus had the key to finding me, but didn't put it in the lock for fear of getting herself into trouble?

And there it was; the decider. I got onto bus number two with the certain knowledge that I was going to do this, no ifs or buts.

The Weatherby Road bus stop came up far too quickly for my liking. As decided as I was, I really wasn't ready to take my investigations to the next level.

I got off the bus and began to walk away up Weatherby Road, for appearances sake only. I really couldn't see this gap in the foliage and fencing, as reported by the slimy Dirty Harry.

To climb down from the bus and immediately start poking around in the bushes would very likely have drawn attention to me. Especially from the woman behind me who had been almost breathing the same air as me as the bus had begun to slow for the Weatherby Road drop.

She was so close, in fact, that if I had stopped abruptly to look around, she would have unwittingly rammed me. To be honest, it would have been something I would have sought to avoid on a good day, never mind a day when I needed to be as stealthy as all get out.

Taking an immediate right as I got off the bus, I had rather hoped Mrs Hot-breath would have gone left. It was a total gamble, and one which I lost. As I strode with seeming purpose along Weatherby Road, Mrs Hot-breath was right behind me. I was already sick of her.

Anyway, I kept going, keen not to draw any sort of attention; I don't know why, but I kept imagining one of those Crimewatch reconstructions on the telly.

Some gangly fool of an actor who had been forced into a duffle coat would be walking along Weatherby Road, with the presenter urging the public or, indeed, the duffle wearer herself, to make urgent contact with the Police on the following number.

I realise that it was far-fetched, and that there would be no reason for anybody to be looking for the gangly fool sporting the duffle coat, but I was suffering from a hugely guilty conscience at that moment in time.

Not to mention the fact that I had *the fear*. Not just any old fear, but big, stinky, relentless fear. I was also wishing that I wasn't the only person in the bright, shiny twenty-first century who still wore a duffle coat. From an identification point of view, it rather singled me out.

Finally, I came to a junction. I was fairly certain that if I took a left, followed by two more lefts, I would be heading back towards the bus stop and the fated gap in the fence. Perhaps it would be a good thing after all; everyone who'd got off the bus, or been in the area when the bus had stopped, would have cleared out by now, and there would be nobody left to wonder why the duffle coat was making a reappearance.

Unless, of course, old Hot-breath was going my way. If she did, I had more or less made up my mind to challenge her about it all. She was ruining my day.

Happily, Mrs Hot-breath and I parted company as I turned left down Carter Street and she continued on along Weatherby Road. I picked up the pace a little, keen to get on with it. However, as I strode along, I couldn't help but worry about being seen.

There were houses on the opposite side of Weatherby Road, not to mention the fact that it was a busy street for traffic.

As predicted, my continual left-turn-taking brought me within a few yards of the bus stop once more. I looked around, pleased to see that there was nobody about on foot. I looked over to the houses opposite.

There really was no sign of anyone in the gardens or windows, and I tried to bolster my flagging confidence with the idea that it was a weekday and everyone would surely be at work. Whatever keeps you sane, right?

When I reached the bus stop, I did a fair job of nonchalantly leaning against the bus shelter, as if waiting for a bus. I turned to look back into the foliage and, after a good few seconds, could see the gap. I could only see the gap in the foliage; I couldn't actually see the fencing behind it.

Again, I looked all around me. There was nobody about; this might be my one and only chance. Taking a deep breath, I ducked a little and scooted up to the gap. With a final look over my shoulder, I threw myself into the dense bush.

I did, as it turned out, have the right spot. There was that kind of loopy wire fencing behind the foliage. It was the kind that the Council puts up everywhere. Anyway, the bushes had grown tall, covering most of it, and the leaves and shoots were quite well intertwined with the wire.

The gap in the wire fencing had been cut, no doubt about it. The edges were sharp and, as I darted through, I caught on the sleeve of my coat. The *duffle of ages* suffered some minor cosmetic damage as a result, but nothing that I couldn't sort with a bit of rough needlework.

Once I was in, I stood as still as a statue as I looked about me. I was in an area of ugly wasteland, that was for sure. It was thoroughly screened off from the rather nice Weatherby Road, so well done to Grantstone Council for that shrewd move.

There were two old wrecks of buildings, one of which seemed to be barely holding its own. The closest one to me had very little by way of a roof, and most of the tiles were scattered far and wide throughout the overgrown wasteland.

The second building was one of those rather utilitarian squarelooking affairs with a flat slab roof. I realised that I had seen the flat roof from the bus before now, but had never really paid it any heed. Why would I?

Beyond the buildings was a little more wasteland, fenced in by a thick swathe of trees. I tried to get my bearings, and wondered what was on the other side of those trees, but I really couldn't place it.

I was tempted to get out my smart phone and check mapping, but I realised immediately that I was procrastinating. I just didn't want to take another step.

Not a thing had moved since I had been staring about me, not even me, so I felt reasonably certain that I was on my own. After all, who else would be wandering around in what looked like a bomb-site on a Friday morning?

I took my first tentative steps, watching very carefully where it was I placed my feet. This was the sort of place where unidentified sharp rusty objects protruded from the earth with no good reason, ready and waiting to pierce the foot of a plimsoll wearing interloper.

I reached the first building and looked up at it doubtfully. It really did seem to me to be too dangerous to enter.

What was left of the rafters were dangling precariously and I didn't much fancy being on the wrong end of one of them if it broke free. I kind of thought that Dirty Harry and Trixie Sunday might well have come to the same conclusion.

I therefore decided to have a poke around in building number two first. If I found nothing of note, I'd risk my limbs in the first building; or, at least, I might.

I wobbled my way through the hard, dry grass and bits of tile and rubble to the next building. As I stood at the door of it, I could see that it was certainly not fully closed. My mouth went a bit dry.

After all, if I had made my way through the gap with ease, no doubt countless others had gone before me, and I was not keen to breath in, or step on, whatever they had left behind. But there was something else gnawing at my senses too. Had Hannah really been here?

I noted somewhat inconsequentially that a squinty plaque on the wall next to the door indicated that this building once belonged, or even still belonged to, the water company. For a brief moment, I hoped they wouldn't mind my intrusion.

I pushed the door cautiously, and it swung inwards. At that moment I would have given anything for it to be locked; I could have gone home convincing myself that I'd done everything I could, right?

Feeling myself begin to shake a little bit, I had to forcibly put one foot in front of the other and keep walking. The whole place had that tower-block lift smell; you know the one, the *caughtshort-after-a-few-pints* eyewatering stench. I winced a little, but knew I couldn't let a little thing like a vile pong hold me back.

As I looked around, I could see that the building must once have been used as an office base of some kind; maybe for the water company workers.

I took the first opening on the right. I say opening, because the door was totally off its hinges and laying in the corridor outside. I had to walked over the door to make my entrance.

Apart from yellowing papers and other such similar debris scattered all over the floor, there was nothing else to see. I didn't hang about; I knew I had to keep moving before my nerve went altogether.

I went through room after room. Some had old desks and chairs in, all had the carpet of old papers everywhere. None had anything of note, at least, as far as an untrained and rather bumbling private detective could see.

I made my way to the stairs. They were of the pre-cast concrete variety, so I could not back out of it all, claiming the stairs might give way at any moment.

I set off really slowly, almost creeping up the stairs one by one. My heart was thundering and, as I reached the final few steps, I could smell something vaguely unpleasant, and very different from the smell downstairs.

It wasn't terribly strong, it has to be said, but it was enough to make me cover my nose and mouth with one of my woollen mittens. It was a weird kind of a smell; like nothing I'd ever smelled before, and it gave me an appalling sense of dread. I had never been frightened by a smell before, and had no idea that something like that was even possible. Breathing hard, I reached the top of the stairs. The odour was growing stronger, although it was still not strong. Perhaps if it had been the middle of summer, instead of January, then things might have been a little different.

I stood on the landing at the top of the stairs for several minutes. There were four doors to choose from, all of them slightly ajar. My heart was pounding harder still, and I almost thought I could hear it in the deathly silence.

And it *was* silent; I couldn't even hear a bird signing anywhere, despite the fact that one or two of the windows were broken.

Knowing that I couldn't just stand there all day, I wondered how the hell I could coax my trembling frame to take a look in the rooms. I really was frightened, and I don't mind admitting it.

I knew that, whatever that smell was, it could *not* be good. It was a decaying sort of a smell; maybe a dead animal of some kind, or even worse.

As I set off bravely for door number one, and entered at speed as a means of making myself do it, I realised that it was, in fact, *worse*. There, laying in the centre of the room was Hannah Davenport, and she was very *definitely* dead.

Chapter Thirteen

It's weird, but I didn't do any of the things you might imagine happen when a person finds a dead body in a deserted building. I didn't throw my hands up to either side of my face and scream right into the camera for an hour and a half.

I didn't scream briefly, and then run from the room, tripping and falling as I went. I didn't collapse to the floor in a dead faint.

I just stood there staring. I was kind of staring in wonder for what must have been a minute or more.

Hannah looked like a wax-work figure from Madame Tussauds. Her eyes were open and staring up at the ceiling. The strangest thing was that she didn't look to be uncomfortable. I know that seems like a dumb thing to say, but she looked more like she was resting, you know?

She was just laying, quite neatly, on the floor. She didn't look like she'd been flung there, or even landed there after a struggle of some kind. It was almost as if she had just laid down, and that was that.

It oddly reminded me of the portrait Matty Jameson had painted of her; it was as if she was there, but had forgotten something. In the painting, she had forgotten that she was not dressed. In that abandoned building, it was almost as if she had forgotten she was alive. She had forgotten to keep breathing.

I was still standing very much in the doorway. I knew what I had to do next; call the Police. I was so shocked that I couldn't even think of a self-preservation story to furnish them with when they arrived. Unfortunately, the truth would have to do.

Still, before ringing them, I thought I should take a closer look at things, in case there was anything of note that I needed to know later on; something that might turn out to be useful.

I stepped towards Hannah, marvelling at the fact I was still able to stand, let alone walk. I walked carefully over to her, watching my step in case I was treading on evidence.

I decided against walking around her, but chose instead to get close enough to be able to see all around without having to move.

Hannah seemed to be fully dressed, and her clothing did not look in any way disarranged. I realised that truly might not mean she had not been molested in any way, I just hoped that was the case. She looked unharmed, barring the dark bruising around her neck. *Had she been strangled?*

Her hair was as glossy as ever and, apart from her pallor, bruising, and blank expression, she was still very like the girl in the giant photograph on the tripod in the middle of the Grantstone University Quad.

But as I got closer, as I studied the sightless eyes, I could see that Hannah's expression, her very demeanour in death, was very much like that of her naked oil portrait. That unknown sadness was there, even if life was not.

Hannah had died with as much sadness in her as when she had sat for the portrait. It struck me as a pain that was beyond the reach of whatever physical and mental anguish was visited upon her in her last moments. It was a pain that remained; unchanged by any other which had been heaped upon it afterwards.

Something about her eyes made me think of betrayal. *Betrayal?* I don't know why, but the feeling was strong.

Everything seemed to be sinking in all at once. Hannah was dead. Hannah, not yet twenty years old, had been stopped in her tracks. Her life would not go beyond this point. Its crowning conclusion had not been a successful university career, a job in the arts, a family, or any one of a million routes a person's life can take.

Instead it had been an untimely death at the hands of another in a stinking old water company office building, two hundred yards back from a busy bus-stop. Nobody should end this way, no matter who they were.

No matter how they had treated me and my friend. No matter how our lives and views differed. Hannah was just a young woman; a young woman like me. I felt sick and suddenly devastated, not only by the horror of it all, but the sadness; the tragedy.

After so many minutes alone in a room with a dead girl, the tears, when they came, were strangely unexpected. I don't know if it was simply the shock wearing off, or if it was the very tangible realisation that no life should be extinguished by another.

Maybe it was the guilt of knowing that I had never truly liked the girl laying lifeless at my feet. And yet, I could not change that. It was a fact, and one that was already in existence.

I couldn't go back now and change it. And maybe, just maybe, I didn't need to. I could feel sadness, anger and horror at Hannah's murder without having to mentally re-write history. I didn't have to like Hannah to be devastated by her death.

The tears began to flow faster, and my breathing was uncontrollably ragged. I was sobbing; actually sobbing in a way that I hadn't done since I was a child. I needed to get out of that room but, at the same time, I didn't want to leave Hannah there all alone.

After some minutes, I realised that my sentimentality was futile; Hannah was dead. She was beyond caring whether or not I stayed with her.

Once outside the room, I took my phone out of my pocket and dialled with trembling fingers. Not 999; it was too late for that. I called Grantstone Constabulary switchboard and asked to speak to DI Malcolm Thorn.

By the time Thorn arrived, I was starting to feel really, seriously unwell. Initially, he stormed past me and straight up the stairs of the building. It was as if he needed to see Hannah for himself before he would ever dream of taking my word for it that she was dead.

He was gone for some time, leaving me to sit on a grasscovered mound of earth outside and silently watch the uniformed constables cordoning off the area, the gap in the fence included.

Briefly, I wondered how I was ever going to get out.

I had been somewhat relieved to see the first wave of uniformed officers arrive. Clearly DI Thorn had mobilised them before he, himself, was able to attend. An officer, who had been instructed to get a first account from me, was staring at me, pen and small pocket notebook poised, as he had waited for me to answer his questions.

I was very shaken, and the poor guy had to ask everything at least four times before it would sink in.

I knew Dale and Betty were on nights, so there was no hope they would turn up. They would both be sleeping peacefully.

"Do you want a cuppa or something, love?" The officer asked.

He was a man of about fifty with grey hair and kindly blue eyes. I looked around somewhat confused; where on earth was he going to magic a cup of tea from?

"No, but thank you for asking." I said, letting him off the hook with gratitude, but wondering what he would have done if I'd said yes.

"Just sit tight, love. The DI will be with you soon." He smiled, as if the idea that the DI was coming might actually bring me comfort.

Still, the kindly officer had no idea of the history between Thorn and me.

"Thanks." I smiled genuinely at him.

It was my default setting when someone was nice to me, even if they didn't actually make me feel better. Still, as he wandered away, I instantly felt his loss. I felt it acutely actually, in a hanging-on-to-his-leg kind of a way.

With the kindly officer gone, my next human contact would undoubtedly be the awful DI Thorn.

"Miss Cloverfield." I nearly tumbled off my grassy knoll; my nemesis had crept up on me.

"Detective Inspector." I said, summoning up every molecule of respectful behaviour I had in me.

"You have a lot of explaining to do young lady." He started off almost kindly, probably taking in my pasty chops, but could not help but taper off into the arena of the condescending by the time he got to the whole *young lady* part.

"Yes, I suppose I do." I said, as flatly as I truly felt.

"But not here. You'll have to come down to the station."

"Yes, of course."

"And I hope you haven't contacted your friend Liam." I could see the beginning of the old antagonism, and I had no doubt it would be back up and running on all four cylinders by the time we reached Grantstone nick.

"No, I haven't." I said, truthfully. In fact, in amongst all the shock, I had barely thought of Liam.

Not in any kind of dismissive way; I was just so disorientated by everything that all I could do was stare at the cops as they went about their business.

"Well, I can check your phone for the truth of that, can't I?"

I stopped myself saying *under what legislation can you seize a witness' phone and interrogate it?* Instead I simply looked blankly at him. Let him seize my phone if he liked; it would give me much needed ammunition at a later date.

"Let's go, young lady."

Ok, you patronising fool.

Chapter Fourteen

"So, tell me again, how was it you realised that Hannah Davenport had an extra Facebook address?"

"Account." I could not help myself; I just kept correcting DI Thorn by some sort of self-destructive instinct.

"What?" DI Thorn, despite being maybe only somewhere in his fifties, was clearly one of the countless thousands of the terminally confused middle-aged when it came to the basics of email and social media.

"Hannah had an extra Facebook account, *not* an address. She had an extra *email* address. It was the one linked to the Facebook account."

Thorn rose from his seat in a kind of elderly way, grunting a bit, followed by a long sigh before he wordlessly left the room. I was left with one of the CID Neanderthals of canteen fame, who stared at the desk without saying a word, almost like I wasn't there at all. It was like he was unplugged from the mains just because his boss had gone out for a wee.

"Let's start at the beginning, shall we?" Thorn said, riding the wave of a truly massive sigh as he re-entered the room, as if his total lack of understanding was entirely my fault.

I had to fight a really strong urge to let my head drop down onto the desk; the man was completely exasperating.

"DI Thorn." I began, and instantly regretted my talking-downto-a-five-year-old tone of voice. "I found a notebook when I was out the other day. It had no name and address in it, so I put it in my bag to hand in at the police station enquiry desk when I was next passing."

"Did you know there's an offence of Theft by Finding?" Thorn said, as if his lack of IT know-how had spurred him on to find some other form of victory over me.

"Yes, of course." I said, totally lying through my teeth but had a fair idea I could wing it, as it were. "But, of course, for that particular offence to be complete, you would have to prove that I had absolutely no intention whatsoever of taking the notebook into the police station. Since it has been only forty-eight hours since I found it, and since it was stolen from me in less than twelve, I think you might struggle to prove that my intention was to keep the thing. Still, you must do what you must, Detective Inspector."

Why oh why could I not speak to this man without patronising him? What the hell was wrong with me? Talk about keep digging, Josie.

"So, you found this notebook, *did you?*" He said, with an accusatory tone.

"Yes." I said simply, since it was the truth.

"Where?"

"On the canal footpath, just at the back of Westmorland Drive. I was out for a walk. I saw it kind of wedged in the hedgerow there."

"Out for a walk, *were you?*"

"Yes."

"Found it in the hedgerow, *did you?*"

"Yes." I really couldn't begin to fathom what exactly DI Thorn hoped to achieve with his rather parrot-like style of questioning.

I mean, just repeating what a person said and adding a *were you?* or a *did you?* to the end of it was hardly likely to make anyone crumble and suddenly confess.

"And then it was stolen from your house?" He said, raising his eyebrows.

I was waiting for the *was it?* and, when it didn't show itself, I have to admit to feeling a little cheated.

"That's correct, Detective Inspector. It was stolen from my house by an intruder who broke in whilst I was in the bath. In fact, I think they were still in my house when I came out of the bathroom and realised it was gone."

"And you didn't call the Police?" "No."

"So, having an intruder in your home isn't an unusual occurrence then?" Thorn said, with a superior little smirk.

"Of course, it is. It was extremely unnerving, as it happens."

"Why, then, did you not call the Police?" Thorn looked like a man who felt sure I was lying but wasn't convinced he'd ever get to the bottom of it all.

"Because just that morning, two of your officers frog-marched my friend out of the university canteen."

"And?"

"And, despite neither of us having a criminal record, both Liam Attwood and I are horribly used to being treated in a certain way by some, not all, of the Grantstone Constabulary." "Really?" He said, and had the gall to look incredulous.

Seriously, and him the main offender!

"Yes, really. So, it's fair to say that my faith in the local police force was at an all-time low at that moment. So much so that calling the police for help when I was scared out of my gourd was absolutely the furthest thing from my mind. In fact, I ended up hiding for a while, then going downstairs to take a look for myself, armed with nothing more than a heavy thermodynamics text book." I was slowly but surely reaching furious again. The man just pushed all my buttons. "But the intruder had fortunately gone."

"Well, that all strikes me as rather odd. Really, for you to have such a problem with the Police...."

"For me to have such a problem with the Police, bearing in mind I am an innocent member of the public, is not *my* problem, is it? If you have sections of the community so alienated that calling the police for help isn't a consideration, then I rather think that is *your* problem."

Josie Cloverfield, for the love of God just shut up!

"So, the notebook was stolen, *was it?*" *Oh, here we go again.*

"Yes."

"So, how did you know about the email *address* and Facebook *account?*"

"Because I had read snippets of it on the bus, looking to see if there was a name anywhere in the book. Then, I would have been able to return it."

"And you wrote it down? The email address, I mean."

"Yes."

"Why?"

"Just as a quick reference."

"So, just run me through the *Emjay* bit again? Presumably you wrote this down for quick reference too?"

"No." I said, feeling too ropey to keep thinking up lie after lie.

"I think you'd better tell me the whole lot, don't you? Start at the beginning."

I could have howled with anguish. As intellectually challenged as Thorn was, he wasn't entirely stupid. There was only so much skirting around the whole issue of withholding evidence that I could feasibly do.

I came to the very sorry conclusion that I would actually be better off in the long run if I told the truth.

So, in the end, that's exactly what I did. I didn't mention that I knew there was a police search on at Hannah's home, and the whole idea of me being on the canal path for a walk seemed to pass muster.

As for the rest of it, I was too tired by the stress and haunted by the sight of Hannah's dead body to do anything other than tell the whole truth.

"You're telling me that Hannah Davenport was a stripper, *are you?*"

"No. I'm telling you that Matty Jameson told me she was a stripper."

"And you found a mucky painting of Hannah in his office at the university?"

"No, I found a nude painting. It was just a nude painting. Not mucky."

"But with no clothes on?"

"Detective Inspector Thorpe! There is a difference. Nude is art and mucky is tabloid."

"And you didn't think to tell the Police about this?"

"No."

"Why?"

"Because for one thing, a portrait sitting is between the adult sitter and the artist. It's not a Police matter, unless, of course, you now keep a register of that sort of thing. For another thing, after the way you treated Liam with absolutely no grounds, I thought that Matty Jameson would get the same treatment. Just a whiff of suspicion at a place like Grantstone University would be likely to lead to Matty Jameson's contract being ended. His whole life! It is bad enough that Liam Attwood feels he can no longer attend university, without another person's life being ruined." Obviously, I refrained from telling him that I did not want to cast further suspicion on Liam by providing DI Thorn with a rather excellent motive.

I didn't want to bring it to his attention.

"And you think that's a good enough reason to have kept it to yourself?"

"Yes, I do. If you want to throw suspicion on people without even a moment's discretion, then it's nothing more than public humiliation. If that's how you do things, then you really should have something approaching evidence before you do it. Instead, you drag people through the mud publicly without evidence. In fact, with nothing more than a bit of cheap tabloid-style suspicion."

"And you don't think it might have saved Hannah's life?" He added, delivering an appalling and very cheap shot.

"Hannah has been dead for days. Hannah was dead already by the time I spoke to Matty Jameson so no, I do not think I could have saved Hannah's life." I hated his guts.

Lazy policing, lazy investigating, lazy interviewing. How I wished I could have said it all to him.

"And how do *you* know Hannah had been dead for days?" He asked.

Thorn was having an *a-ha* moment, predominantly because he was just about the most spectacular fool I'd ever met. He thought for a moment or two that he'd caught the killer! *My suspicions were first aroused, your honour, when Josie Cloverfield claimed certain knowledge of the time of death……..*

"Because of the…… smell." The last word caught in my throat and I felt tears suddenly making my eyeballs sting.

I hated saying it; it felt like I was being mean; making nasty comments. *Hannah smells! Ner ner na-ner ner!* I knew it was ridiculous, but there it was.

The strangest moments were the ones which reminded me that Hannah was very, definitely dead, and that I had found her. I had smelled her body beginning to decay.

"Oh." Thorn said, buying time while he thought of his next clever move. "I wonder why it was that you were on the canal path at the back of Hannah's home at the time of the Police search." His next move….

"No idea. Just one of those things, Detective Inspector. After all, how would I know when a search was taking place? I'm not privy to that sort of information, am I? I also have never been to Hannah's house. I didn't know her address."

"Liam Attwood could have told you it."

"He could have, but he didn't." I'd had enough of his fishing.

"I have told you everything I know. Am I a witness or a suspect?"

"A witness. For now."

"Meaning?"

"Well, let's not forget you kept back this diary. Yes, you say you weren't sure of its exact provenance, but you still could be prosecuted for Withholding Evidence."

"And you're going to charge me with that, are you? Bearing in mind I have the photocopy I described to you and intend to deliver it to you?"

"You still withheld evidence."

"I think that might be open to wider interpretation than you have a capacity for. Still, you must do what you must." I said with a smile, hoping that the return of my mobile phone would give me the armour plating I needed.

"Don't you push me, you little runt. If you think anyone is going to give a damn about a council estate kid's complaint that a nasty policeman was rude to her, then think again. I've got you around the neck, so to speak, so you can stick your university vocabulary where the sun don't shine." Wow! He could be seriously nasty!

Good job it wasn't a taped interview!

"I'd like my mobile phone back now."

"No."

"Have you seized it as evidence? I mean, officially?" "No." He said, shifting a little awkwardly in his seat.

"Then I'd like it back."

With a disgruntled snort, Thorn rose to his feet and left the room.

After some minutes, a uniformed constable came into the room. My heart nearly boomed with joy; the phone was in a police evidence bag. Thorn was busy with some mumbled conversation or other just outside the room.

"Can you just sign the bag, love?" The constable smiled at me.

He'd dated and timed the return and there was a space on the bag for me to sign for it. Also, there was an Evidence Related Property number. *Oh dear oh dear!* This efficient and ethical young officer, fresh from very thorough training and seemingly above any sort of corruption, had booked the phone into the police systems as evidence. All very proper.

"Thank you." I said, smiling warmly at him and really, really meaning it.

The officer smiled and left the room, just as Thorn and his CID Neanderthal lumbered in behind him, almost like an ugly big old boxer dog following his master's lead.

I had left my phone in the bag, but was able to check my messages through the clear plastic. Oh happy day! I found exactly what I had prayed for.

I knew Thorn would be a good, old fashioned, not-exactly-bythe-book type of police officer. The sort that jokingly quoted the *Ways and Means Act*. I'd heard it all before, but this was the first time it was going to work in my favour.

"Oh dear, DI Thorn." I said, looking at my phone and smiling. He looked at me, his eyes flying to the evidence-bag-wrapped phone in my hand. "Not only has the uniformed officer bagged my phone, as should be done with all seized items, he actually booked it into your Evidence Related Property System. Look." I said, holding the bag out for him to inspect. "Here's the Property Number." I was smiling and being a git and I knew it, but nobody deserved it more than the man in front of me. "Which means that there is an electronic audit trail. So, no denying that my person property was seized then."

"So what? Something can be seized and returned. I can easily explain the fact that I thought it might be evidence and decided to hold it until I had spoken to you properly and was sure it was not. It was then returned. Simple."

"No, not simple."

You see, some good, long while ago, I had completed a piece of coursework at school. It was for the social science GCSE. Our course had a rather political bent, and I had chosen to study the Interception of Communications Act.

Now, please believe me when I tell you that I do not go to sleep wearing a tin foil hat lest the evil powers-that-be download the contents of my swede overnight. However, I have always had a healthy suspicion of government agencies, so I really went for it with my coursework.

I was a geeky kid, what can I tell you? And that is why I didn't kick up a stink when he took my phone. I was feeling like a bit of an evil genius; white suit, fluffy cat – the works! And I was thoroughly enjoying it. Holding my tongue had paid off.

"Because, *Mr* Thorn, a text message has been opened."

"So?"

"It was previously *unread*. I had not opened it. It was sent at a quarter to one this afternoon. That's an hour after it was booked into your evidence system, and an hour and a half before it was returned to me. It was opened fifteen minutes after it was sent. About the *same time* that you popped out of the room, in fact. Honestly, I just assumed you'd nipped out for a wee." I was totally loving it.

Really, endless rides on the big-dipper couldn't come close.

"So?"

"The message was read *before* I had opened it. You opened an un-opened message without the relevant authority in place. That is contrary to the Interception of Telecommunications Act 1985." "What?"

"Think back to your days at police training. The thing is, it doesn't just apply to opening someone's physical mail. It also includes messages sent via a public telecommunications system.
Text messages, *Mr* Thorn."

"Stop calling me Mr Thorn. It's DI Thorn to you."

"Not if you get two years for the offence."

The look on his face was worth all the insults and insinuations that had been heaped on me from the moment Malcolm Thorn got me back to the police station.

"So, Detective Inspector Thorn, it's a little bit more than a council estate kid's complaint about a nasty policeman, isn't it?"

"Now look here…." He said, but couldn't find a way to finish it. I had him good and proper, and he knew it.

Even the CID goon knew it, and was squirming like a landed fish in his seat, clearly wondering if he would be guilty by association; he looked like he wanted to evaporate right out of the room.

Well good. He'd been one of two officers who had humiliated my best friend. If Detective Constable Neanderthal was clicking his heels together under the desk and thinking *there's no place like home, there's no place like home*, like Dorothy in the Wizard of Oz, then he deserved it.

"So, don't you ever threaten me again, Detective Inspector. Unless you have truly professional business to do with me, you stay the hell away." I said, rising to my feet in a way which made the chair scrape horribly. "Because it very much looks like it is *I* who has *you* around the neck, as it were. *Not* the other way around." And with that, I started for the door.

"Actually," I began, wincing a little. "You'll have to show me out. I can't remember how we got to this room."

Chapter Fifteen

I almost cantered away from the police station. Very quickly getting over my bout of childish but good self-satisfaction, I realised I needed to act quickly. I needed to get the photocopy photocopied, if you see what I mean.

A police officer was going to be sent to meet me in an hour and a half to take possession of the photocopy. It would take me about an hour to get to uni, and that was with both busses turning up on time.

I still wanted to read the rest of Hannah's diary; I had a horrible feeling that things were going to somehow get worse, and I wanted to at least have the ability to keep detecting.

So, I needed someone to get into my locker, take the photocopy, and photocopy it. I needed a spare.

I had been about to ring Liam when I realised that he did not yet know that Hannah was dead. I was having trouble getting to grips with it myself, and I'd seen her. How could I ring Liam and say *Hannah's dead, please can you pop into uni and photocopy the photocopy*?

Apart from being pretty cold, it would most likely be pointless. Liam was probably still at home, so it would take him as long to get there as it would take me.

Taking my phone out, I ran through my contacts. All seven of them. Rich Richard. There was nobody else. I knew Richard would be there today, since he'd told me so the night before.

Could I trust him? I had no choice really. He already knew about the diary, and already knew his name was in it. I had to give it a shot.

"Hi Josie. Are you in uni?"

"No, Richard. I've just come out of the police station. Look, I really need your help. Thing is, I need it fast and don't have time to explain."

"Ok, what is it? I said I'd help if I could." He sounded sort of pleased, as if I was Alan Sugar giving him the chance to stay in the Apprentice for another week.

"I need you to photocopy Hannah's diary; well, the photocopy."

"Ok, but why?"

"The Police are coming for it in an hour and a half. You'll need to go like the clappers. It's a big photocopy."

"Alright." He said, amazing me a little bit.

"Richard, I'll explain everything when I see you."

"So, which is your locker?" No small talk. He was taking me seriously!

"Its 147. And the combination is GS32QT."

"Your postcode?"

"Yes. So, if you're going to do it, just make sure it's back in my locker with a good ten minutes to spare. Is that ok? I don't want to put you in danger of getting into trouble, but I don't know what else to do."

"No problem. I'll wait in the canteen when I'm done. Come and meet me when you're free of the police."

"Thanks Richard. I seriously owe you."

"I'd better get on with it." And with that, Rich Richard hung up.

Honestly, I felt pretty guilty for not telling him about Hannah, but what good would it have done in that moment?

Once I was on the first bus, I sat near the back, more or less alone, and called Liam.

"Hey Josie." He sounded extremely rattled.

"You ok?"

"Not really. A police van has just pulled up outside my house. I've got a horrible feeling they're here for me. Thorn is with them."

"Liam. I'm really sorry to make this so brief and blunt, but Hannah is dead. I followed a lead from the Trixie email address and ended up finding her in a derelict building on Weatherby Road."

"What? Josie?" Liam sounded winded, like he'd been punched in the belly by a very much bigger bloke.

He was so shocked, and I wished I could have done or said anything in the world to help him at that moment.

"I'm sorry Liam."

"What happened? I mean, was it bad? Was she in a bad way?" I heard his voice choke away into a strangled kind of a sob.

I could barely speak. My eyes were filling with tears and my throat felt really, horribly tight.

"No. I mean, she wasn't in a mess. She just looked like she was sleeping. I'm so sorry, Liam."

"And how did you find her again?" Liam said, almost panicking. "Look, hurry. The Police are knocking at the door now."

"Liam, it doesn't matter how I found her. Look, I told them everything about the diary and the Emjay thing, so all you need to do is be honest. Don't try to work things out or hold back. It will make you look guilty."

"Josie!" He yelled, sounding scared and desperate. God, I was crap at this!

"Liam, what I mean is, don't stress yourself trying to think how I found her. Just tell the things you know and don't worry about the things you don't."

"Ok." He said, quietly. "I have to go." And with that, Liam hung up.

I felt appalling; obviously, Thorn had come to the conclusion that Matty Jameson and the nude painting and the whole stripper business gave Liam one hell of a motive.

I felt very much that it was unfair and yet, when you looked at it in the cold light of day, the Police could do no other than take Liam in for questioning. They had a motive now that went far beyond the lazy *well, he's the boyfriend, after all* theory.

I couldn't exactly blame them, but it didn't stop me hating DI Thorpe harder than I'd ever hated anyone in my life.

A very large part of me wished I had never gone looking for Hannah. I wished I'd just left her there for someone else to find. And yet, when I thought about DI Thorn's lack of imaginative investigation skills, not to mention the effective remoteness of the derelict building, I knew that Hannah would have laid there for a very long time.

Her family would have been left dangling over the hellish fires of pointless hope and very real fear. And Hannah would have continued to disintegrate; I just couldn't get away from that. The smell would not have been the suspicion of decay that I was struggling to forget, but something very much more awful.

And her family would have had to deal with that when they identified her. As much as my discovery had shredded their hope, at least it would allow them to identify a daughter who still looked like their daughter.

I let out a strangled sob; why the hell was I thinking about the very worst things imaginable? Why was my mind taking me to places I didn't want to go?

By the time I reached uni, I could see that a police car was already parked way over in the top car park. It had to be whoever was coming for the diary.

As I sped through the quiet corridors, I was silently praying that Richard had got the photocopy back to my locker before the police had arrived. They were at least ten minutes early, if not more.

There really was only going to be so far I could dangle the Interception of Communications Act in front of DI Thorn before it finally became simple blackmail.

When I reached the locker room, two officers I'd never seen before were talking to a member of university staff.

"Hello." I said, speaking directly to the officers and ignoring the inquisitive stare of the admin assistant.

"Josie?" The first of them said, in a much friendlier way than I was expecting.

"Yes." I said, smiling maniacally as my heart pounded. "Shall we?" I cast a look at the admin lady and the second officer caught on and duly thanked her for her help.

Man, was she peeved to be shooed away before getting an eyeful of the latest gossip.

"I'll just open it up for you." I said, hoping they wouldn't see my hands shake as I punched in the combination.

If Richard hadn't made it back in time, my locker would be empty and I would undoubtedly find myself back at the police station. My throat was so dry and raw that every breath hurt.

With the combination punched in, the electronic keypad gave a happy little beep of recognition before the lock released. Seriously quivering, I pulled the door open. I nearly dropped to my knees with relief; I really did owe Rich Richard big time. Perhaps I would take out a bank loan and buy him a newer Peugeot.

"There you go." I said, smiling in a bright and odd way, kind of like a shop window mannequin, as I handed over the great wedge of paper.

It was nothing like as neatly stacked as I had left it, so I knew that Richard had done his bit. It was either fully or partially copied, depending on how fast he'd been.

"Thanks." The first officer said. "Can you just sign here?" Yet another evidence bag to scrawl on. I signed it with a smile.

"You're welcome." I said, as genuinely as I could manage.

"We'll be off then."

"Ok." I said. "Take care." *Why? Why did I say that?* I really was not good under pressure.

Richard was sitting alone in the canteen when I finally got there, all red and sweaty and finally beginning to feel like hell on earth.

"What's happening?" He said, as I plopped down into the chair next to him.

"Really bad news." I spoke quietly, almost whispering; you see, glaring with full intensity from across the canteen was Fliss, Amelia, and the two insipid hangers-on they had picked up the day before.

"What?" Richard said, the colour starting to drain from his face.

"I found Hannah. She's dead."

It took a considerable length of time to recount the entire tale, since I was whispering and Richard was doing what he could to fight emotion.

It was not common knowledge, and I was in no doubt that DI Thorn expected me to stay silent until the official announcement.

"You went alone?" Richard whispered. "You should have called me." Then, thinking better of it. "But I'm glad you didn't." "I know." I said, and reached out to take his hand.

In that very moment, there was a shriek and a horrible clang as Fliss' chair tipped over. She had stood up at high speed and was thundering over to where Richard and I were sitting. God, could this day get any worse? Hurriedly, I let go of his hand.

"So, not content with hanging out with Liam Attwood, now you're trying your hand at a bit of boyfriend stealing!" She yelled, drawing huge attention from all around. Richard was not wrong; this girl had a dangerously short fuse.

"What?" I said, playing for time.

"You heard me, you scruffy little peasant!" She hissed.

"Shut up, Fliss. You're out of order." Richard looked truly furious with her. He'd had a terrible shock, it was true, but he seemed as if he was totally angry at the way she had insulted me. "And I'm not your boyfriend anymore, am I? So, mind your own damned business and get out of my face!"

Stuff like *get out of my face* always sounds really odd when coming from someone who speaks with that kind of Radio 4 received pronunciation. It was funny; kind of like if EastEnders was re-made but with the Queen and Prince Philip in it. For an awful moment, I thought I was going to let out a nervous and highly inappropriate laugh.

"So, you weren't already seeing her then?" Fliss demanded, turning her back to me, and not for the first time.

"No. Again, not really any of your business. Your nasty little rages are totally out of line, Fliss. You need to get a grip of yourself."

"You expect me to believe that you've only just started seeing her today?" Again, I had no name and no presence in the room.

To be honest, it sort of suited me just fine at that particular moment. I decided not to insist on proper inclusion.

"I'm not seeing Josie." Richard snorted, not losing any of his quiet, contained fury.

"So why were you holding hands?"

"None of your business. Now get lost."

"No. I'm not going anywhere until you answer me."

"Oh, get over yourself!" Finally, I was back in the room. "Who do you think you are? I mean, do you really think we'll follow your demands meekly like Amelia does? Reality check, Felicity." And with that, I got to my feet.

"Good idea. Let's get out of here, Josie." Richard said, smirking as he reached for my hand and began to walk me away through the canteen.

"Sorry, but she deserves this." He whispered, still holding my hand, as Fliss burst into angry tears behind us.

"Fine by me, as long as she doesn't follow me home and boil my bunny rabbit. She's off her gourd." I was getting faster and faster.

"You've got a rabbit?"

"No, Richard." I said, and I would have laughed if I wasn't so horribly out of breath.

By the time we reached the student union bar, right over on the other side of the campus, my face was like a damp, shiny beetroot. I hadn't known where Richard was carting me off to, and sort of expected him to stop at any moment, so I just kept running and hoping.

Had I known we were going to run so far, I'd have refused. I'd have stopped in my tracks and told him to go on without me; I'd meet him there. I just don't like running. I'm not a sporty type. In my world view, running should only be used as a mode of escape when your life is under some sort of serious threat. You know, lions, tigers, muggers and what-have-you.

"At least you didn't have to run carrying this great wad of paper." Richard said, patting his rucksack to indicate the photocopy of the photocopy when he saw my shiny face and winded expression.

"Was Fliss chasing us?" I said, between gasps.

"No, I don't think so." Richard said, looking a little confused.

"Then why were we running?" I said, almost cross eyed as I tried to get my cantering heartbeat under control.

"Oh." Richard said, starting to chuckle in an embarrassed sort of a way. "I don't know."

What I was to athletics, Richard was to common sense. "Anyway, I think you owe me a gin and tonic." He said with a grin, patting the rucksack once again for good measure.

"A gin and tonic? What are you, like sixty?" I said, doubling over with laughter. "Are you sure you don't want a nice drop of sweet sherry?"

"Oh, very funny." Richard said, but he laughed all the same.

In fact, just outside the doors of the student union bar, Rich Richard and I laughed like drains. It was a weird sort of laughter though. It was almost desperate and determined, and about two minutes into it, big, sad tears were streaming down my face.

"I know." Richard said, reaching out for me. "Come here." And he sort of gathered me in, like you do with a sobbing child.

"I'm so sorry." I said, suddenly remembering that I really didn't know Rich Richard too well. In fact, beyond a few stilted lunchtime conversations in the weeks of the Hannah and Liam romance, any real knowledge of each other was literally only as old as the week itself was. It was odd, though; so much had happened that I felt almost as comfortable with Richard as I did with Liam. "I wasn't expecting to cry."

"Why ever not? You found Hannah dead, all by yourself, then your best friend is arrested for it. I'd be crying if I was you. In fact, I'm not entirely sure I won't have a little weep myself at some point, when the fact that Hannah is dead finally sinks in and becomes real. Cry all you want." He said, and gave me an extra little squeeze, sort of strong, like wrestling style, just for emphasis.

Once we got inside the bar, I made my way to get Richard's G&T. Even the girl behind the bar gave a little smirk.

"It's not for me. It's for him." I told her, inclining my head to where Richard was sitting, just for clarification purposes.

I myself had lime cordial, for three reasons. One, I like lime cordial. Two, it's, like, twenty pence if you have it with tap water. Three, I don't drink alcohol. I never have and I never will. I never needed to experiment with it, you see, because I had daily proof of exactly what it could do to you.

I'm not sanctimonious about it; other people can drink what they want, smoke what they want, I'm not a preacher. I just choose not to. As suspected, my order of lime cordial and tap water drew an even bigger smirk from the girl behind the bar, leaving me wishing I hadn't been so openly judgemental about Richard's choice of beverage.

As I walked back over to Richard, I couldn't help but smile. Despite being better off than me, he hadn't patronised me in any way. He hadn't been making a silly joke when he said I owed him a gin and tonic; he meant it, and he followed it through without batting an eyelid.

All in all, I was starting to think that Richard could very well end up being an actual friend. He really was turning out to be what I had been expecting when I went to uni. In truth, I though the whole place would be riddled with people who didn't have a prejudice to their name and fought voraciously against those who did.

The reality had been not quite as I had expected. Maybe I was just too late? Maybe I needed to have been a nineteen-year-old in the sixties for that kind of passion. Maybe centrist attitudes had blunted people's sense of fairness after all, even student-types.

"Thanks Josie." Richard said, before taking a great gulp of his gin and tonic.

"And thank you, for doing the photocopying and risking getting caught out by the police." I responded in kind. "Did you manage to get it all?"

"Yep." He said with a big grin. "The whole thing. I finished with twenty minutes to spare, and passed the cops on my way back out of the locker room after I'd returned it. They were seriously early." He said, with an excited roll of his eyes as he remembered his exploits.

"When I saw their car parked in the top car park, I thought it was all over." I said, reliving the whole thing.

"So, what's next for you?" Richard said, all interest. "I mean, I take it you're going to keep investigating?"

"Well, I guess so. Liam's really going to need my help now, for what it's worth. To be honest, I don't really know what I'm doing."

"Are you kidding, Josie? Seriously, if I was locked up for a crime I didn't commit, I'd want you on my side." "Thanks." I said, smiling a bit sadly.

"I'm not just saying it, Josie. Look at what you've done. Using your brain and a stray email address, you managed to find Hannah. Did the Police do that?"

"No, but to be fair, they didn't have the email address to work with."

"And if that DI Thorn *had* had the Trixie email address, what do you think he would have done with it?"

"I dread to think." I said, giving an embarrassing little snort as I started to laugh.

"Exactly. So, stop looking down. Lift your head up. You're ace. If anyone can get to the bottom of it all, it's you Josie. And I'll help you, whatever you need."

"You actually enjoyed the whole clandestine photocopying thing, didn't you?"

"I did." He said, with a big cheesy grin. "But I like Liam, too. I don't want to see him suffering any more than he has already. I mean, the poor guy, trapped in there, wondering if he's going to end up charged with murder." Richard said, and I winced as I rather wished he hadn't. "And I like you too, Josie. I have from the first. You both seemed to just accept me."

"In the end, I did. Be honest, I didn't exactly cover myself in glory in the accepting stakes."

"Just a hiccup. Means nothing." He said with a wink. "I really liked you and Liam straight away; I always kind of wished that Fliss and Amelia would get lost. Hannah too, if I'm really, horribly honest." He looked down into his gin and tonic.

"It's ok, Richard. I've been trying to come to terms with a few guilty feelings of my own. I was never Hannah's biggest fan. I know I was a bit jealous when she started seeing Liam. I don't mean I fancy the big silly goon, but I thought he wouldn't be my best mate anymore."

"Understandable." Richard said. "And Hannah didn't like you one little bit. I was there, remember? I used to wince at some of the bitchy comments the three of them would come up with."

"Yeah, me too. I suppose, in the end, you can feel sorry and sad for what happened to a person without having to pretend you used to like them, or even blame yourself for not." "I'll drink to that." Richard said, draining his glass.

"Do you want another?" I said, starting to rise.

"No thanks, Josie. I'm driving."

"Oh yes. The Ferrari." I said, with a cheeky grin.

"The very same. Do you need a lift anywhere?"

"Yes please. Would you drop me home?" I said, fighting panic as I tried to kick down one or two of my inferiority barriers.

"Of course."

I have to admit that inviting Richard in for a cup of tea was very close to one of the hardest things I had ever done. Sounds silly, right? But it was a really big step for me.

The only friend I had invited in for many long years was Liam, and only because he knew the score. He knew the score, and he lived it, after all.

In the event, once he was inside the house and drinking his tea, things were suddenly easy-peasy. Richard really was a very different sort of a dude, and he had a kind of cheeky way about him.

He made himself at home, lolling about on the couch and roaring with laughter when I explained that the sudden lack of a television was very likely due to Snatcher Harris.

He even wandered out into the kitchen and asked if he could have a packet of the Euro-Saver crisps from the multi-pack I'd left on the worktop. And he ate them without a moment's hesitation.

Everything about his manner, as posh as he sounded, totally put me at ease. Yep; Rich Richard was very definitely friend material. I just wished I could entirely scrub him off my list of suspects.

Chapter Sixteen

After I'd picked at a nutritious meal of Euro-Saver noodles, followed by their honey-less honey clusters by way of desert, I decided to try Liam's mobile. I was kind of hoping against all hope that he had finally been exonerated entirely and was already on the bus, making his innocent way back home.

It went straight to answer phone, of course, and my naïve optimism was crushed like a grape. Wondering if PC Dale Webb might have the inside track, I put in a call to him next. Once again, I was thwarted by an instant answer phone message.

I huffed loudly; I really needed to know what was going on. Choosing not to leave a message, I hung up and stared down into my bowl. There was a tiny piece of cluster that I had chased around with the spoon, but had been unable to pick up. In the end, I reached in and rescued it with my bare hands.

I popped it into my mouth and rose to take the bowl out to the kitchen. As I washed it up and placed it on the drainer, I suddenly thought of Betty. Could I ring Betty instead? Of course, that would only work if she was on duty. I didn't have her mobile number as I did Dale's.

Feeling a little bit apprehensive, I dialled the Grantstone Constabulary Communications room and tremulously asked if PC Elizabeth Butler was on duty, giving the crime number Betty had handed me the night before in relation to my mum's affray.

"Hi Josie." Betty said, startling me so much that I gave a little gasp. "How are you doing?" I had been put through to Betty at top speed, and the call taker had obviously given my name and crime number and what-not.

"Oh, hi Betty. I'm not too bad, all things considered." I felt suddenly very stupid.

I hardly knew Betty, and I was certain that I should not be asking her to tell me what was happening with a live police investigation involving my closest friend.

"I know; I heard." Betty said, clearly indicating that she was up to date with the whole me finding Hannah business. "You must be feeling pretty rough." There was just something about Betty.

She was certainly an officer you wouldn't tangle with, but she was as caring as any mum should be. Like a fool, I started to cry.

"I do feel rough, to be honest. That's why I called." In for a penny, in for a pound. I was already making a fool of myself, so I might just as well ask inappropriate questions and blame it on the stress. "Is Liam still there?"

"He is, Josie, love." She said, lowering the volume considerably.

I suddenly realised that Betty was unlikely to be alone in the police station, and maybe couldn't really talk.

"I'm sorry to ask, but do you know if he's ok? Or if he's coming home soon? I know he didn't do it Betty. I tried to call Dale, but he's not answering. I'm sorry to hassle you instead."

"It's ok, Josie. Dale is tied up in custody interviewing a shoplifter. I was getting a bit of paperwork out of the way in the meantime. Look, are you at home?" Betty was practically whispering.

"Yes." I whispered back, then almost laughed at my own buffoonery.

"No problem, Miss Cloverfield. I'll just pop round if I may and get you to check over your statement from last night." She said, in a suddenly loud tone which made me jump.

"No idea what you're talking about, but I'm guessing that's for the benefit of the room." I said, with a watery giggle. "I'll be here all night, Betty. And thank you so much."

"No problem, Miss Cloverfield. I'll pop round now." She said, and rang off.

Betty was at the door before the kettle had even boiled. She was a woman of her word, and those were in short supply in my life.

"Hi, Josie. Sorry about the weirdness and the subterfuge. It's just that my Sergeant was hovering, so I had to make it sound like we were talking about your mum's case."

"Thanks so much for coming. And I'm sorry again; I know it's totally inappropriate of me, but I just don't know where to turn. That DI Thorn is a complete fool, and I'm so worried that he'll find some way of fitting Liam up." I realised that I should probably not have said that, and really didn't want to sound like my mum. *All cops are liars.*

I hurriedly told her about the Interception of Communications business. I was glad I did, because Betty was duly disgusted by him.

"Between you and me, I'm not a bit surprised by what you're telling me. Thorn has just been in the job too long, and he's one of the old-school coppers who thinks things like human rights and surveillance laws are a total waste of time and only there to hamper him personally. He wants a result at any price, and doesn't care who is affected by his methods." Betty nodded gratefully as I handed her a steaming cup of strong tea. She'd asked me to leave the bag in; I like a lass who can stand to drink a really deep-tan shade of brew. "But if anyone asks, I didn't say any of this, Josie."

"Understood. And you can trust me. I have a great deal to be grateful to you for already, and I've only known you a few days."

"You're more than welcome." She said, gulping down scalding hot tea in a way which made me even more in awe of her.

"Betty, do they really think it's Liam?"

"Thorn would probably like to think so. It makes his job easier, you see. But he'll still have to find evidence, and that's what you have to hold on to."

"Like forensics?" I asked, hoping that I could ease a bit of info out of my hero.

"Exactly. Look, Hannah was strangled, apparently. Now I really shouldn't be telling you this, so you keep it close to your chest, ok?"

"I promise."

"She was strangled." Betty resumed. "And that's not an easy thing to do to somebody. There's usually a real struggle to it all. There's a possibility that her attacker would have left a bit of DNA behind. Skin cells or what-not."

"What about *other* types of DNA?" I said, looking down into my own cup, mortified. "I mean, when I read the private messages between the two Facebook accounts, it very much seemed as if they were going to meet up at that old building to…well….you know." *Josie Cloverfield: Total prude.*

"No. There was no sign of sexual activity whatsoever" *Ok, why couldn't I have just said that?* "It looks like she was lured there to be killed." Betty shrugged kind of helplessly, and I totally got her mood.

"Oh Betty, that's awful." I said, feeling sadder than ever. "I mean, it's awful that she was killed, no matter what. It just seems worse somehow that *that* was the killer's intention. I mean, it obviously isn't ok for an argument or something to end in violence and death, but it's just the thought that

Hannah set off for what she thought was a bit of fun, only all the time she was making her way to her death. Like, it had all been decided already, and she didn't know." I knew I was babbling. "I'm sorry, that makes no sense at all."

"It makes perfect sense, Josie." Betty said, and reached out to pat my shoulder with such force that I was left hoping she didn't have any small pets at home. "It makes it the more tragic, somehow. Like, if only something had happened on the way to stop her making her rendezvous." Betty totally got it.

"So, if there's no forensics, will Thorn have to let Liam go?"

"Well, he'll keep him for as long as he can, badgering him in the hope he'll confess. He'll only be able to hold Liam in custody for twenty-four hours without charge. Then he'll either have to bail him with the idea that further enquiries need to be made, or release him without any further action. Most likely, it would be bail for further enquiries. If there's no forensics or anything even vaguely solid, then there will be little point in Thorn applying for an extended custody period. He just wouldn't get it, unless he has something a bit stronger. Then, he could apply to hold him from thirty-six to ninety-six hours."

"Thank you, Betty." I said, and I meant it.

It just felt better, somehow, to truly know the ins and outs of what could happen to Liam, and to have that information straight from the horse's mouth, as it were. Still, the idea that Liam could be held for ninety-six hours made me shudder. Four whole days.

"And I'm told that the search at Liam's place turned up nothing." Betty said, in a conspiratorial whisper which spoke volumes about the fact she was really telling me far too much.

"His house has been searched?"

"Yes. This afternoon. You see, Hannah was missing her gold necklace. It was the only thing missing. She still had her phone and purse in her pocket, and all the clothing her mother saw her go out in was intact. Everything but the necklace. And she definitely had it on, because the coroner stated that there was a mark on the back of her neck which was entirely consistent with having the necklace pulled off her whilst still done up." "Oh God." It was an all-encompassing *Oh God*.

It was everything; the fact that Hannah's family now knew, the fact that Liam's home had been searched, and the fact that Hannah's murderer had taken a souvenir.

"I know. But they found nothing. And for what it's worth, Josie, my gut tells me that Liam is innocent. In the end, that will come to the fore. Motive alone isn't evidence."

"Motive?" I said, looking at Betty with big, scared eyes.

"Yes. Thorn is working on the theory that the nude painting gave Liam a good motive. Still, he has yet to prove that Liam could have even known anything about it." "Has Thorn spoken to Matty Jameson?"

"Yes. He called him and asked Jameson to come into the station. He's actually just treating him like a witness instead of a suspect." Betty said with an incredulous shrug.

"And you think he should have arrested him too?"

"Well, I guess I just think that Thorn should have kept an open mind. I don't know this Matty guy, so I can't really say what I think of him. I don't have an actual opinion of him, as such."

"Well, if Matty is innocent, at least Thorn didn't wreck his career by marching into the university and carting him off like they did Liam." I thought of Matty with his silly scarf and his cockapoo puppy hair and just couldn't imagine him hurting anyone.

Still, that probably counted for absolutely zero, and was not exactly an informed line of reasoning.

"Look, I'm going to have to head back to the nick in a minute, Josie. Dale's probably out of custody and wandering around the office banging into stuff." Betty said, with a smile that just made me feel that little bit better.

"Thanks for everything, Betty." I said, rising to show her out.

"Now listen to me, Josie. You did amazingly well to find Hannah the way you did. Honestly, Thorn couldn't have got there in a million years." Her smile began to fade. "But please be careful. I'm not going to tell you to stop looking, because I reckon I'd be doing just the same thing in your shoes. But just watch your back. Not just DI Thorn, but, well….. there's a killer out there, Josie, and there's a really good chance that he was the one who came into your house and stole the diary."

Thanks Betty. That was very look-behind-you. I was suddenly a bit unnerved.

"I'll be careful, I promise."

Chapter Seventeen

My Saturday shift at the dry cleaners dragged horribly the next day. I know that it probably seems odd that I turned into work when I'd found a dead body the day before and my best friend was in clink, but I didn't really have much of a choice in it.

I needed the money, not to mention the fact that I needed to cling on to this job. It wasn't the best pay ever, but they only wanted a Saturday shift out of me, and it never really interfered with my studies.

The meagre income was just manageable for a long-practiced economiser like myself, so, in I went.

The dry cleaners was not a shop as such, but rather an alcove in a supermarket, next door to the key cutting concession. That was its only redeeming feature, really; I could gaze at all sorts of folk as they wandered past the dry cleaners in the direction of the shampoo aisle of the supermarket, and they were so intent that they didn't know I was staring. Sad, but true.

"And can you get the bobbles off it, love? You know, with one of those bobble remover things?" For a scary few seconds, I had no idea what the woman in front of me was talking about.

"Erm…." I began, stalling like a pro. "Yes, of course. Let me get the full price for you."

"Finally." The old duck said, waspishly. "I thought for a minute it would be quicker to serve myself." She went on, turning to say it to some imaginary person behind her, but obviously aiming her snark at me.

Working at the dry cleaners had taught me much about just how irritating the population at large truly was.

How dare I falter for two seconds? How dare I be a human being with a life and troubles of my own, whose concentration wandered for just a heartbeat?

I was just a green overall and an unreadable name badge to her. What was worse, she looked like one of the adorable old ladies on the cereal advert where the little squares of wheat were allegedly knitted by nanas.

Yeah, right; this snappy old goat would be too busy poking new-born babies' eyeballs out with her knitting needles to do anything as mundane as lovingly hand-crafting cereals for a grateful nation.

Just goes to show that anyone, even a snowball-haired, doughfaced old nana, can have that vile sense of entitlement which gives them the erroneous impression that they and their inconsequential wants are so much more important than anything else on earth.

I gave her the price for dry cleaning and de-bobbling the heavy fleece jacket depicting an intricate scene of wolves out on the prairie. She clicked her false fangs and glared at me as if I personally were entirely responsible for a nationwide dry cleaning chain's price list.

"Don't you think that's a bit much?" She barked at me.

"Yes." I said, glaring at her and getting ready to ditch my principles as far as abuse of the elderly went.

"Oh." She said, a little on the back foot.

She had been expecting me to apologetically defend the price. Instead she got a flat one-word answer that seemed impossible to argue with. She looked at me, as if she was expecting me to say something; it was my turn after all. I remained silent. The old duck squirmed a little.

"Well, I don't suppose I have a choice." She spat, determined to have her row.

"Yes, you do." I said, keeping it flat and starting to enjoy myself.

I'd sunk her, and I wanted to cheer.

"Here you go, love." She said, handing me her bank card with a really tight smile that would loosen her dentures if she wasn't careful.

"Thank you."

I was supremely glad to see the back end of Grandma Nasty and, as I lifted my gaze from the cash register to the next customer, I was horrified to find it was none other than Fliss Hardcastle.

"What can I do for you?" I said, keeping hold of the flat tone, despite the sudden thundering of my heart.

Don't get me wrong, Fliss didn't scare me; I just wasn't expecting to see her there and I really, really didn't want her making a scene of some sort at my place of work.

"Oh no, really, I couldn't." Fliss said, looking disdainfully into the alcove and shuddering, as if there was something shameful about dry cleaning. "I would never use such a place."

"Oh really? You just throw your stuff away when it gets dirty, do you?"

"I can't believe you're making jokes." She hissed. "You're in enough trouble as it is."

"I'm not in any trouble, actually. If you don't want dry cleaning done, you need to move on. I'm working."

"Aren't you just." She said, with a derisory laugh. "Working your little socks off to pay for your second-hand clothes and cheap snacks!"

"Go." I snapped.

"No, I won't. You're going to pay for what you've done."

"Which is?"

"You found Hannah. Everyone knows it now!"

"And I'm going to pay for that? I'm going to pay for looking for her and finding her as opposed to leaving her there? You really are an idiot, Fliss."

"Is everything alright?" Bunty, *yes Bunty*, the weekend manager called over to me.

"Yes, thank you." I said, giving her what I hoped was a mindyour-own-business look.

"Look at you!" Fliss went on. "You couldn't care less, could you. If you did, you wouldn't even be able to work! I wonder why it is you don't care?" She was leaning over the counter, her seriously pinched up face just an inch from mine. "Because you either put her there, or you know who did. Liam's going to swing for this, and hopefully you will too."

"Swing for it? No such thing as public hangings anymore, you ignoramus."

"Are you sure everything's alright?" Bunty sounded twitchy.

"Yes, Bunty!" I said, with a little more harshness than was perhaps required.

"Did you watch Liam do it?" Fliss said with a sort of horribly excited relish. Her eyes were wide and she was actually smiling, albeit garishly. "Or did you help him?"

"Neither, because Liam didn't do it. Now please just go away. You're out of order."

"No, you're out of order. You really think you're somebody, don't you?"

Just because you got your paws on Richard....."

"Ah, now I see." I said, and chuckled like some kind of Bond villain; suddenly I was back in my white suit and stroking a big Persian cat.

I must say, however, that I was feeling nowhere near as confident as I was sounding. In truth, I felt sick. Fliss was going to lose me my job if I didn't think of a way to get rid of her.

"You see what?" She snarled.

"You're not here because of Hannah. And as for not caring, you're wrong. I do care, I just can't afford to lose a day's pay. But you? You are awfully dry-eyed for a best friend, aren't you? All perfect hair and make-up, out shopping just hours after you find out your best friend is dead! Seriously, can't you see that your own double standard is showing you up as having the IQ of a cornflake!" I was having a bit of a cereal themed morning. "And that performance at the vigil! Nobody was fooled by that! It was all about you, and all about you getting into the local papers. You make me sick."

"Josie. What's going on?" Bunty squeaked.

"Oh Bunty, give over!" I raised my voice.

"Hannah was my best friend!" Fliss wailed.

"And even now, not a tear in sight. You're not here having a go at me because you think Liam killed Hannah. You're here because you think I took Richard from you. Seriously, your ego is limitless!"

"Oh, don't flatter yourself! Richard's not interested in you! He'd go with anybody! He even....." And there, she stopped dead.

"He even slept with Hannah. Yeah, I know." I said, feeling a really unsettling mixture of the chills and victory. Chills, because I'd realised she had known Richard had cheated on her with Hannah all along, and victory, because I'd got her to give herself away. "But Richard hadn't realised you knew." I went on, desperate to hurt the hell out of her. "Well, well, well.... smells like a good motive to me. No wonder you've been so keen to throw mud and spiteful looks across the canteen."

"You're dead." She said, so vehemently that she spat a little bit. *Man, I hate that.*

"Don't threaten me." I said with an antagonistic smirk, despite feeling a little freaked out.

"I'm watching you." Fliss came very close to actually evaporating me with her sizzling eyebeams, as my own imagination helped her out with a flashback to the message in the steam on my bathroom mirror.

Suddenly, my mouth went a little dry. Could Fliss really have strangled Hannah to death? Was she even strong enough? I remembered Richard's description of her vile temper, not to mention the face scratching that Amelia had suffered.

"Move along, Miss Hardcastle." A voice I recognised snapped me back into the here and now. It was Dale.

"What? No!" Fliss clearly didn't recognise Dale in his everyday-human-wear.

"Now, or I'll lock you up." Dale held his warrant card out in front of him; so close to Fliss that I had a sudden mental image of him actually inserting the stiff badge into her left nostril.

"Oh, I….." Fliss suddenly faltered. How cool was it to have a cop buddy! She looked a little panicked. "Look, officer, I was just questioning her, that's all." Fliss sniffed importantly, and I almost laughed.

"Oh, I see. I'm sorry, I didn't recognise you from the nick. Which department?" Dale said, totally sarcastic.

"I'm not a police officer. I just wanted to….."

"I know what you wanted to do, Miss Hardcastle. You wanted to vent spleen and harass Josie. You wanted to entertain yourself with a bit of spiteful sport instead of mourning the loss of your friend."

"How dare you?" Fliss tried to be assertively outraged, but was looking satisfyingly unsure of herself.

"Oh, I dare, Miss Hardcastle. If you're not careful, the same people who saw you flouncing about like a self-important reality TV celebrity at Hannah's vigil will see you flouncing about causing trouble just hours after she was found dead. You don't look like best friend material to me, and the rest of the world won't be fooled for long, either. So, I suggest you wind you neck in and go and find something else to do." Dale spoke in a low and vaguely menacing tone.

Clearly this was not uniformed officer procedure, but more like something that DI Thorn might say behind closed doors, out of the gaze of the public. However, on this occasion, I was all for it. Double standards, but still, Fliss deserved it.

And Dale was pretty magnificent! I mean, I'd never heard him playing bad cop before, but he did it really well. He looked even taller and broader than normal, not to mention just a little bit hot somehow.

As she spun around to walk off, Fliss gave me the sort of look that could blister gloss paint. I kid you not, my stomach flipped. It was the sort of look that said *you're next*.

"Are you ok Jose?" Dale said, leaning over the counter at me just as Fliss had done, but without any of the negative connotations.

"I am now." I said, breathing a big old sigh of relief. "Apart from being jobless."

"Huh?"

"Bunty has disappeared off out the back." I said, inclining my head sharply. "Presumably to ring head office to get me fired off."

"*Bunty?* Are you serious? *Bunty?*" Dale said, his eyes wide like saucers and the corners of his mouth turning up.

"Yeah, I know. But don't make it worse with any Buntyrelated guffawing. I'm in enough trouble as it is."

"Don't worry about it. I'll talk to Bunty." Dale said, getting ready to rescue me for the second time that day. "Just as soon as I come to terms with her name." Dale took a couple of comical, steadying breaths before ducking under the counter and joining me on my side. "What's her second name?" He whispered in my ear.

"Golightly." I said, my heart dropping like a runaway lift plummeting its way towards the ground floor. *I was about to be jobless.....*

"Oh, please."

"I'm serious."

"How am I supposed to deal with that?" Dale said, his shoulders starting to bounce with conspiratorial mirth. "Oh well, here goes." And he strode off to the door at the back office and knocked loudly.

Five minutes later, Dale emerged with a rather smitten looking Bunty sweeping along behind him.

"Thanks so much for your help, PC Webb." Bunty crooned, and I almost laughed.

"No, really, thank *you*, Miss Golightly, for your understanding. It's always a great help to receive support from members of the public, particularly in a case of harassment."

"Oh yes, of course. Well, it was a pleasure."

"I'm very grateful, as I'm sure Miss Cloverfield is." Dale said, winking at me as a cue for my overt gratitude.

"Yes, thank you Bunty. It really was very embarrassing. It was a good thing that PC Webb happened by." I said, so keen to get her back onside that I almost curtseyed.

"It certainly was." Bunty said, gazing up at the new star of her every fantasy.

"Well, I shall leave you to it." Dale said, giving me a *get-me-the-hell-out-of-here* smile.

"Thank you, PC Webb." I said, wanting to chat a bit longer, but knowing that there would be no shaking Bunty off now.

As it happened, the rest of my shift was spent talking about PC Dale Webb to an over-excited Bunty Golightly. By the end of it, I was totally sick of the man. *PC Webb said this, PC Webb said that, isn't PC Webb attractive?....* you get the picture.

I was desperate for Bunty to bite through her tongue, because I was starting to get over my shock at Fliss showing up, and I wanted to turn my brain back onto the investigation, especially since I felt sure that Fliss was now a legitimate suspect.

I needed to speak to Rich Richard. I don't know why, I just felt he needed to know that Fliss had known about Hannah all along. I knew it was right that Richard should know, but I was being thoroughly Bunty'd to death, and couldn't think straight enough to work it all out.

I was also having other ideas poking and prodding at my tired brain. If Fliss was the killer, was she also Dirty Harry of Facebook fame? Was that even possible? I mean, it very much seemed as if Trixie Sunday and Dirty Harry had already met.

So, did you enjoy the show? Surely, she can only have meant the strip show? Or had she? She hadn't exactly been explicit, after all. Things were not making sense.

Unless Dirty Harry wasn't the killer. I mean, he'd arranged to meet Hannah in that building, but could it be possible he hadn't been the one who strangled her? They could have been followed.

Or Hannah could have been followed and killed before Dirty Harry even arrived. Oh, for God's sake! I was just confusing myself and Bunty's blithering wasn't helping one little bit.

I needed a plan. I needed to find out more. Somewhat controversially, I really *was* starting to think about a trip to the Duchess of Devonshire. Pub, not aristocrat. Maybe there was something to be found out there.

Maybe someone there would be able to describe Dirty Harry? Or anyone who'd paid any kind of interest in Hannah. I know, it was a strip-pub.... There was likely to be a great list of goggling turnip heads who'd fit the bill.

I looked at my watch. It was nearly two o'clock. My six-hour stint was drawing to a merciful close.

"Oh look, here comes Dave." Bunty said, smiling as the twotill-eight guy appeared. "You might as well get going, Jose." Bunty smiled at me. *Jose? Really?* Well, I never. Finally, Bunty liked me. Good old Dale Webb.

"Thanks Bunty." I said, resisting the urge to respond in kind and shorten her name to *Bunts* in the interests of new found friendship. "I'll see you next Saturday."

As I struggled out of my green overall and unreadable name badge and grabbed my rucksack from the back office, I realised that I had told Bunty nothing of my last twenty-four hours.

Even the most reticent of people would surely have told the person they were stuck with for a whole six hours that they'd found a dead body the day before. I smiled at Bunty as I ducked under the counter and sped towards the door, wondering all the while if there was actually something wrong with me.

Not medical, but like psychological, or even just social. Was I actually normal? In truth, I wasn't overly concerned. But maybe that's all part of the condition.

Before I tied myself in knots with inconsequential nonsense and hypochondria, I decided to head straight over to the Duchess of Devonshire and see what I could find out.

After all, it was Saturday, not Sunday. I'd be perfectly safe and, if my outfit was anything to go by, none of the punters would mistake me for the new girl.

Chapter Eighteen

Fortunately for my dwindling coffers, the Duchess of Devonshire was only a twenty-minute walk out of the town centre where the dry cleaners was. I didn't have an actual visual memory of the outside of the pub.

I'd seen it before, but had never been in and certainly never paid it any heed. It was kind of like the council offices or something; I knew they were there, but had never been interested enough to commit the finer details to memory.

Of course, when I pitched up outside the crusty old pub, it seemed suddenly familiar. I'd be a terrible witness to a crime. I'd be making up outfits and hair colours.

Everyone would be *medium height* and *medium build*. I had a great memory for facts and figures, and even great swathes of conversation. But faces and places, not so much. I don't know why; it just is as it is, I guess.

Well, it has to be said that even my mum and Snatcher Harris might think twice about spending quality time in the Duchess of Devonshire public house. It was just about the most run down looking place imaginable without it actually being abandoned and derelict.

To say that the paint on the doors and window frames was peeling would be a huge understatement. There were great curls and strips of bottle green paint snaking their way down the woodwork.

The exposed wood underneath looked grey and dry and almost as if it was shrinking somehow. Not all of the windows had glass in but, for the ones which didn't, somebody had thoughtfully nailed slabs of plywood right across the frames.

As I said, it looked more run down than a derelict building. In fact, to begin with, I thought either I'd made a big mistake, or Matty Jameson had mixed up his pub names.

I hung about outside for a few minutes, looking incredibly suspicious. My heart felt a bit skippy, and I had serious doubts about my courage. Honestly, if you'd have seen it, you wouldn't have wanted to go in either.

Finally, the door opened and someone came out. For an awful moment, I thought it might be the proprietor coming out to see what I thought I was doing. I think, perhaps, the word *proprietor* is maybe lending the place too much of an air of respectability.

Anyway, this guy came lurching out through the doors. As he did so, there came the faintest waft of music on the air. Country and Western music to be really, truly, and *horribly* precise.

As the man carried on past me, I breathed a sigh of relief. He wasn't the proprietor, and the slow closing of the front door put an end to the Country and Western.

So, now I knew that the pub was open; there were people inside and, presumably, drinks being served in the normal way. Bracing myself for the sight of the interior, I forced myself in through the doors.

I walked with as much confidence as I could muster, and hoped I was going in the right direction to finally meet with the bar; it was really very dark, you see.

I tried not to look left and right as I went in. The fact that they had a stripper in the place on a Sunday seemed to have tainted it for the entire week in my eyes.

I'm not too judgy about folk as a rule, but the idea that some or all of the people in the pub now would happily watch a young woman whip her gear off in such maudlin surroundings did, for good or bad, make me think a little less of them.

I finally made my way to the bar. The young woman serving at it stood with her back to me for ages, but I didn't want to try to aggressively get her attention.

I have to admit that I felt horribly out of my depth in the Duchess of Devonshire pub. It just had a very rough feel to it; even worse than the Dalton Arms where my mum and Snatcher tended to go. Also, there was the whole deal about being totally out of place. As much as I detested the Dalton Arms, it was not entirely unfamiliar to me so, as unpleasant as it was, it didn't make me feel afraid to go into it.

The Duchess of Devonshire was very different; I didn't know the place and I didn't know anybody in it. There was a horrible uncertainty creeping over me, having much to do with not knowing what would happen next.

As I continued to actively shrink into the bar, lest I anger the bar tender for trying to get her attention, I decided to un-clench just enough to have a quick look around. The pub did, as I had long suspected, smell of the worst kind of cooking; school dinners.

Also, if you closed your eyes and took in a really deep breath, you know, like a wine connoisseur but in vastly different surroundings, you could isolate various aromas. In the case of the Duchess of Devonshire, these were beer-soaked carpet, cigarettes, despite the ban, and, I almost *wince* at telling you, urine.

I tried to limit myself to nothing more than shallow breaths as I continued to look around and noted, with a certain amount of horror, that the door to the gents' toilet was wide open, affording the casual observer a superb view of the urinals.

Mercifully, they were not currently being used. I was having enough trouble staying on the high-up barstool as it was.

The seat was covered in that shiny mock-leather stuff in a grim shade of pub-furniture-green, and I was slip-sliding about. Had I clocked some brazen chap piddling freely, I would most likely have slipped right off and plummeted towards the beer soaked carpet.

All in all, I could not begin to imagine anyone stripping in this vile place, much less someone as prim and pristine as Hannah Davenport.

Once again, I had to wonder if Matty had made some mistake with pub names. That was until the girl behind the bar turned to finally look my way. This time, I really did come very close to falling off my stool, for there, right in front of me, stood Hannah Davenport.

I gasped, well, shrieked, actually.

I was instantly sweating from head to toe and my scalp was tingling so furiously that it felt almost sun-burned.

"Are you alright, love?" The girl said in an even rougher regional accent than my own. Despite the kindness of her words, her expression spoke volumes about how she actually couldn't have cared less if I was alright or not.

The voice alone told me it wasn't Hannah, and my brain backed it up with an unwanted mental image of Hannah's dead body. However, the knowledge didn't make the likeness any less shocking.

This girl was the spitting image. I quickly did a top to toe of her; very much in the same way that Hannah, Fliss and Amelia used to do to me when we all met up in the canteen.

Still, I comforted myself that my gawping was definitely not spite-related; more shock related. However, the more I studied her clothes, the more I could see the differences.

This girl had not been raised with the same attention to detail that Hannah's family had undoubtedly insisted upon. This girl did not have the barely-there expensive jewellery. Instead, she wore cheap, dangly earrings that were supposed to look like silver.

They were a bit tarnished and just a bit too big to be anything other than coloured metal. Her outfit was all a bit revealing. Her skirt was on the short side and tight side, although it has to be said it suited her.

Her top was a cheap stretchy thing, cut pretty low. Over that she wore a sleeveless gillet which was fluffy and mink coloured. I'm not being a clothes bitch, I'm just describing her.

The difference between this girl and Hannah in terms of style and, more than likely, disposable income, were obviously huge. However, the differences in face structure and eye colour and beautiful glossy brown hair were non-existent.

They could have been sisters. I was feeling really very confused, but something still told me that Hannah Davenport and the bar tender at the Duchess of Devonshire were unlikely to be sisters. Oh, but they were related, and there was no doubt about that. It was giving me the creeps.

"Erm…." I said, pretty much still shocked to the core of my being and doing my best to get on top of so, so many questions that were all bouncing around in my skull.

"D'you want a drink or what?" She said, losing patience faster than a mean old lady with a wolfy fleece in need of de-bobbling.

"Yes, please. Could I have a gin and tonic?" I had not dared ask for my customary lime cordial and tap water; not in a place like that, they'd probably kill me and make a necklace out of my teeth.

"A what?" She said, with a sneer.

I don't know why I picked Rich Richard's tipple of choice. I don't normally buy alcohol, so I stupidly didn't have a drink in mind when I trotted into the Duchess of Devonshire. The words *gin and tonic* just rolled off my tongue.

Judging by her expression, I might just as well have asked for a mug of Ovaltine. I decided to stay firm in my choice; if I changed it to a beer or something socially acceptable in that place, this woman would undoubtedly lose whatever tiny shreds of respect she might have for me, and I would be able to get *nothing* out of her.

As it was, my hopes weren't high.

"There's no ice or lemon. It ain't that kind of place." She snapped, thrusting the glass across the bar at me and holding out her hand. "Four twenty."

"Thanks." I said, when what I really wanted to say was *What? Four twenty for a warm G&T in a dive like this? You're stiffing me!*

I handed her a fiver, praying that tears would not spring to my eyes as I parted with the note. I calculated that drink to be more than half an hour in Bunty Golightly's company. At least this wasn't the sort of place where you felt obliged to leave a tip.

"Look, do you mind if I ask you a couple of questions?" I said hurriedly when the Hannah look-a-like seemed set to turn her back on me once more.

What about?" She said, scowling. "About a girl who used to work here." "Hannah." She said, flatly.

"Yes."

"Are you press, then?" She said, her eyes lighting up a little. "'Cos if you were, you'd have to pay me for information."

"No, I'm not press."

"Copper? You lot have already been. My dad told me as much."

"I'm not a copper." I said, keeping my voice low and wishing that she would do the same. It struck me that, rather like the Dalton Arms, this was not a place where you would want to be mistaken for a police officer.

"Who the hell are you then?" She seemed to sneer and the effect struck me as far more menacing than anything Hannah could have slung at me in the canteen.

I must admit, I felt a little bit scared of this girl.

"My name's Josie. I was at uni with Hannah."

"Oh, la-di-bloody-da!" She said, starting to laugh, but not in a humorous way.

"No, actually, not *la-di-da*. Well, not me, anyway." I said, instantly regretting the little snap in my temper.

I was so used to being sneered at for being a wee bit on the poor side that I bridled inexplicably at being accused of being quite the opposite.

I guess it doesn't actually matter where you are on the socioeconomic scale; if someone is being rude to you, they're just being rude to you. Not on, in either direction, apparently.

The result of my snippy retort was that the girl raised her eyebrows a little defensively. I wasn't expecting that at all. I decided to capitalise on it.

"And Hannah Davenport didn't mind pointing it out one little bit."

"Oh." She said, seeming to thaw a little as she looked over the counter and gave me a top to toe. I shivered; it felt so horribly familiar. "I see it now. You're a bit, well…. charity shop, aren't you?" She smirked and I felt insulted once more.

A girl in a fluffy gillet was taking the mickey out me. I wonder what she would have made of the wolves-on-the-prairie fleece that was all set for de-bobbling.

"Yeah, that's right." I said, with a scowl of my own. "And I don't give a damn what you think of my clothes, any more than I did when Hannah used to give me the once over."

"Yeah, well, she could be bitchy." She said, with a shrug. *And you can't?* "So, why are you asking questions then?"

"Because for one thing, I found Hannah's body, and for another, my friend is currently in the nick being questioned about it."

"Oh, the boyfriend, right?" She said, eyebrows raising with keen interest.

"Yes, the boyfriend. And my best friend. My innocent best friend."

"Are you sure? I mean, it's normally the boyfriend in these cases, isn't it?" I didn't like what she was saying, but at least she was talking to me.

"Well, not in this case. He had only been seeing her for a few weeks, and neither one of them was really that interested in the other. He's just been dragged in because we come from the Moss Park Estate and the copper in charge is too damn lazy to investigate properly. The DI in charge couldn't even find her. I did!" I felt a little bit puffed up at that point, before I remembered that there was a very real dead girl at the root of all this.

"So, how did you find her?" She said, leaning over the bar, totally hooked.

"Well, she had a spare Facebook account in her stripper name from here."

"Trixie Sunday?" The girl said, her eyes wide with inappropriate excitement.

Yes, anyway, I hacked into it and found a string of messages from someone who wanted to meet her in a derelict building on the day she disappeared."

"So, you went and found her?"

"Yes." I could feel it getting away from me; I felt like I was the one being interviewed by an amateur private investigator, not the other way around.

"Cool." She said, her admiration grudging but obvious.

What did puzzle me was her seeming lack of feeling for Hannah. Surely, they were related.

"Are you related to Hannah. I mean, you really look like her." "Cousins."

"What's your name?" I said, with a smile. Seeing her scowl suspiciously, I added, "You want a drink?"

"Oh, go on then. I'll have a lager." By which she meant a full pint.

She started to pour me out another vile gin and tonic before I had a chance to protest. It wasn't so much that I couldn't choke the awful stuff down, I just didn't want to pay for it.

"Seven forty." She said, and thrust her hand out again. I wanted to dissolve with grief.

"Here you go." I said, smiling in what was probably a weirdly frozen way as I handed over yet more cash.

"Kellie." She said, without explanation.

"Huh?"

"Me! I'm Kellie. But most people just call me Kel." She smiled and I suddenly warmed to her.

"I'm Josie." I said, still smiling.

"You already said."

"Oh, yeah, I did, didn't I." I chuckled as best I could. "So, did you and Hannah not get on too well?"

"I didn't kill her, if that's what you mean."

"Noooo." I said, starting to laugh. "That's not what I meant." Unbelievably, she started to laugh too.

"It's funny, you sort of feel guilty in a weird way when something like this happens." She shrugged. "No, we didn't get on. She was proper snooty, and she lorded it over me a bit."

"So, did she work here for long?"

"No, just a few weeks, eight maybe. She wanted to get back at her snobby old hypocrite of a mother."

"Why?" This was warming up; I was getting the good stuff. "Oi! Kel!" Came a great booming voice from God alone knew where.

I looked all about me for the source and, to be honest, I was glad when it didn't materialise.

I looked back to Kellie and was shocked to see just how scared she looked. In that moment, I felt awful for her.

"Who was that?" I whispered.

"My dad." She said, her eyes wide and wild looking.

"Are you ok?"

"Not if he catches me nattering. Look, the pub's filling up now. You'd better go."

"Kel, I need your help. There might be something that the police didn't ask your dad. They've been really sloppy. Please." I could not have been more beseeching if I'd thrown myself to the beer-soaked carpet and clung to her legs.

"Oh, there was loads he didn't tell them. Dad's like that; he hates the police. They're always locking him up. They don't even know that my dad was married to Hannah's aunt."

"Really?"

"Yep. They didn't ask so he didn't tell. That's what he's like." "Kel!" The voice came again. I was already getting up off my seat.

"Look, I've got to go. Just get out of here." Kellie looked truly troubled.

"Meet me tomorrow."

"No."

Please. Look, when can you get out? Meet me at Mama Mia's pizza place."

"You'll buy me pizza?" Her face lit up a little as my heart sank utterly.

"Yeah, of course. What time?"

"Three o'clock. That's when the stripper's on. Nobody buys beer then, they're too busy goggling. I get two hours off." "Kel! Get down here now!" The voice seemed to be growing louder.

The only people in the pub who seemed perturbed by it were Kellie and me. The rest of them couldn't have cared less. I wanted out as soon as possible, despite the fact I felt terrible about leaving the poor woman there.

"I'll see you there." I said, and smiled before dashing off for the door.

Chapter Nineteen

By the time I'd made it back home, I was feeling pretty low about Kellie. She looked so much like Hannah, yet their lives could not have been more different.

Hannah had been brought up with everything from gymkhanas and Labradors to jewellery and the best clothes. Kellie had a fluffy gillet, a dad with a mangy old strip-pub, and something of a *kicked-around-the-world-a-bit* attitude.

Still, I suppose Kellie was the one who got to live, in the end.

It was way beyond teatime when I shrugged my duffle coat off and listened intently for any signs of my mum in the house, breaking her bail conditions. Silence; a silence I was most grateful for.

I was hungry and keen to eat something substantial enough to soak up the awful gin and tonic. I didn't actually feel like it had touched me, but it had given me something of a headache and an empty feeling in my belly. I opened all the usual cupboards and, when I saw the customary array of dried noodles and crisps, I knew I needed something with a little more heft to it; the chippy was calling me.

To be honest, I normally eat a little better than I was doing. Not expensively, but pretty well. But, somehow, everything in my world seemed to have been swallowed up by everything in Hannah's. Had it really only been a week?

Well, less than that, really. Hannah had last been seen on Monday afternoon, and it was only Saturday. It felt like forever. This cloud of uncertainty which had turned into sadness and horror, had clung to us all, somehow permeating everything that was once normal.

I vaguely wondered if I was slipping behind in my classes. In all honesty, I hadn't missed much, and I knew I'd catch up easily anyway. Still, that wasn't really the point. Sooner or later the world would have to return to normal.

As I hung on the cupboard door and continued to stare pointlessly in at the Euro-Saver noodles, a kind of melancholy crept over me. So, that's what happened in the end; a person died and the world kept turning.

All that promise of a life snuffed out, then that was that. Everyone else just kept going, and all that promise turned to dust in the very act of forgetting. You see, I'd seen news reports before.

Young people, women and girls mostly, it has to be said, murdered. Everyone is full of outrage and pain and promises never to forget; lessons must be learned. And then, they're gone.

That young life which so affected you with its sudden cessation, becomes a distant memory or, worse, forgotten entirely. Everyone else goes on with their lives, whilst they are stuck there; frozen in time. Left behind at the point their lives were taken away from them. No promise come to fruition, or achievement; only ever remembered for being a murder victim.

I started to feel a bit nauseous and honestly didn't know if it was fatigue, delayed shock, or the gin and tonic on an empty stomach.

With a sigh, I shut the cupboard door much harder than it was really built for, and headed off upstairs for a shower. I'd liven myself up a bit, then head off into the early evening darkness to the chippy.

As I stood in the shower, I wondered what, if anything, I could do that night. I knew I had Kellie the next day, but was there something else I could be looking at? Was there a vital bit of investigating that I could be doing in the meantime?

Maybe I'd got as far as I was going to get when I'd found Hannah. But then, I wasn't looking for Hannah anymore; I was looking for her killer. I shuddered a little at the thought.

I mean, I'm bright enough, and the thought had been there ever since I had decided to go on with my own investigations after I'd found Hannah's body, it's just that I hadn't exactly acknowledged it.

In trying to clear Liam's name, all I could really do was find the person who had actually killed Hannah.

As I wrapped myself in the least thread-bare of our bath towels, I hoped that I would be able to find the killer in a passive way; you know, just find irrefutable proof and send it DI Thorn's way.

Above all things, I did not want to come face to face with the person who had choked the life out of a young woman. I so very much did not have the stones for that kind of caper.

So, after firstly depressing myself, then frightening myself, I switched on every light between the bathroom and my bedroom.

It was like Christmas on the first floor, without any of the spirit. I almost wished my mum was there. Almost. I certainly wished that Liam was there. As I wandered about my bedroom, pulling clean clothes from the wardrobe, I felt a bit teary again.

I wondered what Liam was going through and just when he would be released. Hadn't Betty said they could only hold him twenty-four hours without charge? With a possibility for up to ninety-six if they had something a bit more than groundless suspicion.

As much as Betty had made me feel better with her explanation, I started to think about the sort of copper DI Thorn really was. I doubted he'd lose too much sleep if he over-egged something to a judge just to get his ninety-six hours.

If Liam was going to be held for ninety-six hours, I wouldn't set eyes on him again until Tuesday afternoon. That was if they didn't charge him with something. Something?

If they were going to charge Liam with anything, it could only be Hannah's murder. What else was there to charge him with? I felt a horrible swooping sensation in the pit of my stomach.

I knew I was making things worse; dwelling on the worst-case scenario. I wouldn't be doing that if I had company; if Liam was here. I started to cry, all the while trying not to. I hadn't cried when Betty was here.

I hadn't felt so very negative in Rich Richard's company, despite a tear or two. I supposed that was because their very presence staved off murky thoughts such as the ones I was running in my head.

As I pulled my plimsoles on, I heard a noise from downstairs.

"Oh, not again!" I breathed almost silently. I listened hard. Someone was trying the back door handle in the kitchen. Surely not the intruder again? What could he want this time?

He already had Hannah's diary, and didn't know about the photocopy….. at least, I didn't think he did. My heart began to race as the noise from the kitchen door grew louder. Whomever was trying to get in was really intent about it. Well, this time, I didn't have to worry about calling the police.

I had nothing to lose. I got to my feet and searched silently through my rucksack. I was shaking like a leaf and couldn't find the phone anywhere. In sheer panic, I tipped the contents of my rucksack out on the bed.

My phone wasn't there. I continued to stare at the collection of objects, almost as if my panic was blinding me somehow to the phone's very real presence. Then, with a truly sinking feeling, I remembered that I had been checking my emails on the bus ride home and, when the bus had pulled up on the edge of Moss Park, I'd slid the phone into the pocket of my duffle coat.

The very same duffle coat that was hanging up downstairs on the pegs by the front door.

In a heartbeat, I was up on my feet and running downstairs. I needed to get through the kitchen, through the living room, and out of the front door before the intruder finally burst into the kitchen.

If I didn't get out right then, I'd very likely be trapped inside the house with him or her.

With just one plimsole on, I sprinted for the stairs.

I ran down them so fast I almost lost my footing. Breathing harder than an athlete at the end of a 10-K, I wheezed my way through the brightly lit kitchen.

As I passed the door, it flew open and a figure fell in; a great big figure who took me down to the floor as he fell. I hit the ground hard and tried to scream, but every ounce of air had been forced out of my lungs with the impact.

I tried to draw in a breath, knowing that a big scream was very much going to be needed here, but just couldn't. For some reason, I just couldn't get the air in. I felt my head start to pound painfully, and had the awful feeling I was about to die.

Not at the hands of the intruder who had me down on the floor, but because my own body was going to let me down when I needed it most.

Without the air I needed, I could feel myself start to get weak. Maybe it was just the panic, who knows? I couldn't even struggle against the intruder although, in truth, he didn't seem to have a hold on me anymore.

The person who had knocked me to the floor was grumbling and trying to get up. Even though the light was on in the kitchen, the intruder was behind me and I just did not have the strength left to even turn around.

The room was starting to darken, and I thought I must be about to pass out. In the very moment when I stopped trying to breath, I was taken seriously aback by a great rush of air which shrieked in through my throat, making the most awful noise.

It was a scream, but on the in-breath, rather than an out-breath. It was the worst and most eerie sound I'd ever heard in my life, and I could hardly believe it was me making it. Seriously, the makers of horror movies need to try this one out as a sound effect; it is truly horrible.

Anyway, after that first breath went in, there came a series of shorter ones, and I was panting like a pooch. As a phenomenon, being winded is not something I hope to ever repeat and, to each and every one of you who has experienced it and survived, I salute you my friend.

The room was bright again and I regained a fully functioning, if somewhat shocked, body. I scrambled to my feet, ready to fight like a lion for my survival.

My head was still pounding and I felt suddenly furious. I was not going to be strangled in my own kitchen, and that was that! I spun around, fist pulled way back, hay-maker style.

"Oi!" Came a great shout, and slowly, *very slowly*, I took in Liam's face.

"What the hell….?" I said, finally getting the shakes and gasping again.

"Just turn the lights out Josie." Liam said, racing for the switch and plunging the kitchen into darkness. "And the ones upstairs." I couldn't speak, and instead just made curious guttural noises.

"Are you alright, Josie?" Liam said, as if the whole bundling me to the deck thing hadn't happened. Without waiting for an answer, he shot off upstairs and, suddenly, it was no longer Christmas on the first floor.

I was still standing in the kitchen, doing my best to work things out and let go of my suddenly murderous anger towards my best friend when he trundled back down the stairs by the torch light on his mobile phone.

"Where are you, Dude?" He whispered.

"In a shambolic state in the middle of the kitchen floor where you left me, half-wit." I spat.

"Dude, that is *harsh*." Liam said, and I could hear a bit of a chuckle developing in his voice, most inappropriately in my opinion.

"They released you then?" I said, doing what I could to hold my tone in check.

"I've been released on Police bail. Pending further enquiries, apparently."

"And you're alright?"

"Yes, all things considered Dude, I'm ok."

"And you couldn't just ring me, or knock the door like a normal person?"

"No, I couldn't. Well, I suppose I could have called you if I'd thought of it, but as for knocking the door, no way."

"So, there was a bonafide reason for you to break into my house, scare the living daylights out of me, and chuck me to the ground, causing the near-death experience of winding?" I was actually scaring myself with my Clint Eastwood calm-yetmenacing thing.

"Yes, there was." He began, all serious. "Winded? Was that why you made that horrible screamy noise? Seriously, Dude, that noise gave me *chills*." Even in the darkness, I knew he was grinning.

I knew every nuance, every change of tone, and every facial expression that accompanied it. I knew all of this because Liam was my best friend and always had been.

"Are you really alright?" I said, and felt myself soften to blancmange.

"Yeah, I'll be ok. They had nothing on me, Josie, and they knew it as well as I did. But still, it was pretty rough. They treated me like dirt, Dude. Not like physically, but just their attitude. As far as Thorn is concerned, I did it. I am the sort of low-life scumbag who would strangle the life out of his girlfriend." Liam faltered for a moment, and I knew the facial expression that went with that sound too.

I knew it so well that tears sprang to my eyes. I could barely see him in the darkness, particularly since he seemed to have the torchlight aimed at the linoleum, but I shuffled over to where he was, nonetheless.

Once I'd safely reached him, we fell into each other's arms. We were silent for the longest time, but I knew that Liam was crying, just as I was.

How the hell did we get here? Liam's biggest crime, as far as I could see, was going out with a girl whom everybody, the girl included, thought was far too good for him.

As we held tightly to each other in the darkness, I decided that I did want to be the one to find the killer.

I didn't want to be in the background, doing nothing more than piecing together all the clues; I wanted to be the one to chase them down the street and rugby-tackle them to the floor, before giving him or her the most vicious beating they could ever have imagined. Liam had done nothing to deserve having his life pulled apart, but the ones doing the pulling didn't know him.

They'd never seen into his heart, or witnessed his six-year-old self bravely standing up for a little girl he didn't know.

I could feel Liam reaching around the back of my neck to surreptitiously wipe his eyes, and I decided to stay silent and just hold him until he broke that silence.

Chapter Twenty

Like a mole, I began to get used to the darkness. I had to, Liam's aptitude with a torch was shocking. He was a bit excitable, which was probably understandable all things considered.

Still, the way he wafted the torch about reminded me of really fast disco lights, and I was just thankful not to be an epileptic.

"So, why are we hiding out in the dark?" I asked, when we'd both finally got on top of our own emotions.

"Because the front of my house was crawling with press when I got home. I thought about sneaking around the back, but I just couldn't face it. I thought they might see me and, if they did, even running to your place wouldn't help. They'd have followed me."

"Oh, I see. But why didn't you knock?"

"It's hard to explain."

"*Try*, old bean."

"Well, I could see all the lights on upstairs. *Why,* by the way?" "I'd spooked myself and needed a bit of sunshine."

"Fair enough." Liam said, before going on. "Anyway, I knew you were upstairs, not down, judging by the lights. I didn't want to bray on the door, in case there were any press wandering about near your place. So, since the kitchen door is almost always unlocked, I went for it."

"Only to find it was locked." I said, remembering my heightened security measures after the intruder had broken in.

"Yeah. I was getting more and more agitated, and in the end, I just put my shoulder too it. A bit too hard, as it happens. That's how come I ended up on the floor."

"Knocking me to the ground and emptying my body of vital oxygen, lest we forget." I added in a slightly pinched tone.

"Soz, Dude." Liam said, and I could hear the hint of mirth in his tone once more. "And oddly, it's not actually broken! The springy bit just boinged back when I pushed the door. That's why it flew open the way it did."

With technical terminology like that, Liam, it's just as well you took art."

"Now is not the time for Liam-bashing, my weirdly practical little friend." He was still amused, and I was glad of it.

It had almost torn me in half when he had cried in my arms in the darkness.

"So, do you think they'll come here?" I didn't like the idea of being a media sensation. I was no Fliss Hardcastle.

"If someone tips them off that we're best buds, Dude, I reckon they will." Liam said, sounding suddenly agitated. "You should have seen them, Dude. There were just loads of them hovering about outside. Cars, vans, not to mention half the street out having a nosey. One of my neighbours will tell them about you soon enough. That's why we have to keep the lights out. And no noise whatsoever."

As if by magic, my mobile began to ring loudly.

"Light my way to the front door, Liam. It's in my duffle pocket." Liam did as I asked, and I was able to answer the phone and put an end to the horribly loud ringing in quick time.

"Hello."

"Hi Josie, it's Richard."

"Oh, hi Richard."

"Any news on Liam yet?"

"Yes. He's just got out. He broke into my kitchen and scared the living daylights out of me."

"Sounds like fun." Rich Richard laughed. "Is he ok?"

"Yeah, he's fine." Once again, I had to push away the emotion of just minutes before. "They've bailed him for further enquiries."

"In other words, they have nothing." Richard said, and I remembered why I liked him so much.

"Exactly."

"So, where do you go from here?"

"To the chip shop, if I can get out of my darkened house without any members of the press seeing me."

"What? Seriously?"

"Well, they might end up here. They were all outside Liam's place when he got back, so he came over here and broke in. Did I mention he scared the living daylights out of me?" I heard Liam snort in the background, and I was glad he was returning to his old self.

"Oh wow."

"Yep. We're in darkness and starving in a house with nothing but dry noodles and crisps."

"Look, stay where you are. I'll sneak over to your place. I'll be really careful, I promise. And I'll stop at the fish and chip shop on the way. I'll be about forty minutes."

"Oh, that's great. See you then. And come around the back of the house."

"Will do." And with that, Rich Richard hung up.

Liam was simply relieved that someone, *anyone*, was coming with chips. It was then that I realised there was a lot of catching up to do.

There were things that neither Liam nor Richard knew, and I would probably be better off waiting and telling them the ins and outs of my further investigations when I had them both together.

Except, of course, that I needed to tell Liam about Hannah and Richard. I laid heavy emphasis on the fact that their one-night stand had happened before Liam and Hannah had ever met.

"Don't worry, Dude. I'm not going to go all Neanderthal right here in your kitchen. I told you before, I just didn't have that really big feeling about Hannah, you know?"

"I know, but I wanted to get it out of the way before Rich Richard got here. I didn't want it to come as a shock, you know?"

"Yeah, I know." Liam said, quietly. "I know I wasn't really into Hannah that much, and we would have lasted about five more minutes, but I still feel sick that she's dead."

"I know, Liam."

 Hey, you don't think Rich Richard did it, do you?"

"I doubt it. But you never know, I guess."

"Funnily enough, I can't see it either. I quite like him. He's alright for a toff."

"He's not a toff, Liam. He's like us, but with more money."

"Really? So, you've got to know him then?"

"A bit. He's been really helpful while you were away. He photocopied the photocopy before the police went to the university to seize it. He made it with, like, seconds to spare. He's been pretty cool. I think we can trust him."

"And he *is* bringing chips." Liam wasn't even joking.

As far as he was concerned, it was stuff like that upon which one could truly rate a man.

"So, what else has been happening?" Liam went on.

"Oh, let's wait until Rich Richard gets here and we're eating. Otherwise I'll have to repeat some of it, and I'm knackered already."

"I know you are. You just kept going, didn't you? I mean, you just carried on investigating, looking for the killer."

"I had to. I didn't know what else to do."

"Thanks, Josie. I really love you."

"I really love you too, but don't call me Josie. It's weirding me out."

"Alright, Dude."

Finally, Richard arrived with the chips. The chips came with fish and battered sausages, so Richard became our new hero on the spot.

We were kind of bonding over the batter, and I didn't really want to end all that by starting with Fliss at the dry cleaners, but unfortunately that was the beginning.

"So, Fliss knew all along." Richard said, sounding more awkward than concerned.

"Yes." I said, feeling a little of the awkwardness myself.

"Why do you think she didn't mention it? Do you reckon she was saving something up for you? I mean, hatching some sort of plan?" Liam was feeling no awkwardness whatsoever, and both Richard and I relaxed.

"Like what?" Richard asked, sounding more concerned about Fliss.

"Well, didn't you say that Fliss had a face-scratching sort of a temper?"

Liam went on, and I could hear that his mouth was crammed to capacity with chips, and was glad we were eating by torchlight so that I didn't have to bear witness. "Not to mention the whole *you're dead* threat she gave to the Dude here."

"That must have been rough. Sorry you had to put up with that, Josie." Richard said, his chip etiquette miles better than Liam's.

"It's hardly your fault. She's just a nasty piece of work." I reassured him.

"Nasty enough to kill?" Liam more or less said what we were all thinking.

"Nasty enough, yes, but actually capable? I don't know about that." I said, thoughtfully. "And then there's the whole business of Dirty Harry. Surely Fliss wasn't Dirty Harry. And it seemed to me that Trixie and Harry had already met at the strip-pub."

"That's if Dirty Harry was actually the killer." Liam said.

"I've thought about that too, but it all seems too coincidental."

"But what if she met Harry and they….. you know….." Liam was as curiously prudish as me, evidently. "And then Dirty Harry left and Fliss came along."

"Still kind of complicated. Fliss would have to have been following Hannah." I said.

"Or Harry." Richard added.

"Yeah. It does seem kind of out there." Liam gave in.

"But not impossible. None of it is impossible." Richard added. "Like, we shouldn't exactly close the door on that one."

"Ok." I said, wanting to move things along. "Let's keep Fliss on the list."

Who else is on it?" Richard asked, innocently.

"Well, I thought I'd better keep an open mind about MJ. Well, Matty Jameson, you know. Just in case."

"He's always been on my list." Liam said.

"Oh, you've got a list too?" I said, chuckling.

"Yeah. You're on it Dude, so watch what you say." He chuckled back, and Richard joined in.

"Am I on the list?" Richard asked, quietly. It totally took me aback.

"*Noooooo.*" I said, with way too much vehemence to be anywhere near casual.

"Does that *noooooo* mean yes?"

"No. No, it really doesn't." I knew I was scarlet, thank God for torchlight.

Rich Richard, however much I liked him, was still on my list, and he knew it as well as I did.

"It's ok, Josie. If you're doing this right, then my name should be there, shouldn't it?"

"And mine, Dude." Liam added. He always knew what to do. "Don't leave me out. I'm on bail, after all." He wailed plaintively, and we all burst out laughing.

"Ok, so you're both on my list." I said, chuckling and kind of knowing that neither one of them could possibly have killed Hannah Davenport.

"Anyone else?" Richard asked, when we'd all got over the chuckles.

"Well, I'm not sure yet. I should have a better idea by tomorrow afternoon."

"Oh?" Liam said, and I could feel both of them suddenly straighten up, waiting for the next bit.

So, I told them all about my encounter with the Hannah lookalike in the Duchess of Devonshire.

"Dude! You went in there on your own?" Liam almost dropped his chips. "Seriously?"

"Yes." I said, feeling kind of badass and full of myself. They didn't have to know I had quivered like frog spawn in a jam-jar.

"No way!" Liam started to laugh. "Dude, did they make you wear a feather boa?" Liam was snorting hard, and Richard joined in.

For badass read *butt of everyone's jokes!*

"You utter fool!" I was trying to be annoyed, but couldn't find the right spot. Liam was just too funny, and I was sunk. I started to laugh. "And anyway, Sunday is stripper day, not Saturday. Shame, really. It probably pays more than the dry cleaners." The boys were still giggling like….well….boys.

"So, was she really like Hannah?" Richard asked, pulling himself together long before Liam.

"I nearly fell off my barstool." I said, honestly. "And then she spoke, and they were poles apart." I went on to tell my thoroughly engrossed audience about all the differences of dress, voice and mannerisms.

"When are you meeting her?" Richard asked.

"Three o'clock in Mama Mia's. I'm buying her a pizza."

"Do you think you should really go alone, Dude?" Liam asked, suddenly sounding concerned.

"Yeah, she's fine. To be honest, despite her spikey ways, she's strangely likeable. I mean, I feel a bit sorry for her. Her dad sounded awful. He was bellowing from the cellar, and Kellie just looked terrified. I'm guessing she hasn't had an easy life."

"That's a shame." Richard said a little sadly, and I wondered if he was comparing Kellie and me.

"So, what are you hoping to get from her?" Liam asked as he screwed up his empty chip papers.

"Well, a bit of family background. Exactly how they are related would be interesting. And if there were any regulars who might actually fit the profile of Dirty Harry." "More suspects." Richard said.

"Yes, more suspects."

"Cool." He went on. "So, what can we do to help tonight? Googling or Facebooking or what-not?"

"Yeah. Put us to work, Dude." Liam said, and he seemed kind of warmed up by the fact that he had at least two people on his side, willing to do whatever it took to clear his name.

"I don't think there's any online stuff to look at yet. Hopefully Kellie will give us something tomorrow that we can dig into." I said, and I began chewing thoughtfully at my bottom lip.

Suddenly, the torchlight was full in my face and I blinked and ducked.

"Dude! I totally knew you were doing that munchy bottom lip thing! It cracks me up; you look like a lama or something when you think hard. Do it again, so Rich can see it." I think I've already mentioned that Liam is not possessed of a robust attention span.

"We have to find out who the killer is, fast." Richard said, quite seriously. "Because this numpty won't last five minutes in prison."

Once again, the three of us were laughing. Liam appreciated Richard's line so much that the two of them hi-fived in the semidarkness.

So, my best friend had bonded with my new friend. To be honest, I couldn't help liking that a lot. There was something about Rich Richard which sort of marked a turning point in the way I viewed the world around me.

I really, really hoped he didn't turn out to be a killer.

"What about the photocopy? Did you get through that yet?" Richard asked.

"Oh, no, not yet. I'll go and get it." I shot off, taking Liam's phone for a light and plunging my pals into darkness as I trotted off upstairs for the photocopy.

Well, photocopy of the photocopy.

We read through several pages with very little on them but the odd appointment or lecture change. It was not easy by torchlight, it has to be said and, in the end, we took turns reading out a few pages each.

Before long, we were almost in the present day. There was no more talk of rebellion or random email addresses. There was nothing else regarding Emjay or nudity or anything of that nature.

The closer we got to the end, the more I realised that the big clues were very much at the beginning of the diary.

Something about that was kind of niggling me, but before I could get to the bottom of what, Liam started reading something a little bit different.

"Sooner or later the Chav is going to realise he isn't fit to polish my shoes. I actually think he knows already, after I turned up at his house." Liam paused for a moment. I really didn't want him to read the rest. Judging by the look on his face, he'd gone on a little in his head. *"I've been in nicer sheds than that vile house. Still, he couldn't really do any other than let me in. It was all so funny, and worth every boring day I've spent with him. Sure, he's hot, but he's so far down the food chain. As we sat on his bed in that bare, awful room, I felt him slowly shrinking beside me. I don't know how I kept a straight face. Enough rebellion, huh? Time to let the poor, sad creature go."* When Liam had finished, you could not have heard a pin drop.

The three of us just sat in silence, all slowly digesting the spite in written form. Why did it have to be the page Liam was reading aloud? Why couldn't it have been mine? I would have made something up.

I risked a look at Liam's face in the dim light, and saw something I'd never seen before; hatred. Real hatred.

"I'm struggling to feel sorry for Hannah right now." Richard broke the silence.

"Yeah, me too." I said, in solidarity.

"Well, at least I'm hot." Liam said, although not with his usual humour.

"Oh, totally, mate." Richard said.

"Smokin'." I added.

"For a Chav." Liam sounded so defeated.

My friend, dragged over hot coals and accused, all for the sake of some nasty little snob who had only dated him to feel better about herself. In that moment, I could have strangled Hannah Davenport myself.

Every time I started to feel sorry for her, something would come up and I'd despise her all over again. Confusing times, I can tell you.

"I didn't know she turned up at your house." I said, wondering if I was doing the right thing by still talking about it.

"Yeah. She did just show up. It was Sunday night. I totally was not expecting her. I never invited her to my place because…well….you know." Liam tailed off.

"And was she really so awful?" I went on.

"I don't know. Maybe. I thought she was just being nosey or determined or whatever, but then she became really keen to have a good look around. And honestly? Yeah, I did shrink. I suppose I realised that she knew it, too. But then, Monday came and she was all chipper at uni and stuff. It seemed to me like maybe she didn't care about that sort of thing. Maybe she was different." I snorted involuntarily. "I know, Dude. Naïve, right?" "No, not naïve." I said, sadly.

"Just human, Liam." Richard finally spoke. "And Hannah did not deserve you to look twice at her. Man, I knew she was a snob. I'd always known that. But….wow….I had no idea she was so deeply rotten."

"It's all tied up with this *rebellion* thing. The one-night stand, Liam the Chav boyfriend." I said nonchalantly, and was pleased to hear Liam chuckle. "The nude portrait, the stripping, Dirty Harry. What the hell had happened in Hannah's life to spark it all off? What was so damn big that she needed to rebel?"

"Let's hope you find something like an answer when you speak to Kellie tomorrow." Liam said, seeming to have recovered.

"Yes. Anything to find who really did this and get the Police off Liam's back." Richard said, sounding kind of flat.

I knew he was having one of those struggles; the kind of thing that kept blasting me in the beginning. I didn't like Hannah. Richard didn't like her either, but that had only just happened. "Guys, none of this is easy. Trust me, I've had some guilty moments over the last few days, especially when I think back over my opinions of Hannah before she went missing. But don't let it eat into your soul. We're humans, with human feelings and opinions and yes, even judgements at times. So what? We're still doing the right thing. Right now, we might not feel like finding the person who killed Hannah but, in a day or two, we'll all come to the conclusion that being a totally spiteful snob is not actually punishable by death. But, in the meantime, until we each get to that point, we just need to feel what we feel without getting all guilty about it." I finished my long-winded point to be greeted by complete silence. It went on for ages.

"Did either of you hear me?" I said, wondering if they'd tuned out about four sentences back.

"Yeah." Richard said.

"Yeah, Dude. I'm just, like, taken aback or what-not. I didn't realise you knew this kind of stuff."

"What stuff?" I said, a little defensively.

"Like feelings and stuff. I totally thought for years that you had Asperger's, Dude. I didn't think you thought that way. I thought it was all just numbers and straight lines and blunt comments."

I could just make out Richard's outline beginning to bob with mirth.

"Richard, don't you even think about laughing at this fool." I said, trying not to laugh myself. Liam was a complete donkey. "He doesn't need any kind of encouragement here."

"Sorry Josie." Richard said, before booming with laughter.

As the two of them carried on laughing like kids, I looked down at the photocopy. I turned the last couple of pages and realised that the entry about Liam was the very last that Hannah had made.

To be completely honest, I don't know how I felt about that.

Chapter Twenty-One

By the time I had waited in Mama Mia's for twenty minutes, I had myself convinced that Kellie wouldn't be coming.

She'd changed her mind and, after all, why wouldn't she? This was just pizza for her. There was nothing much more for her to gain than that. I was the one doing all the wanting, so I could hardly blame her for ducking out of the arrangement.

Still, I hardly slept all night thinking about this meeting; going over and over exactly what I should ask Kellie.

And I suppose having two snoring men in my room had quite possibly added to my sleeplessness. We had talked over the whole investigation until the wee small hours, and I could do no other than invite Richard to stay.

In a weirdly unspoken way, none of us had wanted to venture into my mum's empty room to sleep. We all just kind of gravitated towards the neat and tidy little oasis that was my room.

Nothing sordid, I might add. I slept on my bed, and the lads had blankets on the floor. It was like a bizarre indoor camping expedition.

I had been about to nod off when Richard, still messing about on his phone said, "Oh, The Catcher in the Rye! I haven't read that for ages!" It took me a moment or two to realise that he had swung his phone enough to see by its light *exactly* which books were currently propping up the lower end of my bed.

"Well, don't try to re-read it now, or we're all in trouble." I said, surprised that I found it amusing for once, instead of humiliating.

Well, who knew? There really was more to life!

Finally, the door of Mama Mia's swung open and I looked up to see a familiar mink coloured fluffy gillet hove into view.

I was not surprised to see it was Kellie who was wearing it; there was seriously not another garment in the world quite like that gillet.

"Hi, Kel. Thanks for coming." I felt a bit odd calling her Kel.

It felt too personal. Yet, at the same time, I knew if I called her Kellie, it would somehow close down the lines of communication.

You know how school teachers always used your proper name, even when your own parents didn't; it drove a wedge, kind of thing.

"Hi. Sorry I'm late. Dad was being a bit…well…." She didn't finish, she simply sat down opposite me and picked up the menu.

My pauper's heart was so hoping that she liked a nice cheap and cheerful margarita pizza.

"I'll have a large Hawaiian with extra cheese, garlic bread, and a big coke." Kellie said. *Don't cry, Josie Cloverfield. Just grin and bear it.*

"No problem." I said, smiling really hard. I caught the waitresses' eye and gave her our order before the part of me that religiously packed that flask every day took over and made a fool of me right there and then.

I thought fondly of the Euro-Saver's wonderful range of flat and floppy pizzas, and wished that they were what we were having now.

"So, what do you want to know?" Kellie said, quite unguardedly. I was pretty thankful, since I hadn't quite come up with a line which would take us from pizza order to direct questioning.

"You said that your mum was Hannah's aunt."

"That's right. She's dead, though. She died years ago, when I was really little."

"I'm so sorry." I said, and meant it.

How this young woman's life had differed from Hannah's was pretty distinct. So far, it seemed like Kellie had received all the rough breaks; except, perhaps, for the final one.

"It's ok. I don't even remember her."

"Kel, was your mum Hannah's mum's sister, or Hannah's dad's?"

"Hannah's mum and my mum were sisters."

"I see." I said, "Did they get on? I mean, did your mum and Hannah's mum stay in touch?" It was the only way I could think of to highlight the obvious differences in the two households.

"Nah!" Kellie started laughing. "Once Hugh Davenport had whisked her away from my Dad, Hannah's mum never looked back. She became one of *them* overnight. Total fake!"

"Sorry….." I said, confusion about to swallow me. "Hannah's dad whisked your aunt away from….your Dad?" I had that Jeremy Kyle feeling.

"Yeah. Aunt Sharon was engaged to my dad before my mum was. She worked at the Duchess with him." "Worked?" I said, dubiously.

"Well, stripped." She laughed. I was obviously not wearing my poker face. "Yeah, that's right. Mrs *hoity-toity* used to be a stripper in my dad's pub. You wouldn't know it to see her now. And to hear her! Wow, she sounds like the flaming Queen!" Kellie was getting kind of loud; she was suffering a mixture of amusement and outrage. "And she's not called Sharon anymore. She calls herself Sian! Sian Davenport. Total fake."

"Oh, my Lord!" I said, almost as if I was reading from a gossip magazine in the hairdressers. Really, what would Miss Marple have said about my obvious manner? "So, how did Hugh Davenport come into things?"

"He was a punter at the Duchess! Dad said he used to be there every Sunday. Always got in early to get a seat with the best view, if you know what I mean. Dirty git!" Kellie almost spat the last.

Of course, our pizzas just *had* to arrive at that very moment, didn't they? The waitress almost dropped Kellie's Hawaiian onto the table.

"And they make out they're so above everyone. Her an exstripper, and him a dirty old git who used to cart his posh carcass around the worst pubs and clubs in Grantstone."

"Well, that has surprised me, I've got to tell you." I said quietly, as I watched Kellie take a huge bite of pizza.

"Yeah. I bet none of their posh friends and neighbours ever get to hear the story of how they first met!" And with that, Kellie burst out laughing.

"So, Hannah knew all this? I mean, she ended up working at your dad's place herself."

"Oh, she didn't know it for years. She didn't know any of it. She was totally in the dark about the whole thing." Kellie's face was screwed up tightly, and I couldn't tell if she felt sorry for Hannah, or scornful of her.

"So, how did she find out?"

"My Gran died. It was her funeral in the summer."

"Oh, I'm sorry." I said again, realising that I was actually really bad at this sort of thing.

I just didn't know what else to say. Maybe my donkey-brained best friend had a point after all.

"It's ok. I never knew her. Once Aunt Sharon, or *Sian* should I say, made her way up in the world, she made sure her own mother was looked after. Dad says that Gran became someone else altogether. They put her in a nice little bungalow far away from us."

"Oh, that sort of stinks."

"Yeah, it does. Hannah had the lot. She even got my Gran to herself."

"So, you didn't see your Gran then?"

"No. Apparently, there was some kind of row after my mum got it together with my dad. She worked at the Duchess too, you see. Anyway, that was all done and dusted before I was even born. My mum, dad and me were kind of cut off from the rest. Like we were some kind of guilty secret."

"That *really* stinks." And it did. I meant it.

"Yeah, it does."

"So, you went to your Gran's funeral?"

"My dad was determined. Obviously, my mum was long gone before then. But dad said it was a public place and they couldn't ban us from it."

"True." I said, thoughtfully. "But why would he want to go to the funeral of an old woman who'd turned her back on her own daughter and granddaughter?"

"Oh, because he thought that the old crow might have left me some money. He wanted to go to the funeral to see if he could find out when the reading of the will was going to be." Kellie spoke as if it was the most normal behaviour in the world.

There was something about Kellie's father's attitude which reminded me uncomfortably of my own mother. It felt weirdly familiar.

"And you saw Hannah, obviously." I went on, not wanting to dwell on or judge Kellie's dad.

"Yeah. Her mum tried to keep her away from my dad and me. Man, you should have seen her face when she realised we had shown up at the funeral." Kellie was displaying a certain amount of almost justifiable glee at the memory. "After my mum had died, I suppose Sian thought she'd never set eyes on me and my dad ever again. She'd probably forgotten we even existed." Kellie shrugged. "And she was desperate, *desperate*, to keep

Hannah away from dad and me."

"Without success?"

"Too right. Hannah could see how alike we were. Dad said he'd have struggled to tell us apart if we wore the same kind of clothes. And it was true too. Anyway, I could just tell she was dying to find out more. She looked pretty shocked when she realised she had more family than she knew about."

"So, you talked?"

"Yeah, in the end, Sian had other people to attend to, and Hannah soon made her way over to me."

"What did she say?"

"She was mostly looking me up and down to start with. Her clothes were really swanky. You know, like good quality and stuff. Anyway, she seemed pretty pleased with herself. She tried it on, but I soon squashed her." Kellie took another huge bite of pizza and sat back in her chair, also seeming a little pleased with herself.

"Tried it on, how?"

"Lording it over me. Wincing at the way I speak and asking where I lived and stuff. Then she told me where she lived and all the stuff she had. She was so posh, you know?"

"Yes, I know." I said, with a shrug. "So, you squashed her?"

"Yeah. I lost it a bit. I don't like people looking me up and down. It's rude." Kellie said, very much on her dignity. Obviously, her own habit for looking people up and down in an appraising way was an unconscious one. It was the one mannerism which made my flesh crawl, it was so like Hannah's had been. "Anyway, I told her to pack it in and she just laughed. Man, I was angry. I just gave her every bit of history I could think of. I told her everything! She looked shocked, but I could tell she didn't believe me."

"But eventually she must have." I said, wishing that Kellie would speed along to the point.

"It took a few days. She flounced off at the funeral, and I thought that was the last I'd see of her. Then, at the end of the week, she just strides into the pub. I couldn't believe it. I thought she'd come for some sort of showdown, you know?"

"And had she?"

"No. She was all calm and stuff. I think the stuff I'd told her had begun to sink in, and she wanted to know all of it. Every detail."

"And how did she take it?"

"She was quiet. It took the wind out of her sails alright. I felt sorry for her then, to be honest."

"I suppose everything she took for granted in her world was proved a lie, kind of."

"That's exactly it. Anyway, she kept coming back, you know. She was a bit snotty and always snobby, but it seemed like she wanted to hang out, you know? Well, at first it did."

"Why, what happened?"

"She only wanted one thing."

"What?" I was on the edge of my seat, my tiny margarita pizza practically untouched.

"She wanted to be the Sunday stripper! She was desperate to do it."

"I don't get it. Like mother like daughter kind of thing?"

"No. More like revenge. I think she wanted to do it and somehow have her mother find out about it. She even said what a laugh it would be if her dirty old dad still went to the Duchess for a show and found himself looking up at his daughter! Twisted, if you ask me."

"I suppose it had all really hurt her." I said, feeling really, horribly sorry for Hannah.

Even if she did have a bad attitude towards others, it would have been impossible for her not to be so wounded and humiliated by the secrets she had learned.

Her ever-so-nice parents must have suddenly seemed like strangers to her, and everything in her world must have felt so phoney.

"Yeah, it did hurt her. Still, she soon got used to the stripping." "Did her parents ever find out?"

"I don't think so. Well, I suppose they know now. Everything will have come out, won't it? My dad wouldn't have held back about that bit when he spoke to the police."

"Did Hannah ever seem to regret it?"

"Not at all. She was a bit of a show-off really. I reckon she liked the attention."

"Did she get attention from anyone in particular?" I asked, remembering the main questions I had rehearsed the night before. I needed more credible suspects.

"From everyone! They all fawned round her, and she loved it."

"But did she seem to get on with anyone more than the others?"

"Yeah, there was some big-haired bloke in a stupid long coat. He looked like either he was an artist or a homeless man. Older than her though, not a really young bloke, you know?" I almost laughed; it had to be Matty Jameson. "He stuck out like a sore thumb in the Duchess, I can tell you."

"And, anyone else?"

"No, I don't think so." She said, staring down thoughtfully at the great pile of pizza crusts which she clearly had no intention of eating. Seriously, the waste was making me feel a little bit sweaty. "Oh, hang on, there was someone else she used to natter to. A younger bloke. He was quite nice looking, what I remember of him. He had dark hair, maybe nineteen or twenty."

"And he was interested in her?"

"No, I don't think so. I got the feeling they didn't get on too well. I saw him a couple of times and he seemed a bit annoyed." "Did you know why?"

"No. I don't even know if he really was annoyed, it just sort of seemed like he was. Body language or what-have-you."

"What did he look like apart from the dark hair? Would you recognise him again?"

"No, I didn't really get a good look at him. Like I say, he only came in a couple of times. Not like the older one; he came in just about every Sunday that Hannah was on." Kellie finished with an amused sneer.

"Was there anyone else? Did she ever arrange to meet up with anyone that she met in the Duchess?" It was such a long shot.

"Not that I know of. Hannah liked the attention, but she was way too snooty to actually fall in with anyone who went in the Duchess on a Sunday. Or any day."

"So, I guess the two of you kind of made up your differences in the end. After all, she did work at your dad's pub."

"Yes and no. She would cosy up to me now and again, but mostly she let me know just how much better than me she was and always would be."

"I think I got that myself from time to time." I said, in solidarity.

"What did *you* think of her?" Kellie asked, and I was a little taken aback.

I was just wondering if there was any way I wouldn't have to answer her, then I saw how intently she was eyeing me, and I knew I had to.

"Honestly, Kel, I didn't like Hannah. Some of it was my own fault; my own hang-ups and insecurities about my fairly rough upbringing. But mostly, it was Hannah. She had a way of looking me up and down and she always had a one-liner designed to make me feel about this big." I indicated a tiny gap between thumb and forefinger. "So, I guess we would never have been friends. Still, when I found her in that building, I couldn't have been more sorry."

"Really?" Kellie looked incredulous at first, then her face softened into something I couldn't quite describe. "Even after she made you feel like crap?"

"Yeah. You see, I realised that nobody should have their life ended that way, even people I don't particularly like. One day, Hannah might have grown out of the self-satisfied stuff; the entitlement and the spiteful attitude. But we'll never know. She never got the chance, did she? And that's really, really wrong."

"You sound like a saint or something." Kellie was smirksneering again.

"Far from it. I still don't like Hannah Davenport. I just wish that she hadn't been murdered."

"I wouldn't mind another coke." Kellie's countenance had returned to normal, and I reckoned I'd got about as much out of her as there was to get.

Chapter Twenty-Two

As I wandered away from Mama Mia's, rattling the thirtyseven pence I had left in the whole world, I thought about all I had learned and where it might get me.

The question of Hannah's rebellion had finally been answered. She had wanted to devastate her parents by acting in much the same way as they had done in their own youth.

To be honest, I'm not really sure how stuff like that works. How do you really punish someone by acting in the same way as they did?

Obviously, as a psychologist, I would make an exceptional window cleaner but, at the same time, I still wondered if Hannah's reaction to the revelations had been strictly normal.

I hate the fact that my mum was a stripper, so I'm going to be one too. That way, I can very much register my distaste and disappointment. Mmmm.

I too have moments of sweeping disappointment in my own parent, but acting just like her couldn't be further from my mind. Maybe I'm just too simplistic?

Maybe I lack the necessary layers to be a truly complicated human being? I mulled that over for a while and, in the end, I had to admit that it seemed quite likely. No doubt Liam would understand it all.

As I made for the bus stop, I switched my phone from silent mode. As I'd been in Mama Mia's, Liam had sent me two messages.

"Dude, we've snuck out and gone to Rich Richard's place to watch films. Rich says to come over when you're done. Hurry up, I want to know what you've found out."

I was just about to wonder exactly how I would get to Rich Richard's place when I had no idea where it was, when I saw text number two.

"Oh yeah, he's at 26 Kenton Gardens. Google it. Lx"

So, I googled it. It was just one bus ride out of town and a short walk. Thank God for bus passes!

As the bus rumbled its way along the quiet Sunday streets, the dusk of early evening was falling. I hoped I'd be able to get to Rich Richard's place before it was dark, since I'd be less inclined to get lost or knock the wrong door.

I looked down at my clothing, hoping that my old duffle coat, jeans and plimsoles would pass muster at the front door of 26 Kenton Gardens.

Still, if they'd let Liam into the house, then I was hardly likely to come as a shock to the Allencourt family. At least I hoped not.

In the event, I was not at all shocking. And why would I be? Mrs Allencourt was just lovely. She was a bit older than my own mum, and a lot nicer to strangers.

She was clearly expecting me and pulled the door back wide for me to enter before I'd even spoken.

"Hi. You must be Josie. Come in, love, they're upstairs in Richard's room. Just follow the noise."

"Hi Mrs Allencourt." I said, smiling brightly.

In the right circumstances, I could be very appealing to other people's parents.

"Do you want a drink to take up?"

"Oh, yes please." I said, partly not wanting one, because I would have to hold it together with Richard's mum long enough for her to make it for me.

"Tea or coffee? Or coke?" She said, wandering away towards the kitchen.

"Tea please, Mrs Allencourt." I said, and followed along behind her.

We went in through the already open door into what might well have been the most untidy and shambolic kitchen I'd ever seen in my life.

There was loads of really nice stuff, like a coffee maker and one of those instant boiling water things which made kettles a thing of the past, but everywhere seemed crammed with stuff.

There were multi bags of crisps spilling out across the counter and a chopping board covered with crumbs. The fact that Rich Richard's mum was not a happy house-worker kind of made me relax a little bit.

"Have you eaten?" She asked, and seemed genuinely prepared to feed me. I just hoped Liam hadn't taken liberties with that question. He was a total pig at times.

"I've just had a pizza, thanks, Mrs Allencourt."

"Oh, call me Sheila." She said, and I watched in happy amazement as she made me a cup of tea without having to boil the kettle. So cool. So *very* cool.

"Sheila." I said, a bit experimentally. I sometimes forget that I am an adult. Well, technically, you know?

"Well, take some crisps up with you." And with that, she thrust the multi bag at me. "No doubt the boys will be hungry again." "Thanks." I said, smiling as she thrust the mug into my free hand.

"Richard speaks very highly of you, Josie." She was smiling so enthusiastically at me that I couldn't help but smile back. "He says you're so clever that if anyone can solve the case, it's you."

"Oh, that was nice of him. I'm not sure it's true, exactly." I felt quite glowy.

It was a nice feeling. It was also nice to meet a mum who was interested in the goings-on in her offspring's life. I couldn't imagine telling my mum all the ins and outs of the investigation. She wouldn't be a bit interested.

By the time I got upstairs, whatever film Liam and Richard had been watching had come to an end.

Liam looked totally content for a man on police bail on suspicion of murder. The film and the new friend had taken his mind of it for a while, and I was so, so pleased about that.

"Dude, what are you doing with all those crisps?" Liam said, eyeing the huge multi bag.

"Oh, you know, I was just peckish."

"Funny, Dude. Very funny." Liam said, nodding in appreciation of what he thought was great humour.

"So, what happened?" Richard pointed to the bed. "Have a seat." I put my tea down and shrugged off my duffle before making myself comfortable enough to tell the tale.

I was no longer surprised to see that Richard took after his mum in terms of disorganization and untidiness.

It had never occurred to me that posh people could be messy. I must admit, I quite liked it. It narrowed what had been a chasm of a gap into something more like a slither.

I told my appreciative audience the whole thing, and got many *oohs* and *ahhs* along the way as each revelation unfolded.

"I wonder who the younger bloke was?" Liam said, seeming to cling to what he thought was a new lead.

"No idea, unfortunately. Just that he was younger and dark haired. That's it." I said, shrugging.

"That could be you." Richard said to Liam, laughing.

"Oh God, it could. Best not tell DI Thorn, or he'll bring back hanging." Liam grinned.

He really was the most resilient person on earth. I knew just how awful he had felt the previous night, and yet he had done everything in his power to get back on his feet again.

Indestructible little donkey-brain.

"And the other guy just has to be Matty Jameson." Richard said, thoughtfully.

"Yes, without a doubt. But I was surprised that Kellie said he was such a regular. He really gave me the impression that he wasn't. He more or less said he went in to study the female form for his art work." Both Liam and Richard burst out laughing.

"Yes, alright!" I said, laughing too. "I didn't buy it either, but I did believe that it wasn't a big thing with him. A big pastime, you know?"

"Maybe he lied?" Liam said.

"Maybe he was just embarrassed?" Richard added.

"Well, I guess he stays on the list. With interest." I said, wondering if I'd got the man so very wrong.

Richard put on another film, but all three of us talked over the entire thing with theories and suspects. In the end, it seemed as if we were all at a loss as to what to do next. Where else was there to look?

By the end of the evening, I felt a little flat. Richard seemed to mirror my sentiments, and Liam did a really good job of appearing to be fine with it all.

By ten o'clock, we left Richard's place. Richard planned to see Liam's lecturer's the next day and collect whatever study notes Liam had missed. Liam was so touched; he went kind of quiet for a few minutes.

Still, once he had regained his equanimity, he arranged to meet Richard in town at around half ten. I was getting more and more pleased by their friendship. It was exactly what Liam needed right then.

Our journey home was all but silent, and Liam didn't really speak until we were walking back through Moss Park. He had a hat, hood, scarf and balaclava type of a thing all wrapped about his head in an attempt to conceal his identity.

"I hope nobody recognises me." His muffled voice drifted out through several layers of wool.

"I doubt it. They'll just think you're a mugger." I laughed.

"Dude, what if this is it? What if we never find out who killed Hannah?"

"That doesn't mean you'll be charged with it. They have no evidence against you."

"That's kind of not my point."

"Oh?"

"Even if I don't get charged with murder, I'll always be under suspicion if the real killer is never caught." He stopped for a moment, looking around. "I'll always be hiding, won't I?"

"No, you won't." I said, with grim determination. "Because I'm going to find the killer if it's the last thing I do."

"Thanks Dude." Liam said, so quietly, I almost didn't hear him. "No probs." I said, and took his gloved hand in my mittened one.

"Dude, don't you find these hard to wear?" Liam's woollen head nodded down at my mittens. "I mean, it's like having just one big finger and a thumb. It's kind of mutanty, Dude."

As I've said before, Liam has a really short attention span.

As we got closer to my house, we slowed down a little and became very much more aware.

"No sign of any press outside. I guess your house is still a safe one." Liam said, seeming greatly relieved.

"You speak too soon, my friend." I said, on the wave of a great sigh. I could see lights on in my house.

"Why?" Liam asked, and I just pointed at the brightly lit windows in response. "Oh, Dude, they broke in!"

"No, Liam! It will be my mum."

"But she's breaking her bail conditions."

"Like she'd care, Liam."

"You could call the police. They'd lock her up for that, especially since it's domestic violence related."

"But it will cause a big scene. If there's any press on the estate, they'll be here in a heartbeat."

"Good thinking." Liam said, sounding hunted. "But now we've nowhere to go."

"Let's try your place. We'll sneak through the alleys and go in through the back garden."

"Yeah, come on, Dude. It's worth a go.

In the event, the mainstream media of the United Kingdom were not outside Liam's place.

We'd managed to canter through some of the shadiest alleyways in the country, if not the world, and, after a couple of fences which I scaled without any hint of grace or skill, we were in Liam's back garden.

We hovered for a bit, barely daring to breathe lest we alert anyone to our presence. In the end, we just went in through the kitchen door.

As always, Mrs Attwood was parked up at the kitchen table, staring miserably at the small television on the worktop.

"Hi mum." Liam said, cheerfully. He bent down to kiss the top of her head.

"Hi Liam." She said, really vaguely. "Hi Josie." And that was it.

No concern for the bright young son who had been to hell and back in the last few days. No outrage for the fact he had been arrested and detained for a really horrible crime which he had not committed. Nothing.

I thought of Sheila Allencourt. She was practically a stranger to us both, yet she had shown more interest in our lives in ten seconds than either one of our mothers had in a lifetime.

And still, Liam kissed the top of her head. Still he loved her. I probably loved my mum too, somewhere deep down. Very deep down. Instigating her arrest for Affray notwithstanding. "We're gonna go up, mum." Liam said, after grabbing some snacks.

"Ok." She barely lifted her eyes from the telly.

In that moment, I nearly cried. Why didn't Liam and I have mums like

Sheila Allencourt or Betty Butler? Why was it that we would go through life not knowing what family life was really like, even for just a day?

"Come on, Dude. I'm knackered." Liam said, tugging at the sleeve of my duffle coat.

Like a true gent, Liam took the floor and let me have the bed. We were settled down in no time, and I realised that I was truly shattered.

I felt guilty about Liam sleeping on the floor for a second night running. There was room for both of us on the bed, and we were good enough friends for it not to be weird.

I could hear him crunching away on his crisps as he watched YouTube clips of people falling over on his phone, giggling like a fool.

I just lay there, staring up at the ceiling, wondering how the hell I was going to keep to my promise of finding Hannah's killer if it was the last thing I did. Poor Liam.

I would have done just about anything to clear his name and ensure a happy future for him.

As I was about to tell him that there was room enough on the bed for us both, I heard the first of what turned out to be an entire night's worth of loud snores. Liam had gone out cold.

Chapter Twenty-Three

Liam woke me really early the next morning. I was suffering from that slightly scared confusion you get when you wake up somewhere you weren't expecting to be. When he prodded at my shoulder, I yelled.

"Seriously, Dude! What's up with you?" Liam's face loomed down, just inches from mine.

"Do that to yourself in the mirror one day, and you'll have your answer." I said, squinting at him.

"I'm going to set off now."

"What time is it?"

"It's only half-seven, but I want to get off the estate before it gets light."

"Liam, you're not meeting Richard for ages."

"I'm just going to hover about in town until he meets me. I don't want to risk being seen here."

"The press have gone."

"Maybe. But the neighbours haven't. You know what some of them can be like. They won't need evidence to find me guilty, will they?"

I sat up in bed. Liam was absolutely right. It sort of strikes me that the vast majority of humanity fits into the *there's no smoke without fire, the boyfriend must have done it* category.

I couldn't help but think it was a very good thing that we've got rid of capital punishment in this country. Murkily, I wondered how many people were wrongly hanged over the years.

Yeah, I know, not helpful.

"Ok. Well, keep in touch. I'm going to go into uni this morning, so I'll catch up with you later. And I'll see if I can get Dale and Betty to get my mum out of the house. Then we can hide out there again."

"Alright, Dude. Well, I'll ring you after I've seen Rich Richard."

"Liam, do you think we should still call him that?"

"Yeah. It suits him."

"You're an idiot." I said, chuckling.

"See you later, Dude." And off he went.

I managed to get another half-hour of much needed sleep and, after I'd tip-toed to the bathroom and back, I was feeling a bit more optimistic than I had done the night before. There would be something else; some other line of enquiry or place to look.

I looked at my clothes and realised I would have to wear them again. There was no way I could go home. It was not yet half past eight, and my mum would still be in bed. There was no way she'd be up and out of the house, put it that way.

I made my way over to the one and only chest of drawers in the room. I could lessen the scruff-bag feeling by borrowing some of Liam's shorts and socks. I knew he wouldn't mind.

As I blundered through the shorts, I nearly laughed out loud when I happened upon a pair of Spiderman underpants. I was very much going to bring that up later, I can assure you. Selecting a very sensible pair of plain shorts, I popped them on.

Opening the next drawer, I began to rifle through Liam's socks. There were way too many of those chunky and horribly thick sports socks for men. I would burst right out of my Converse in a pair of them.

I kept going, feeling sure there must be some normal socks in there somewhere. Finally, I came to a pair of plain black, normal weight socks. With a sense of relief, I sat on the edge of the bed to put them on.

The first one was fine, but there was something scratchy in the second. With a bit of a huff, I pulled off the second sock and turned it inside out to see what the scratchy problem was.

As I did so, something fell out and onto the carpet. I picked it up. It was a necklace. With a sudden sick feeling, I realised that I recognised it. It was Hannah's, and it was broken.

As I turned it over and over in my hands, all I could think of was Betty confiding in me that the Police had searched for it in Liam's house on the day they had arrested him. Hannah's necklace had been ripped from her neck.

The coroner had said that there was a mark on the back of Hannah's neck which was consistent with having it pulled off whilst still done up. Wasn't that what Betty had said? I knew it was, and I wished I didn't have such a great memory for chunks of conversation.

The necklace was gold and quite thin. The clasp was still done up, and the chain itself had snapped. My mouth went dry.

How could Hannah's necklace be in Liam's sock? How had the police missed it? For a moment, I was lost in the investigation again. I imagined a burly cop in big, blue overalls tipping out the sock drawer and going through the contents without actually thinking to look *inside* the socks.

Even a cursory squeeze of a sock or two wouldn't have given the necklace's location away. It was perfectly feasible that it had been missed. *Of course,* it had been missed. I was missing the point and I knew it; I was missing it on purpose. I didn't want to think about any of it, but I knew I had to.

I sat on the edge of Liam's bed, curiously pondering my feet; I had only one sock on. I was almost immobile, apart from my eyes looking around the room that had barely changed since Liam and I were six years old.

How could any of this be real? I knew Liam. I knew him as well as I knew myself; didn't I?

I could feel my hands shaking, and the trembling reached right inside me, making my stomach feel almost as if it was vibrating.

I felt hot and sick and utterly devastated. I must be wrong; there must be some kind of mistake. Liam couldn't choke the life out of somebody.

He just couldn't. And then I pictured his face in the torchlight as he'd read Hannah's last spiteful comments aloud. She'd turned up at his home, and made him shrink to nothing. Liam's face had struck me that night.

I'd seen hatred there for the first time. Had something happened that night? The night before she disappeared, when Hannah turned up unexpectedly and sat on the very bed I was sitting on.

Had she said or done something that night which had brewed the hatred I'd seen on my best friend's face? Had she pushed him?

I couldn't believe I was about to start making excuses for him. Liam wouldn't be any less guilty of murder just because I loved him so much.

Finally, the tears began to make their way through the shock, and they flowed like open taps. I began to shake in earnest, but I knew I had to get out of there. I had to find Liam; confront him. I had to know for sure.

And then it came to me; a way to know for sure. I took my phone and opened Facebook. Not knowing if the profile would still be there, I was amazed to find that the Police had not made any moves to get it removed.

I sent a friend request to Dirty Harry. He accepted it within minutes.

Chapter Twenty-Four

Sitting on the bus, heading for Weatherby Road, I could hardly believe I was holding it together. Sitting at the very back, I scanned the Facebook private messages again and again. Dirty Harry had sent the first message; he'd sent it within seconds of our friendship being confirmed by Facebook.

"Hello Josie."

"I know who you are."

"I doubt that."

"Meet me. Now."

"Where?"

"Where you left her."

"Ok. But no police. I'll know and I'll bolt. You come alone or not at all."

"I won't call them. I want to speak to you. I want you to explain."

"Alright. And remember, no Police. I'm watching you."

That final line; *I'm watching you*. I remembered the morning I had seen it on my bathroom mirror. Liam had been the first person I'd told.

When the intruder had been in my house, I'd assumed Liam was still with the police. It wasn't until the next day he'd told me he'd been released, but had fallen asleep on his bed.

So tired, he hadn't even undressed. And I'd believed him. Why wouldn't I?

Instead, he'd let himself into my house. He'd known my mum was a nightmare when it came to locking up.

He'd gone straight for the kitchen door the night he'd been released for the second time, hadn't he? But was that really possible? Had Liam really done that? Had my best friend really tried to scare me out of my wits?

Everything seemed to add up horribly. I felt sick again.

I knew I'd be safe with him, as strange as that sounds. Even if he had murdered his girlfriend, I knew Liam would never hurt me.

I needed to know why, and I knew he'd tell me. It had to be there, in the place where I'd found Hannah's body. It had to be in the place he'd killed her, because I needed to see remorse.

Liam had to hate what he'd done, or everything in my world would have been built on as much of a lie as Hannah's life had been.

When I stepped off the bus, I was physically shaking. I felt hollow, like my insides had been completely scooped out, leaving me just a husk in a duffle coat.

This time, when I looked up and down Weatherby Road for any sign of a witness, I found myself completely alone; no hovering about or touring around the block waiting for my chance.

I slipped through the gap in the overgrown foliage and fencing with ease. As I strode across the waste ground, I looked at my feet; I watched every step, almost as if I was looking at somebody else's feet entirely.

I couldn't help but think that the next few minutes would change my life forever; if I stopped now, if I did and said nothing, would things go on as they always had? No, of course they wouldn't.

Nothing would ever be the same again.

I walked into the derelict building with confidence. I was quite surprised that the Police had released the scene of crime so early. Maybe there really was nothing more to gain from this place.

I suppose it wasn't like searching a house, with crammed drawers and cupboards and attics. There was nothing here. Apart from the odd chair, bit of paperwork, and occasional desk, there was nothing.

I stopped briefly in the doorway, noting that I was nowhere near as afraid as I had been on the day I had first wandered into this awful place. Stupid, really, since I was about to be faced with a killer. I strode up the stairs, knowing I could not put off the inevitable any longer.

I pushed the door open and looked in. The room was exactly as it had been on that awful day, except that Hannah was not there.

Nobody was there. I stood staring in silence as waited, leaning all my weight against the back wall. I faced the door resolutely, ready to face the killer of Hannah Davenport.

Finally, I heard footsteps downstairs.

I wasn't scared, not for a moment, but I was more heartbroken than I had ever been in my life. It seemed almost as if he was walking in slow motion, and it took an age before he finally appeared in the doorway.

For the last few seconds, I had been hoping to see almost anyone but my best friend. When I finally focused on the person in front of me, the tears flew down my face. It really was Liam. "Dude, why did you come here?" He said, almost scowling at me.

"You know why. You got my message. I know what you did."

"I *saw* your message." Liam said, looking at me oddly. "But I don't know what it is you think *I* did."

"The necklace. I found it in your sock."

"My sock? What the hell are you talking about?"

"Hannah's broken necklace was inside one of your socks in your drawer. I found it when I went in for socks."

"Dude, you're wearing my socks?" Liam's eyebrows rose comically. I almost laughed. It was so very like Liam to pick up on totally the wrong thread. Even now.

"Missing the point, Liam."

"Ok, how did Hannah's necklace get inside my sock?" "You tell me." I said, darkly.

"Well how would I....? Oh, wait a minute..... you think I..... God Almighty, Dude!" He finished on a squeaky high note of the kind I hadn't heard since his voice had properly broken.

"Well, you *are* Dirty Harry. And you're here, aren't you."

"I'm here, you duffle-coated buffoon, because you *contacted* Dirty Harry. I couldn't believe it. I could *actually* kill you for being so reckless."

"What?" I said, suddenly confused.

"Facebook notification pinged on my mobile. *Josie and Dirty Harry are now friends!* Seriously, Dude?"

"Oh, so you're *not* Dirty Harry?" I felt a burgeoning hope.

"Of course I'm not, you *fool*."

"So how did you know I'd be here?" I said, with more accusation in my voice than I had intended.

"Because I hacked straight in to your account and checked your messages."

"How?"

"Duh! You use your postcode for every password, like, ever, for one thing. And for another, you're not the only smarty pants in the whole wide world." Liam started off annoyed, then slipped into oddly interested. "Also, the idea that you were about to get yourself murdered suddenly cleared my brain of the extraneous nonsense that's normally in there. I was, like, *totally focused*. I suppose that's what it's like to be Josie Cloverfield. It was cool, and a bit weird. To be honest, I prefer being me to you. Anyway, the point is, I had a flash of inspiration, Dude, and here I am." "Oh wow! Well done old bean!" I said, and rushed to hug him.

I was so relieved that I can't even begin to explain how it felt. It was like I'd had my whole world handed back to me and I suddenly realised just how brilliant it really was. All of it, from eating Euro-Saver crisps to having a drunken, unreliable parent. I had Liam, and he made everything brilliant.

"You totally thought I was a throat-squeezing murderer, didn't you?" Liam said, as I buried my face into his chest.

"No. I……." What was the point in denying it? "Well, yes, I did. But I was really, really shocked, if that's any consolation?

It's not like I thought it all along."

Absolutely no consolation whatsoever, Miss Marple." Liam hugged me really tightly, until there came a noise from downstairs.

"What the hell?" I whispered to Liam.

"The killer!" He hissed, reminding us both why we were there. "Sounds like he's fallen over! I'm going to get down there before he comes round!"

"Liam!" I squawked at his departing back.

"I'm not going to prison for murder, Josie." And he cantered off down the stairs.

By the time I had made it half way, I heard another dull thump, followed by a crash. I ran, jumping down the last four steps and racing in the direction of the noise. Liam was face down on the floor, blood oozing from the back of his head.

I dropped to my knees beside him and gently tried to prod at his neck for a pulse. As I did so, I heard a step behind me. Slowly, I turned to look at the real killer of Hannah Davenport.

Chapter Twenty-Five

The fluffy mink-coloured gillet was unmistakable. Well, *she* hadn't been on my list of suspects. Standing there, holding a crow bar in one hand and a really big knife in the other, Kellie smirked at me.

Slowly I rose to my feet, and stood to face her. The coolness of her gaze was so horribly familiar and, as she slowly looked me up and down, taking in everything from my plimsoles to my duffle coat, the hairs on the back of my neck stood up. I was so shocked that even my scalp tingled.

"Hannah?" I said, and heard my voice tremble.

"Well done, Charity Shop!" She said, in the cut glass tones of the woman who had allegedly been murdered. "But I must admit, when you sent me that stupid message, I really thought you'd worked it out then."

"No, I hadn't."

"So, who did you think I was?" She said, with a sneer. "Liam." I answered truthfully, because I was just too stunned not to.

My brain was whirring with the possibilities. I looked down at Liam; I couldn't see any movement whatsoever.

As I looked back up at Hannah, I suddenly lost all fear. If my friend was dead, I would find a way to disarm Hannah, and then kill her for real.

"He needs an ambulance." I said, looking back down at him.

"No, he doesn't. Ambulances are for the living." She was smirking again.

"If he's dead, you're dead."

"Oh please, I'm armed and you are useless!" She scoffed.

"So useless that I found your body here?" I realised how daft that sounded.

I also realised that it was poor Kellie who had been murdered and left here. A girl I liked; a girl I had never met!

Yes, and you did it very well. In the end, I was glad that you stole my diary from the canal path. That idiot Detective Thorn would never have worked it out. When I saw my mother throw the damn thing over the fence, I thought it was all over. Trust her. She'd probably seen the rebellion stuff and nudity bit and wanted to keep up appearances. Good old Mummy! Still, I *needed* the police to find it. I'd gone to such great lengths to come up with all the little clues to lead them to my dead body. The Facebook accounts and the email address needed to be looked at, especially after I'd put so much effort into them."

"You *wanted* them to find her?" I said, incredulously.

"It was imperative. I needed Hannah Davenport to be found dead. That was the whole point."

"To make your parents suffer by killing their *daughter?*" I couldn't believe what an appalling human being she really was. "And then you followed me? You broke in to my house?"

"Your house, yes. Eeek. As if it wasn't bad enough that I'd had to follow you from the canal, I had to enter the pit of despair that is your humble abode." Hannah made a huge display of quivering revulsion. "Yes. I needed the police to have the diary. I just didn't ever find a way of getting it to them after I'd taken it from you. Still, never mind. You'd read it, I presume, and worked it out. It probably worked out for the best in the end, huh? Well done again, Charity Shop."

"That's the last time you call me that." I said, and meant it.

My fear was staying away, and I was feeling a bit full of myself.

"Whatever." She said, smirking.

"*Whatever?* Seriously? You act bored and unmoved, but you killed your own cousin! What did Kellie do to deserve that?"

"Nothing. She just really, really looked like me. It was so fortuitous." She was grinning again and turning the knife over and over in her hand.

Alright, I did go a bit sweaty just then.

"And that was it? Jesus! How could you?"

"Well, if she had stayed away from my Grandma's funeral and kept her mouth shut about my mother's past activities, then I wouldn't have needed to punish my parents, and Kellie would still be alive; living out her miserable chav existence in that vile pub."

"You killed Kellie and you're actually blaming *her* for it?"

Suddenly, I caught a flash of movement out of the corner of my eye. I couldn't let Hannah know, or she would lunge at me, so I did a truly sensation impression of a person doubling over in complete disbelief. Really, I did.

As I made a display of pulling myself together, I peered over to the window, and saw the beautiful, slightly terrifying face of PC Betty Butler. Oh wow! She had come to save me. The lioness was coming to rescue the gormless little cub.

Betty worked her hand, almost as if she were operating a glove puppet, and I quickly realised that she wanted me to keep Hannah talking.

"I did her a favour. You saw that place yourself. Oh, and the clothes! She made *you* look well dressed." Hannah gave the braying laughter which had been the audio accompaniment to my lunchtimes for weeks.

Man, I hated her. But no guilt this time. I wanted to strangle her myself.

"You vile, stuck up mad woman. And what the hell did you think you were going to live on? No university degree, no mummy and daddy paying for everything. Pretty stupid plan, Hannah." I spat the words.

"Oh please! I've taken so much from my parent's credit cards; they'll be choking when they get their statements. I'll move away and start a new life. New identity, you see. It's amazing the shady people you meet when you strip in a dive like the Duchess of
Devonshire."

"And when the money runs out?"

"I'll have found someone to take care of me long before then. Class always finds class, my dear."

Oh really?" I said, doing my best Hannah-style sneer. "Like you dad found your mum. Very classy!" That turned out to be a bad move; Hannah took a step towards me, her eyes furious!

"Oh, wait." I said, holding up a flat palm. "The necklace. How did you pull that off?"

"Easy!" Hannah said, almost pleased that I'd shown an interest in her scheming. "I'd planted it the night before I went missing. I'd bought one just like it for Kellie. I yanked it off her before I strangled her. I'd already snapped my own one and hid it in the chav boy's sock the night before." Her manner was so cold; so matter of fact.

"That's the last time you call him that."

"You're just so funny." Hannah said, and gave a spiteful laugh. "Anyway, the Police fouled up again. I thought their search would be more thorough.

Still, Josie Cloverfield to the rescue again, huh? And it worked. You thought Liam had done it."

"You couldn't have known the Police would search his place."

"No, but I had a fair idea. For one thing, I'd left enough clues to make it look like Liam had cause to be jealous and, for another, they always look at the boyfriend first, right? That's why I picked someone from that awful estate. The Police wouldn't take much persuading that somebody so very....well....*downtown*, would have done it. Especially with *his* shady family."

"You *picked* him? You mean, *that's* why you went out with Liam? You had it all planned?" I was furious.

"Yes. He was perfect. Such an idiot, and entirely disposable."

"You know what, Hannah? People aren't disposable. Not Liam, not Kellie, not Matty. You think yourself so above everyone else, that other people are just chess pieces, but in the end, you're just a low rent stripper like old *Shazza* was. Like mother like daughter. You total skank!"

"No, you're the skank."

"No, Hannah, I'm just poor. You had chances thrown at you from all directions, yet you still took your kit off in a urinesoaked pub to make a point."

That was clearly the last straw. Hannah lifted the knife high in the air and advanced. I was so scared I couldn't even close my eyes; I just stared at her in horror.

For a moment, she seemed frozen. Just like the Statue of Liberty, one arm held aloft. Then I heard a determined sort of a crackling noise, and Dale suddenly appeared from God knows where.

He had her around the waist and disarmed before the shock of the taser had dropped her to the floor. In a rather cool way, he let go of her so that she hit the ground with a proper good thump.

Suddenly, Betty was there too, casually unhooking the wires which attached Hannah to her taser.

"Good shot, Betty." I said, with a totally inappropriate chuckle.

"Good talking. Nicely done." Betty replied, making me feel totally cool.

"Yeah, good one." Came a croak from the floor. "Remember me?" I darted to Liam's side.

"You're awake?"

"I've been awake for ages."

"Oh cheers, pal!" I said, scowling at his very, very pale face.

"I didn't want to confuse things, Dude. You know I say silly stuff under pressure." He said, with a really big Liam-style grin. "And anyway, I could see Dale pressed up against the doorway, and Betty sneaking in, all scary rolling shoulders, like a leopard or something."

"What do you see in this bloke?" Betty laughed before radioing for an ambulance for Liam.

"God knows." I said, smiling at him, and also starting to cry a little bit.

"Oh, no way, Dude. This is *happy time!* You spared me a lifetime of balaclava wearing, and the bump on my swede will die down soon enough."

"I know." My voice wobbled.

Come here." Liam sat up as best he could and pulled me into his arms. "Thanks Josie." He murmured into my hair.

This time, I didn't mind him calling me Josie one little bit.

"Oh, by the way." Liam said, pulling back a little and looking at Dale. "How did you know to come here? Are you getting visions and stuff now?"

"No, you plumb!" Dale said, his shoulders shaking with mirth. "I've been following Josie on and off all week." "Why?" I said, a little sharply.

"I don't know, Josie. I just had a feeling. I knew you'd do whatever you had to do to save Liam, so I thought I'd better have your back. I couldn't have anything happening to you now, could I?"

"The library?" I asked. I had to know.

"Yeah, but I didn't think you'd seen me."

"And then the vigil and the dry cleaners?" I said, thawing out with the realisation that I was very much cared about.

"Yeah, alright, I'm not so stealthy. I've not done any surveillance courses yet." He shrugged.

"Nor are you likely to." Betty said, laughing. "Oh, I hear sirens."

Epilogue.

"Nice flowers, Dude." Liam said as I set a bunch of bright little gerbera daisies down on Kellie's grave.

"Thanks, Liam." I smiled up at him. "You know, it's weird, I feel like I knew her."

"Maybe because Hannah did a good impression. She must have made a good study of her cousin to fool Kellie's own father."

"I guess so. Still, some parents just aren't that observant, as we both know very well."

"Dude, people do their best with what they have available at the time. Not just material stuff, but personality and resilience and what-not. It's time to let it go, Dude, or it will cloud your world forever."

"You always take me aback when you act like a man. I'm so used to the boy."

"You can have both, since I *am* both." Liam smiled at me, and helped me back up.

"Thanks. And I'm always here for you too."

"I know that, Dude. You saved my hide." He was grinning.

"I really *did* save your hide, old bean. Me. Josie Cloverfield. Campus Detective!"

"Me and Rich Richard helped. We're detectives too." Liam pulled his affronted face.

"Ok. If you say so." And *I* pulled my sarcastic face. "But it was still *me* who saved your furry butt, my friend."

"Ok, you really did. Although we need to talk about the fact you were so easily convinced that I was the Grantstone
Strangler."

"Oh, Liam!"

"Seriously, I'm not going to forget it."

"You really should forget it."

Nope. Never. In fact, I'm going to go on about it forever. I'll mention it more than the colouring book story."

"I've got two words for you."

"Steady on, Dude. Keep it clean."

"Spiderman underpants." I was victorious. He crumbled immediately. He knew I'd seen them.

"Ok. We're quits." He said, and threw an arm around me as we slowly made our way out of the cemetery. "Shall we track down Rich Richard?" He grinned.

"Yeah, go on. We might be able to turn him upside down and shake the loose change out of his pockets or something." I chuckled.

"Dude, that's so scandalous. You've literally turned into Snatcher Harris right there. That man is like your father-figure now." Liam laughed too, knowing that I truly liked Richard.

He was one of us now, after all. No longer was Richard a part of the old group who dealt out spite and shame.

If I'd been a little less judgemental, I would have seen that he was never really a part of that world in the first place.

Anyway, I'd now doubled my list of best mates to two; a minor miracle in Josie Cloverfield land. A minor miracle that made me really, really happy.

The End

I hope you have enjoyed reading the first of my Josie Cloverfield Detective Novels.

I would greatly appreciate an honest review for my work on Amazon.

Please come by my Facebook Page

http://www.facebook.com/JosieCloverfieldBooks

Leave me a message, your thoughts on Josie and the gang, and to get updates on the progress of the next Josie Cloverfield novel.

Thanks so much,

Jack x

Printed in Great Britain
by Amazon